Praise for Erin Lange

'A compelling read.'
Bookseller

'I highly recommend.'
The Bookbag

'A powerful and courageous novel.'
BookTrust

'Poignant, tough, and rewarding.'
Metro

'The humour of *The Fault in Our Stars* and the poignancy of R.J. Palacio's *Wonder*.'
We Love This Book

'A moving road-movie tale.'
WRD Magazine

'A moving and thoughtful story of friendship and love.'
Crime Review

'A dark and humorous tale.'
Telegraph

'A story for our time . . . an instant page-turner.'
Sunderland Echo

About the Author

Erin Lange writes facts by day and fiction by night. As a former TV news producer, she is inspired by real-world issues. She grew up in the cornfields of northern Illinois, along the Mississippi River, but now lives in the sunshine of Arizona. Her previous books include *Butter* and *Dead Ends*, both of which were shortlisted for the Waterstones Children's Book Prize.

Find Erin on Facebook www.facebook.com/ErinJadeLange and Twitter @erinjadelange. Find out more about *Butter* at www.butterslastmeal.com/

By the Same Author

Butter
Dead Ends
Rebel, Bully, Geek, Pariah

THE
CHAOS
OF
NOW

Erin Lange

FABER & FABER

First published in 2018
by Faber and Faber Limited
Bloomsbury House,
74–77 Great Russell Street,
London, WC1B 3DA

Typeset by MRules
Printed in England by CPI Group (UK) Ltd, Croydon, CR0 4YY

A CIP record for this book
is available from the British Library

ISBN 978–0–571–31747–9

FSC
www.fsc.org
MIX
Paper from
responsible sources
FSC® C020471

2 4 6 8 10 9 7 5 3 1

To Grace & Harper,
the two greatest stories I will ever help write.

air gap *noun*

1. the virtual space between
    a secure computer and an
    unsecured network, such as the
    internet; defined by the absence
    of any connection ever made with
    the secure device

2. the bubble surrounding
    virgin technology; any laptop,
    smartphone, or tablet that hasn't
    popped its internet cherry

3. a safe space but just one
    connection away from total chaos

1

April 1st of my freshman year, I saw something I will never unsee. That was the day Jordan Bishop walked into the Haver High cafeteria and set himself on fire. And even though it was April Fools' Day, it was no joke.

The kid soaked himself in gasoline and lit a match.

On purpose.

And the sickest part is he didn't even die right away. A lunch monitor shot him with a fire extinguisher until he was covered in foam, and two days later, at the hospital, his parents took him off life support.

For weeks, whenever I closed my eyes, I would see a Jordan-shaped wall of flames behind my eyelids. But I was lucky, because I was at the other end of the cafeteria and only saw fire. Kids who were closer saw what the fire did to him, so they'll all be messed up pretty much forever.

We spent the rest of the semester awkwardly avoiding the burn marks in the linoleum and pretending to be surprised that someone at our school could be treated so terribly that he wanted to off himself. When classes started back up in the fall, the cafeteria had a new floor, and every wall in every hallway had a fire-engine red No Bully Zone sign. To the credit of the Haver High student body, some of the signs hadn't even been vandalised yet.

Exactly one year to the day after Jordan Bishop's fire show, I was bleeding under one of those signs in the second-floor East Wing bathroom.

I had felt Malcolm's fist before it hit my face. That moment just before impact was an instant that lasted an eternity, and when Malcolm's knuckles finally connected with my eye socket, I almost welcomed it, because then at least the suspense was over.

Now I was on the floor next to a urinal, pain exploding over my left eye.

Malcolm crouched down and leaned in close until his red hair and freckled face filled my vision. It was some kind of biological joke that a guy like Malcolm Mahoney would get a spray of spots on his cheeks and nose that made him look perpetually twelve years old and innocent.

'You saw nothing, got it?'

He was right about that. I hadn't *seen* anything at all.

He raised his fist again, and I braced for another blow. But at the last second, he opened his thick fingers and gripped one side of my head, pushing me over into the urinal.

'Did you hear me?'

I gagged as my cheek pressed against the dirty porcelain. I'd have preferred another punch.

'I heard you,' I groaned through my teeth.

Heard you pressuring that girl to hurry up and pee on the stick. Heard you accusing her of skipping her birth control pills.

Really, this was partially my fault – well, mine and the bathroom door's. The door of the East Wing toilets always took an annoyingly long time to close, and when it finally did seal shut, it made this heavy suction sound that echoed off all the porcelain and tile.

In hindsight, that meant I had ample time to exit the boys' room as soon as I heard a girl's voice, and I definitely should have turned around and walked out when I recognised Malcolm's voice in the stall with her.

But instead I stood there listening like a creep until the door betrayed me with its big bang. The second Malcolm heard it, he'd flown from the stall, ushering the girl out with one hand while the other slammed me against the wall.

Pro tip for the physically inferior and/or socially awkward nerdling: When questioned by the big dude with the fists about how much you overheard, do not parrot it all back to him.

Malcolm increased the pressure on my skull. 'If you tell

anyone about this, you will be in even deeper shit than I am.'

Unless the name on her paternity test comes up Eli Bennett instead of Malcolm Mahoney, I highly doubt it.

But I kept the thought to myself. Even if I'd wanted to share it out loud, I was too afraid to open my mouth again, for fear of letting something disgusting in. I was so close to the urinal's deodorizing cake I was practically eating it.

A whimper of a sound escaped my lips, and I hated how small and pathetic it made me feel. But it was also effective. Malcolm released me finally and tilted back on his heels, apparently satisfied he'd made his point. When he spoke again, his tone was almost conversational.

'Consider this your sex-ed lesson for the day.' He knotted his hair with his fist, looking smaller than usual for a second, before he seemed to remember who he was talking to. He laughed and slugged me on the shoulder. 'Not that you'd know anything about that, right, Bennett?'

I managed not to roll my eyes, thanks to the newly tenderised area around the left socket.

Malcolm stood up and brushed his hands on his jeans, as if he'd contaminated them by touching me. Maybe he thought my virginity was contagious. 'I'll be checking in on you,' he said. 'Just to make sure you remember this is our little secret.'

4

'Looking forward to it,' I answered. I held up my hand in the two-finger salute I'd learned back in Cub Scouts and held it there until he stood and turned his back to me. When the bathroom door slammed shut behind him, my hand twisted into the one-finger salute I had also learned in Scouts.

Malcolm assumed because I looked a certain way – skinny and slouchy in a uniform of wrinkled jeans and perpetually messy hair – that I must be a book nerd, just like I assumed because he wore sleeveless muscle Ts and had a tribal tattoo on his upper arm that he must be a prick. The difference was, in his case, I was right.

As for me, I was more computer-nerd than book-nerd.

In two years of high school, I had barely cracked a book. And *barely* was all it took at Haver. I was acing all my classes, save one, with minimum effort. But I had no complaints about being unchallenged. I spent most of my waking hours on my laptop, and schoolwork would only be a distraction. Besides, I'd never really had the patience for reading. Some might argue it takes more patience to spend hours in front of a screen coding, but that was different – mainly because I could do it with music blaring through my headphones and Red Bull in my veins.

Although at the moment I was wishing I'd spent a little

less time programming and a little more time learning how to block a punch.

With a groan, I started to peel myself off the floor, but a flushing toilet startled me back onto my ass. I scrambled, unthinking, into the nearest stall and slammed the door shut.

I hadn't realised anyone else was in there. I'd just assumed Malcolm had checked the stalls, but no way could he miss the orange-and-blue Adidas now squeaking across the bathroom tiles.

I dragged myself up onto the toilet, half-embarrassed that this kid had heard me getting my ass kicked and half-worried he would tattle about what he'd heard. I willed the orange-and-blue shoes to move faster, to speed up this awkward moment, but instead they stopped right in front of my stall.

I closed my eyes. *Great, a do-gooder. Probably wants to take me to the nurse – or worse, he'll want to tell someone about the girl.* If Malcolm's secret got out, he'd never believe it wasn't me.

I waited for the kid to say something, but a split second later, all I heard was more squeaking – not his shoes this time but something else. I crouched down to the floor and tipped my head to see under the stall door. His bright Adidas pointed toward the sinks, but there was no running water, no pull of towels from the dispenser, only the squeak – not quite fingernails-on-a-chalkboard awful but still enough to give me the chills. Then the sound suddenly stopped, and the kid and his shoes moved toward the door.

When I was finally alone, I flushed the toilet out of habit and stepped out of the stall to check out the damage to my face. Only it wasn't my reflection I saw in the mirror. It was a smear of black marker scrawled across the reflective surface.

01000001 01100100 01110010 01100101 01110011 01110100 01101001 01100001

It would have looked like gibberish to most people, but my brain instantly clicked into gear, translating. It was basic binary – obviously just letters – but I only knew the first one at a glance, a capital *A*. The others would take me a few minutes to work out, but the more pressing riddle was why the guy left the note at all – and in code I could read. Did he know me? And if so, why didn't he help me out instead of tucking up his feet and hiding on a toilet like a coward?

Better a coward than a cliché, getting my ass kicked in the boys' room by the school thug.

A warning bell blared through the East Wing, and I was out of time for translating. I snapped a photo of the mirror with my phone, then used a wet paper towel to wipe away the message. Or more like smear it around. I only had a minute, and I had to get myself cleaned up too.

Despite the throbbing pain around my eye, there wasn't much visible damage. My T-shirt looked worse. I didn't know exactly how it had happened, but the seam along the shoulder had split and was now gaping open. I untied the hoodie from around my waist and threw it on to cover up the tear. The shirt would go in the trash when I got home. If Misty saw it in the laundry, she might mention it to Dad, and that was a conversation I did not plan on having.

Out in the hall, kids ran in both directions, hustling to their next class. I wove through the crowd, my eyes on their feet, but I didn't see any orange-and-blue Adidas.

2

A few minutes later, I joined a crush of sophomores funneling through the double doors into the auditorium. I spotted Zach at the centre of a long row and climbed over a line of my complaining classmates before dropping into the seat next to him.

'Whoa, Eli, your face,' he greeted me.

So maybe the damage was a little visible after all. Shit. I'd have to think of something to tell Dad.

'I think I just got beat up,' I said in a low voice. It dawned on me as I said it, and I felt a strange sense of pride, like I had survived some rite of passage. 'No, yeah, I definitely just got beat up.'

Zach's eyes widened in alarm. 'What? Who? Where? Why?'

'Malcolm Mahoney. In the bathroom. Just now.'

The *why* was a little less clear.

'He snuck some girl in there to . . .' I lowered my voice. 'To take a pregnancy test, and he got all freaked out that I would tell someone.'

'Which you just did,' Zach pointed out.

'Yeah, but that doesn't count.'

'Because you tell me everything.'

That wasn't entirely true. I might be shit at keeping Malcolm Mahoney's secret, but I'd gotten pretty good at keeping my own.

'Zach,' I said, pausing to let my next words sink in. 'Malcolm Mahoney is going to have offspring.'

His eyes widened in mock horror. 'Mini Malcolms?'

We both shuddered.

The shudder dissolved into laughter as the auditorium lights flickered on and off – a warning to all rowdy teens to get settled.

'I can't believe he hit you.' Zach blew a flop of hair out of his eye, and it fell right back. 'What did it feel like?'

I thought about that for a minute. Maybe I'd blacked out or something, but I couldn't recall how the actual punch felt – only the moment before it.

'Like an air gap,' I said.

'Huh?'

'Right before he hit me, it was all still and then . . . *pow*!'

'Right.' Zach nodded, because only my best friend and fellow coding geek would understand how plugging a secure computer into the internet for the first time is similar to being punched in the face.

'I should really punch him back,' I said. 'Punch a hole

right through his firewall and turn his hard drive to mush.'

My strange pride from a moment ago was sinking into an emotion closer to that time I peed my pants on the playground in first grade. I wanted Malcolm Mahoney to feel the same way. Like a worthless chump.

'Or we could change all his social media icons to big, hairy butt cheeks,' Zach suggested.

I laughed, but I knew Zach would never really do that. He had the potential to be the most skilled hacker I'd ever met in real life, but he was too proud for pranks and too scared of committing a crime. He had no problem obeying even the most ridiculous cyberlaws.

And that's why I had my secrets.

The auditorium lights dimmed, and Principal Givens took the stage to say a few things about respect and remembrance. When he stepped away, a surge of dreary music accompanied a montage of photos on a giant projector screen – each one featuring Jordan Bishop.

The memorial was mandatory for the entire sophomore class. I guess they assumed, since we were in the same grade, that we'd all been friends with him and would want to basically have his funeral all over again every year.

Look, I didn't have anything against the guy, I just didn't know him very well. I knew him the way anyone named Bennett knows someone named Bishop. We got seated in adjacent desks in first grade. It never really evolved from there. And considering half the kids in the auditorium used to call him 'trailer trash,' all this pageantry seemed a little phony.

Tragedy porn, Dad called it. And that was one thing Dad and I could agree on.

There had been a lot of it right afterward. People gathered at parks and lit candles and sang songs and cried for this Jordan guy they'd never even met. And not just here in Haver – not even just in Iowa. Misty said her sister went to a vigil for Jordan down in Florida too.

I wished Misty would go back to Florida – back to that strip club where Dad found her and should have left her.

My eyes wandered around the auditorium and spotted the TV cameras along a side aisle – just a few photographers and only one reporter, who looked bored. It was nothing like before, when big, boxy trucks with splashy CNN and Fox News logos were all over Haver. Famous reporters ate in our diners and slept in our motels for weeks. It was cool for a while, but it was also kind of a relief when they finally packed up and left – like the whole town let out a great big sigh.

I leaned over to Zach, who was not-so-discreetly texting instead of mourning.

'Check this out,' I whispered. I tugged my phone out

of my pocket and pulled up the picture of the bathroom-mirror scrawl.

He cupped a hand over the screen to mute the glow and read the numbers.

'Adrestia? What's that?'

'Hey, you spoiled it! I didn't have a chance to work it out yet.' I shook my head, impressed and annoyed at the same time. Sometimes I wondered if binary was Zach's first language. And who even needed it anymore? It was just a show-off thing to know.

'It's a message. Someone left it for me in the bathroom,' I said.

Zach raised an eyebrow. 'Say what now?'

'In the bathroom with Malcolm … someone else was there too.'

'Who?'

'No idea. They left before I could see who it was.'

A girl one row back scolded us with a 'shush,' and I waited until the music swelled before I spoke again.

'Adrestia. Do you think it's a name? Like maybe … a girl's name?' I asked hopefully.

To Zach's credit, he didn't laugh out loud, but he didn't feed my ego either. 'Sure. A girl hanging out in the boys' bathroom just waiting to send you a coded message of nothing but her name.'

'Okay, it's not a girl,' I conceded.

Malcolm had been right about one thing. When it came to girls, Zach and I had no game.

And apparently we had no tact either. Or at least that's what the girl behind us leaned forward to tell us just then.

I managed to keep my trap shut as a string of students stepped up to the microphone to say kind things about Jordan. It didn't sound like any of them were really his friends – more like nice kids the teachers picked to recite a few anecdotes about how he was a good student with a gentle soul. I cringed. This stuff was so generic it was almost worse than the insults kids used to hurl at him. And I only heard what they said to his face. Word is, the truly terrible stuff happened online. I couldn't imagine what people could say to make a guy want to kill himself, but whatever it was, it had to be even worse than taking a hit from Malcolm Mahoney.

Onstage, a girl was rattling off a list of things Jordan might have been had he lived. MIT student, future rocket scientist, world changer. *No pressure.* I racked my brain, trying to recall whether Jordan had ever struck me as a math or science genius. He was definitely in all my advanced classes, but it was hard to imagine the quiet kid in the back of the class as one of Haver's rising stars.

It occurred to me then that I, too, was that guy acing most of my classes from the back row. Maybe, like me, Jordan wasn't that interested in MIT or any other university. Just because someone got good grades didn't mean their future was ivy-covered. It was so narrow-minded, thinking college was the be-all, end-all. Zach and I had other plans. We were going to develop a game or some other app and sell it for a gazillion dollars before we graduated. We'd made the pact two years ago. We were going to get started any day now.

As if she could read my mind, the girl onstage concluded by saying Jordan's death should be a reminder to not put things off and to start chasing our dreams right now. I slumped down in my seat, wondering what dreams had gone up in flames along with Jordan.

*

'Eli.' Zach nudged my arm. 'Come on. It's over.'

I lifted my head to see students standing and stretching all around me. A tiny bit of drool pooled at the corner of my mouth told me I'd dozed off, and a scowl from the girl behind us told me I may have also been snoring.

Zach slung his backpack on his shoulder and kicked my foot. 'Time to face the doom.'

I groaned. The 'doom' was Spanish – the one subject I couldn't breeze my way through.

Acing Calculus was all about finishing homework assignments, which I did in the halls before class; internet spoilers are your friend for fudging the details of a book you didn't read for Advanced Lit; and I temporarily could cram enough facts about wars and revolutions into my brain to ace an American History exam.

But Spanish? Damn. There's just no way around the memorisation. It took more time than I was willing to spend, and it was showing in my grade. Today would be extra awful, since we were getting our vocab quizzes back. I looked away from the students shuffling up the auditorium aisles to the row of adults lingering down by the stage.

'Maybe we could stay and talk to one of the counselors ...'

'Oh wow, that is low,' Zach said. 'You're going to squeeze out some fake tears just to get out of Spanish?'

'I would squeeze Marty Johnson's back zits to get out of Spanish.'

Zach gagged and laughed at the same time, and I joined him, even though I was only half-kidding.

*

Señora Vega didn't waste any time delivering the bad news. She passed out the quizzes right away and didn't make eye contact when she placed mine facedown on the desk. I guess she was trying to spare me the humiliation, but I could see the red F burning through the page. I leaned over my desk casually, trying to look bored, and made my arm a shield so Zach couldn't see when I turned the paper.

Señora Vega had filled in the spaces I'd left blank, which was about half of them, and in the margins, she had crossed out my scribbled, *I don't know* and *I'm sorry!* notes and translated them to *No lo sé* and *¡Lo siento!*

The only English on the page was a note below the F.

See me after class.

3

I slipped out the side door after school, avoiding the parking lot where Malcolm and his thug friends would be hanging. Truthfully, I was avoiding Zach too. I wasn't really in the mood to recap this shitty day.

I pulled my oversize headphones out of my bag and turned up the volume on a song with a heavy drumbeat to drown out the after-school sounds of chatting students who hadn't gotten a bathroom beating or a lecture from a teacher today. I didn't want to hear them, and I wished I couldn't see them, either.

But then I noticed something that made me glad for my twenty-twenty vision.

Isabel Ortega.

She was leaning against a bike rack in a pink T-shirt that creased where it pulled tight across her chest and jeans that hung low on her hips.

Seriously, it should be illegal for girls to be shaped like that.

She was alone, probably waiting for some lucky guy, braiding her long dark hair in a bored sort of way. And she was right in my path.

I turned down my music the way people do when they're driving past a car crash, like somehow the lower volume will help you better assess a tricky situation. But I kept my headphones on so it wouldn't be too awkward when I walked right by her without saying anything.

Because what could I possibly say to Isabel Ortega? *I love the way you pronounce your name, EE-sah-bell. It turns me on when I hear you speaking Spanish to your friends, because your language is as beautiful as you are, and oh, by the way, I'm flunking because I can't figure it out. Lo siento.*

I ducked my head as I approached the bike rack, partly to avoid making eye contact with Isabel and partly to keep watch on my own feet to make sure they didn't do something embarrassing like trip me. Misty always said girls want you to look them in the eye, but I figured that was just because she'd made a career out of inviting men to look a little lower.

When I was safely clear of Isabel and the bike rack and the noise of my classmates, I finally slowed my pace. I cut through the cornfield across the road from school, picking my way around its tiny, new green buds, laid out in neat rows that narrowed into infinity in the distance.

If only I could put off telling Dad about Spanish for infinity . . . but Haver had a policy of calling parents when students were failing a course. Señora Vega had warned that call would be coming tonight.

'Maybe languages are not your strength,' she'd said.

I wanted to tell her I spoke a language made entirely of ones and zeros that was infinitely more complicated than her language, but instead I had just dug my nails into my palm and said, 'Yeah, maybe.'

I paused now, in the middle of the cornfield. The thought of the binary code had reminded me of the mirror message, and I reached for my phone to study the numbers in the picture.

Adrestia. I confirmed the translation for myself – much more slowly than Zach had – then Googled the word. I couldn't stop a smug grin when I saw I'd been half-right. Adrestia *was* a girl's name. Unfortunately for me, this particular girl was a Greek goddess and not so much a student at Haver.

I made a mental note to do more research later, but for now I needed to leg it home. If I beat Dad there, maybe I could intercept the call from school and delay the inevitable. I had never failed a class. I didn't know if it meant summer school or repeating sophomore Spanish or public flogging or what ... but I knew this much: Dad was going to go completely apeshit.

*

Misty was all over the kitchen when I got home, bouncing around in tiny cutoff shorts, dancing to some song that didn't sync with the one blaring through my headphones. I paused my music and pushed the 'phones off my ears. The tune coming out of the speakers on the kitchen counter was some awful chick-rock anthem with a girl cheering about how she'd crashed her car into a bridge and didn't care.

When Misty came to live with us, my life had crashed into a bridge, and Dad didn't care.

But at this moment, it was better to have Misty home than Dad.

Misty was *always* home. She claimed she wanted to get a job, but Dad said her job was to take care of me and the house, since work kept him away so often. He made it sound like Misty was supposed to be a gift to me. *Here, Eli, I got you a doll. You can call her Mom. Pull her string, and she even talks!* Too bad you couldn't remove the batteries to make her shut up.

Misty gave an embarrassing shake of her butt, spun around, and finally spotted me. She shrieked and jumped back, startled; then she let out that explosive laugh of hers – kind of hoarse and deep, as if years of cigar smoke and artificial fog from the strip clubs had climbed into her throat and never left. The coarse voice didn't go with all her tiny blondness.

'Busted!' she laughed.

She turned off the music, and the silence that settled over the kitchen made it sound like Dad was home, even though he wasn't. Things always went a little quiet when Dad got home. Until Misty inevitably filled up the quiet spaces with her jabbering, which she started doing just then.

'How was school? Are you hungry? I went shopping and got those little pizza-bite things you like.' She reached for the freezer door and pulled out boxes one by one. 'I also got some Popsicles. I can't believe how hot it's getting already. It's only April and feels like Florida in August – minus the hurricanes.' She tossed the boxes of frozen goodies on the kitchen island. 'What looks good?'

I started to answer 'Nothing,' but she cut me off.

'Oh! How was the thing for Jordan? Was it sad?'

I bristled at the way she said Jordan's name like she knew him – like she'd ever even met him. She seemed to think watching his story on TV gave her permission to be on a first-name basis. And she sounded genuinely sad when she talked about him, like she wasn't even aware she was just another one of those gross people who enjoy a tragedy.

'It was fine,' I said. I kept my body turned at a careful angle, so she wouldn't notice the redness still lingering around my eye. Then, hoping to distract her, I added, 'I'll have a Popsicle. It's too hot for the pizza bites.'

'It *is* too hot!' Misty put the bites back into the freezer and started babbling on again about the weather.

Conversation successfully detoured.

By the time she turned around to hand me the Popsicle, I had already left the kitchen and was halfway up the stairs. Behind me, I heard her voice, softer than usual.

'Oh. Okay. Maybe later.'

I paused, a tiny thread of guilt – fragile as a strand of hair – trying to tug me back down the stairs, but I shook it off easily. It wasn't my job to entertain her while Dad was off working all the time. She had to be pretty dumb if she didn't get that those long hours paid for our house and all the fancy clothes and stuff that she liked.

Still, Dad always insisted she was smart. He claimed she'd been on her way to some double-degree in Biology and Communications when he'd swept her off her feet. I couldn't imagine Dad sweeping anyone off their feet – especially not someone who looked like Misty. No offence to Dad, but skinny and bald didn't usually land the beauty queen.

The one thing Dad had was money. Not like millionaire money, but he had enough to live large in a small place like Haver, enough to impress the dancers at Florida strip clubs, enough to make them quit college and move to middle-of-nowhere Iowa.

Misty's lame chick rock started up again just as I reached my room, and I slammed the door behind me to shut it out. I dropped my book bag on top of the overflowing laundry hamper, tossed my headphones on the cluttered desk next to it, and flopped facedown on my bed, wishing the covers would swallow me up.

When my comforter didn't turn into quicksand, I dug around in the bed for the remote control and flipped on the TV.

'... *marks one year since fifteen-year-old Jordan Bishop committed suicide by fire at Haver High School.*'

A picture of Jordan slid across the screen in slow motion over blurry background video of a cemetery while some lady on TV tried her best to sound as sad as Misty about a boy she'd never met.

'*The tragedy triggered a national debate over cyberbullying and whether schools are within their rights to monitor students' online activity ...*'

Monitoring? More like spying. The internet regulations that had popped up in the wake of Jordan's death were oppressive at best and downright criminal, if you asked me. Kids could hardly post a selfie online these days without getting flagged by school cybermonitors.

Actually, maybe that part wasn't so bad. I was pretty sick of selfies.

I turned off the TV and tossed the remote to the end of the bed, but I overshot and it landed in the trash can next to my desk. Just above the trash, my backpack hovered, teetering on top of my mountain of dirty shorts and socks. Somewhere inside that bag, a crumpled ball of paper with a flaming red F was just waiting for Dad's disapproval.

I could already hear the lecture – *too much time on the computer, blah blah, every subject counts, blah blah*. And his favourite – *better to be a jack-of-all-trades than a master of one*.

Personally, I think that's just something people say when they haven't mastered anything.

I dragged myself out of bed and over to my desk, but instead of turning on the computer like usual, I spun in the chair, trying to remember when Dad's authoritarian phase had started. Growing up, he was always the fun dad – *too fun*, according to my aunt, who told him I had no discipline. Then he'd spent a few years burying me in gifts. It was around the same time he'd changed jobs and started travelling so much. *Guilt*, my aunt said. Any gadget or game I wanted back then was mine. Every day was Christmas ... except Dad was never home for the holiday.

I stopped spinning to stare out the window at the big green sugar maples that shaded our backyard. They were all over Haver, and in the fall they turned a million different shades of orange and red, so it looked like our yard and the entire town was on fire. Fun Dad would rake the fallen leaves into piles for jumping. Santa Dad hired someone else to rake them. And this current version of Dad would gladly cut them down to spare himself the hassle, if Misty hadn't begged him not to.

My phone buzzed in my pocket, shaking me out of my backyard gazing. Before I could grab it, it beeped ... then dinged ... then played a song. It was like every alarm was going off at once. By the time I got the thing out of my pocket, I had twelve alerts from text to email and on every single social media account. I clicked through them, one by one, but it only took the first few for me to realise the messages would all be exactly the same.

It was a single line, and despite the warm spring sun streaming through the window, it chilled me to my core.

It wasn't possible. I had erased all traces of it.

But there it was, in tiny text, over and over again … the same string of letters and symbols that would have looked to anyone else like a cat stepped on the keyboard but was intimately familiar to me. Because it *was* me – my digital signature.

```
/*e$b*/
```

I used to hide it inside all my code back when I was a hacker hopeful. I had since realised what a stupid thing it was, to brand your own misdeeds, but ego is sometimes louder than logic, so I had proudly signed my work much like a graffiti artist signs his – at the risk of getting caught.

And the very last time I used that signature, I was damn lucky I *didn't* get caught. It was really dumb, trying to prove myself to some of the coders I looked up to – to show them I was more than just a script kiddie relying on existing programs to navigate the internet's back doors. Looking at it now, I knew I had nothing to prove to those online strangers, probably just a bunch of lonely dudes living off ramen noodles and trolling hacker forums for kids to pick on. But like I said ... *ego*.

Ego is why I wrote a program capable of extracting personnel information from the Haver police department's servers. Ego is why I posted that private information online. And ego is why I didn't realise what a dumb-shit thing I had done.

I mean, to me, it wasn't anything that interesting, really ... just a bunch of phone numbers and addresses for Haver cops. The data was irrelevant. I only posted it to prove my program worked. It didn't occur to me that releasing the addresses of police detectives and their families might be dangerous and insanely stupid.

It wasn't until a crew of gang members from Iowa City came down to Haver to use one detective's home for target practise that I realised what I'd done. Apparently the cop had spent a year undercover with their gang and ended up putting a ton of its members away. When I published his address, I gave them a gift. Fortunately, the detective and his family were on vacation, so none of them got hit by the bullets that shattered their windows, but I was rattled by the *what ifs*.

The shit storm that followed was epic. For months, the hack was the top headline of our little *Haver Herald* newspaper, and at one point, it was even mentioned on TV. It wasn't like the attention Haver got when Jordan Bishop set himself on fire or anything, but it was enough to scare me straight. That, and the fact that I had almost been responsible for innocent people getting shot. It was a pretty heavy weight for my fourteen-year-old shoulders.

I hadn't tried a crack like that since, and two years later, I still spent some nights lying awake wondering if the police or government was coming for me. But they never did, and I suspected this wasn't them now either. I stared down at my phone, flipping through the texts and social media messages, mocking me with my own signature. I knew the police wouldn't come in with guns blazing, like they did in the movies, but I doubted they'd play games like this.

I was sure this was somehow related to the cryptic bathroom message, but I couldn't imagine who at school could have possibly found me out. Not even Zach knew what I'd done. He'd warned me against some of the shadier online hacker circles, saying players who got in too deep always ended up committing crimes. I couldn't admit that he'd turned out to be right, and honestly, I was a little scared he'd rat me out. But even if he'd finally figured it out after all this time, he would come straight to me instead of hiding behind a computer. Plus, he wouldn't be caught dead in orange-and-blue Adidas. We were Converse guys, all the way.

My thoughts were interrupted by the sound of a car in the driveway, followed by a knock at my bedroom door.

'Eli?' Misty opened the door and poked her head in without waiting for an invitation. 'Your dad's home.'

'So?'

She released a short sigh and tossed something small and circular onto my bed. It was a tiny tub with flesh-coloured cream inside.

'Concealer,' she said, pointing at my face. 'To cover that shiner.'

Oh.

I was shocked she'd noticed. There was no bruising, and even the redness had faded to a faint halo of pink.

I closed a fist around the tub. 'I don't want to talk about it.'

'I didn't ask.'

Misty respecting my privacy? That was a first.

'I'm hoping you'll tell me on your own,' she said.

She stood there waiting, arms crossed in what she probably thought was a good 'mom' stance, and I stared back in wordless rebellion. Finally, she dropped her arms and moved out of the doorway. 'Dinner's in an hour.'

Great, another *Misty special*. I could hardly wait to see

if it was burned spaghetti casserole or cold-in-the-middle meat loaf. I missed the days when Dad just brought home a pizza.

I waited until Misty's footsteps faded back to the first floor, then refocused on my phone. All the messages were from anonymous sources or dummy social media accounts. No doubt, if I tried to trace an IP address, I'd just get bounced around a bot network. Hard as it was for me to admit, sometimes hiding behind a computer wasn't an option. I'd have to be direct.

I opened one of the text messages filled with my signature, took a deep breath, and typed back:

Who is this?

The reply was instantaneous.

And cryptic, of course.

It was just a web link.

I decided not to click it and instead set up a sandbox on my desktop computer and typed the address in there. My heart beat a little faster as the site loaded, and I honestly couldn't say if I was scared or excited. The page that opened was nothing but a blank box with a cursor.

Definitely a little excited.

I tried to suppress the jolt of adrenaline. That kind of

thrill-seeking had led me to hack Haver PD, and most likely, whoever this was knew all about it – and planned to use it against me. I'd be smarter to be more afraid than excited, but as Señora Vega had all but pointed out today – maybe I wasn't as smart as everyone seemed to think.

I tapped the mouse a couple times, dragging it around the screen, but there didn't seem to be any hidden doorways – only the box, waiting for me to type. I started with the obvious.

```
/*e$b*/
```

Nope. Should have figured it wouldn't be as easy as entering my own signature.

I tapped my keyboard absently – space, backspace, space, backspace – a pattern I repeated whenever I was stuck on a particular piece of code, a problem I couldn't solve.

What about ...

I picked up my phone, searching for the photo I'd taken of the bathroom mirror. There it was again in black marker:

01000001 01100100 01110010 01100101 01110011 01110100 01101001 01100001

I carefully typed the binary code into the box, but I ran out of room long before I ran out of ones and zeros.

Space, backspace, space, backspace.

I stared at the string of numbers for a few more seconds before it dawned on me. There was a Greek goddess hidden inside that code. I put the cursor in the box one more time.

Adrestia

Instantly, the screen dissolved, replaced by a new page with the words '11PM TONIGHT,' followed by an address. No sooner had the text appeared on screen than it began to fade, and I scrambled to unearth a pen from the mess of wires and hardware on my desk. I had just finished jotting down the street number when the last words disappeared.

5

I pushed the white lump of meat Misty called chicken around my plate, trying hard not to check my phone for the 200th time. I didn't expect any more messages, but the compulsion to check was still there, like if I stared at the screen long enough, I'd be able to see the person on the other end of the connection.

Across the table, Misty had already finished and was now chomping gum with her mouth open. She always said the gum was a replacement for cigarettes, but at least if she still smoked, we could force her to go outside. And maybe I could even lock the door behind her.

'Did you like it?' Misty cooed as Dad finally dropped his fork.

He smiled. 'I always do.'

His plate was still half-full.

Misty smacked her gum in response, and Dad acted as if the sound wasn't the most annoying thing in the world.

'Eli, what did you think?' Dad asked in a voice that clearly said, *Eli, you better tell Misty what a great cook she is, because I have more important things to do than lecture you later.*

I speared a bite of the rubbery chicken and waited until my mouth was full of it to answer. 'I think it would have tasted better in front of the TV.'

Before Misty, Dad let me eat most of my meals on the couch. I would chow down in the living room while he ate up in his office. That was a typical setup for us – both under the same roof but not in the same room. He checked in with me every couple of days to make sure my grades were still good and nag me about spending too much time on the computer, but other than that, he pretty much left me alone. I didn't realise how much it was like not having a dad at all until Misty showed up and started forcing all this 'togetherness' on us.

Eating at the table was one of the things she insisted we do 'together.' She said that was the way normal families did dinner, but if you ask me, she'd watched a few too many old sitcoms, because I knew for a fact that Zach's family ate all their meals standing up at the kitchen counter in between Zach's chess tournaments and his little sister's soccer games. But Dad went along with whatever Misty said made us 'family.'

Funny, I thought we were already a family.

Apparently we were doing it wrong.

'Are we boring you, Eli?' Dad asked. His eyes moved pointedly toward my phone, which I didn't even realise I had checked again. 'You haven't let the screen go dark for more than five seconds all night. Expecting a call?'

'Probably from a girl,' Misty teased.

I flashed on Isabel at the bike rack – her clingy shirt and low jeans, her accent that lingered in the air like music, even after she was done talking. If there was any message I could get tonight that would be more exciting than the one I'd already received, it would be from her.

'A girl?' Dad winked. ''Bout time.'

Misty laughed her husky, smoke-filled laugh, and Dad's chest swelled up in that way it always did when she acted like his corny sense of humour was truly funny. I shoved a piece of broccoli in my mouth, annoyed. She didn't even sound like she was faking it.

'Is there dessert?' I asked, mostly just to stop the flirting. It was even more unappetizing than the food.

'Sure.' Misty stopped cooing at Dad and gave me a pointed look. 'We still have those Popsicles from this afternoon.'

Was that a threat?

I wouldn't put it past her to narc on me to Dad for being rude earlier. And of course, he would take her side. He couldn't seem to see how suffocating she was, maybe because he was out of town most of the time.

He worked in sales and travelled all over the country. A

few years ago, he'd spent more time travelling than usual – mostly to Florida – leaving me with my aunt a lot. And one day he came back from Miami with more than shells he picked off the beach. Apparently he'd been dating Misty for months, and he got tired of seeing other guys pawing her in the strip club, so he brought her back to Iowa where people more or less kept their hands to themselves – if not their eyeballs.

It's why I never had any guys over the house. They would just drool on Misty and tell me how lucky I was that my dad had such a 'hot' girlfriend. I didn't see the appeal at all, and in that way alone, she was like a mom.

Out of the corner of my eye, I saw my phone screen turn off again, but I willed myself to keep my gaze on my plate. Part of me was itching to call Zach and tell him all about the cryptic messages, but another part of me knew he would probably talk me out of going, and I wasn't really in the mood for that voice of reason. Zach kind of took the fun out of things that way, sometimes.

I had already looked up the address – just a house in a normal neighborhood, owned by some couple I'd never heard of with no obvious internet profiles. It all looked pretty harmless from the safety of my bedroom, but now I had to admit I was getting a little nervous . . . mostly about sneaking out of the house in the middle of the night, which

I'd never done, because I never had anywhere to be in the middle of the night.

A shrill ringing interrupted our dinner just then, and I dropped my fork, scrambling to grab my phone.

'Definitely a girl,' Misty concluded as the fork clattered against my plate.

But it wasn't my phone ringing; it was Dad's.

And suddenly I remembered what all the messages had pushed out of my head: Spanish, Señora Vega, the red F seared into my vocab quiz. I watched as Dad reached toward the ringing in his pocket and wondered how to say *don't answer* in Spanish.

Misty's hand closed over Dad's arm. 'Paul, I'm sure it can wait.' Her eyes flicked to my phone too. 'In fact, I've been thinking about a ban on electronics at dinnertime.'

Normally, I'd be annoyed that Misty was trying so hard with her grown-up rules . . . as if, at 27, she wasn't closer to my 16 years of age than Dad's 40 . . . but in this moment, I was grateful.

Unfortunately, it was one rule Dad wasn't interested in following.

'It could be work,' he said, plucking his phone from his pocket and swiping the screen. 'Paul Bennett,' he answered instead of *Hello*.

Misty started clearing plates, and I held my breath as Dad uttered a few 'uh-huh's and 'mm-hm's and one stiff 'I see' before thanking the person and hanging up the phone. His eyes were on me the whole time, and I swear I saw a blood vessel in one eyeball burst.

'Okay, look,' I jumped in before he could start. 'Here's the thing about Spanish—'

'No, *here* is the thing about Spanish.' Dad jabbed a finger on the table with a sound as loud as if he'd punched it with a fist. 'It is an easy pass.'

'I know, Dad, but—'

'High school language courses are a matter of homework and memorisation.'

'I *know*—'

'They do not require complex reasoning or excessive effort . . .'

I tuned out as the lecture launched. I tried to interrupt with my excuses, but Dad rolled over me with his fury and worse – his disappointment. As expected, he managed to blame my Spanish failure on my time spent coding, and he worked in the usual line about jacks and masters. Then he added something new to the spiel:

'I know you think you're smarter than everyone else, Eli.' The bitter way he said it made it clear that by *everyone* he meant him. 'But colleges value more than your IQ. They value hard work. If they see a smart kid failing one class, they know you're just not doing the work.'

And here was the difference between me and Dad. He believed you could have anything you want in life if you just work hard enough for it, but I didn't have to work very hard for most things at all. And maybe he was just a little bit jealous of that.

'So?'

My single-word answer to Dad's lecture pissed him off exactly as much as expected, and this time it was his fist that landed on the table. 'Damn it, Eli. It's like you don't even want to go to college.'

Bingo.

Dad looked startled by my silence, and I thought for a second that his brain might short-circuit.

'Of course, you're going to ... why wouldn't you ...' he blustered.

'I don't need to.'

Misty placed a small plate of something vaguely dessert-shaped in front of me, and I pushed it to the side.

'What do you mean you don't need—'

'Dad, Google pays someone two million dollars a year to hack their cloud.'

'And?'

'And I don't need a college degree to do that. I can do that right now. Why waste four years?'

Misty's nails drummed the kitchen counter. *Click click click click.*

'Two million, really?' she said.

I ignored her. Or I tried. *Click click click click.*

Dad was unimpressed. 'I imagine those jobs are few and far between. Anybody can be a musician. They can't all be rock stars.'

Ouch.

My wounded feelings must have showed on my face, because Dad hurried to add, 'I understand computers can be a lucrative career path, but a lot of people can code these days. It's an extremely competitive market.'

'Good thing I'm smarter than everyone else, huh?'

I grinned, but Dad did not appreciate having his words tossed back at him. His lips met in a thin line, and he stared me down for a few seconds until he figured out how to knock the grin off my face.

'I'm taking away your computer.'

'What?!' I spluttered. 'That's – you can't – that's ridiculous!'

'No more computers until your next Spanish quiz. Then, if I see an improvement, and if the rest of your grades are still acceptable, I will reconsider.'

'But it's too late for Spanish anyway!' I cried. 'This isn't a solution!'

'No, it's a punishment.'

'But, Paul,' Misty interrupted, coming to stand behind me. 'He needs the computer for his other classes. So much of his homework requires the internet now.'

I don't know if it was the way Dad chewed his lip, considering Misty's input when he hadn't considered mine, or if it was the motherly hand Misty put on my shoulder, like we were on the same side, but something in me snapped.

'Don't help me!' I spat, jerking away from her hand and out of my chair. 'This doesn't even concern you. It's a *family* thing.'

'I know I'm not your mom—'

'That's right. You're just my dad's midlife crisis.'

Okay, yeah. Total dick thing to say. But that's what happens when you have to keep all your thoughts and feelings about something to yourself. Eventually it all bursts out in one ugly truth.

I opened my mouth to apologise or at least lie and say I didn't mean it, but Dad's voice filled the room before mine could make a sound.

'Eli, that was out of line!'

'But she—'

'She *nothing*!' He exploded out of his chair, letting it clatter to the floor. 'You don't ever speak to her that way. Ever!'

My mouth flopped open like a fish, and I may have cowered a little.

Dad paced the kitchen, thundering about 'respect' and 'shame' and 'no excuses' and I don't know what else because I was so shocked to see him lose his cool, I missed most of it. Usually, he was the master of the quiet chill. But I did catch one word near the end that surprised me even more than the outburst.

Grounded.

Dad seemed as surprised to say it as I was to hear it, and the room went momentarily silent. We stared at each other from opposite sides of the table, both standing with our heads tilted in a question, as if waiting for the other one to explain what this was, this 'grounded' thing.

Dad could be intense about school and grades, but he was never really one to discipline because I was never one to cause much trouble . . . that he knew of, anyway. I would have blamed Misty somehow, but she looked just as shocked as I did. Or possibly she was still reeling from that shitty thing I said. My lips twitched now with the unspoken apology.

'Yes.' Dad nodded, shaking off his own surprise and

embracing the punishment. 'Grounded. No hanging out with Zach, no after-school activities . . .'

Because I have so many extracurriculars.

He must have seen the thought in my eye roll, because then he added, 'No TV and no computer.'

Misty gave a small cough.

'No computer for anything other than homework,' Dad amended.

'Uh . . . okay,' I said. 'But can we start tomorrow? I have a thing tonight.'

'You have no "thing,"' Dad said, his voice now taking on an icy edge. 'You have *one* thing, and that thing is Spanish. You will spend the rest of this night and every night for the next week in your room thinking up extra-credit projects and ways to persuade your teacher to pull up your grade. And not that you deserve her help after tonight, but it just so happens someone in this house speaks Spanish.'

Was that true? I glanced at Misty, begrudgingly impressed.

'Maybe,' Dad said, 'if you start treating her with a little respect, she'll work with you.'

Misty smiled at Dad with watery eyes. I don't know what she saw when she looked at him, but it couldn't be this sort-of-skinny guy with glasses and no hair and a talent for making people feel small.

'Fine,' I said, trying not to sound defeated. 'I'll start now.'

Then I turned on my heel, took the stairs two at a time, and locked my bedroom door shut behind me before he could ask whether I needed my computer for homework.

Homework was the last thing on my mind. The closest I came to hitting the books that night was when I dug the balled-up wad of my Spanish quiz out of my backpack, flicked a lighter, and watched it burn a stain into a ceramic dish on my desk. I tried to get some satisfaction out of seeing the paper go up in smoke, but the flames took me back to that day in the cafeteria one year ago. I wondered if I would ever look at fire again without seeing Jordan Bishop's outline.

When the quiz was nothing but ash, I set the dish aside and turned to my phone instead. An hour ago, I could hardly wait to find out who was on the other end of my messages, but now it seemed like the wrong night to be sneaking out of the house. I sent half a dozen texts and emails to my anonymous pal:

> Can we reschedule?
> I can't get out tonight.
> Video chat instead?

But the emails bounced back, the phony account they'd come from already deleted, and the texts went unanswered. After an hour, I sent one last message, in case there was still someone on the other end to get it.

I'll be there.

The clock on my phone flashed 7:00 PM. I had four hours to burn before my curiosity was satisfied . . . and my head possibly chopped off by an ax murderer.

I killed the time the way I always did – coding. Nothing could eat up hours like an endless wave of numbers and symbols and extremely focused brainpower. I'm sure to most people programming looked like a mind-numbing chore, but to me, it was more than lines of code on a screen. The string of characters was exploding with energy – a living, breathing thing, constantly growing and changing right in front of you.

It spoke to me – and in more than one language. There was Java, MIPS, C++, binary – though most people just used that last one to show off or nerd out, like Zach. My fingers, which had been flying over the keyboard, paused in sync with my thoughts.

I'd been keeping those fingers busy not just to kill time but also to stop them from texting Zach. Now they twitched toward my phone. It wasn't such a bad idea to let *someone* know where I was going tonight . . .

No.

I wasn't sure how much this mystery messenger knew about me, and I couldn't risk Zach finding out about the police department hack and becoming my accomplice. I'd never burden my best friend like that. And maybe a small part of me still didn't trust him not to narc.

I snatched up my phone before the temptation struck again and tossed it across the room to my bed, where it disappeared into the covers.

A knock at the door surprised me. It was faster, sharper than usual. Dad, not Misty.

Reflexively, I dumped the code on my screen, and in three keystrokes, I'd pulled up a website featuring Napoleon Bonaparte. By the time Dad opened the door, I even had my headphones on, pretending I hadn't heard the knock.

Despite all that, Dad's wary eyes went right to my desktop.

'You're not playing on the computer, are you?'

I tugged my 'phones down with a sigh.

Playing.

Not programming.

That pretty much summed up everything Dad didn't understand about coding . . . about me.

I turned the screen for him to see.

'History,' I said. 'French Revolution.'

'Fine, fine.' He twisted his hands, looking more uncomfortable than usual. 'Look, Eli, I just came up to say, I – I understand if you're feeling ... *conflicted* about Misty. I don't condone what you said, but I do respect your feelings on the matter—'

This was too painful to watch.

'Dad.'

'Yeah?'

One side of my mouth quirked up in a smile. 'Did Misty write this script for you?'

A snort of laughter escaped before he could stifle it, then he ran his hands down his face, nodding. 'Busted.'

I laughed a little too, and for just a moment, there was an echo of something that used to be – something before I turned teen and Dad turned workaholic ... before we became strangers with shared DNA.

'I'll apologise,' I said.

It was a lie, and he knew it.

'Good,' he said, nodding like he believed me. It was easier for him to pretend than to admit there was an elephant in the room – an elephant he'd brought back from Florida and parked in our house.

'You're still grounded,' he said, before leaving the room.

When the door was closed, I turned back to my computer, recalling the program I'd hidden from Dad, but the code snaking down the screen didn't hold my interest anymore. I pulled up an internet search instead and typed in Adrestia.

And instantly wished I hadn't.

My quick search earlier had told me Adrestia was the name of a goddess, but now I could see the goddess of *what*:

Revolt; retribution; the balance between good and evil; she whom none can escape.

I logged off before I could read anything else that might change my mind, and a few hours later, I was on my bike, speeding through the dark toward my date with Adrestia.

*

The glow from a small basement window was the only light on in the little house on the corner of a quiet neighborhood. It seemed like it might be the only light on in the entire town of Haver – already asleep, though it wasn't even midnight yet.

I sat perched on my bike, one foot on the pavement like a kickstand and the other still on a pedal, staring at the tiny rectangle of light cutting through the dark. Good sense told me to turn around and go home, but curiosity warned it would be agony to never know what was inside that basement.

I teetered one more moment on the edge of stay or go, and then my bike was forgotten on the sidewalk as I crossed the lawn and knelt in the overgrown grass next to the window. It was propped open slightly, like an invitation.

I took one shaky breath, pulled it all the way open, and shimmied through.

7

I don't know what I'd been expecting. An underground lair maybe? A hacktivist collective? By comparison, the two guys in front of me were both a relief and a disappointment. They were on their feet, quietly watching my clumsy entrance as I slid through the narrow window into a basement rec room, and on one set of those feet, I saw the familiar orange-and-blue Adidas.

My eyes flicked up to the boy standing in those shoes, and his face was instantly familiar, though my brain couldn't produce a name. He was a sophomore like me, and we had a couple of classes together. He was the short, skinny kid who always bounced around in his seat, looking like he wanted to crawl out of his skin. He was bouncing even now, balanced on the balls of his feet, his body pitched forward as if about to take off in a sprint.

Somebody obviously hasn't taken their Ritalin.

'You got my message,' he said. The words spilled out in a fast clip, and a smile split open his face.

'*Our* message,' the boy next to him corrected.

And here was a name I knew. Seth March was on every

academic list at Haver High, from the honor roll to Merit Scholars. His senior year was winding down, and everyone expected him to go off to an Ivy next year, though he hadn't announced which one yet. The only subject I'd known him to fail was human interaction. Word was he'd gone one entire school year only speaking Klingon or Dothraki or whatever language it is the elves speak in *The Lord of the Rings*.

'Did you like the clues?' The skinny kid asked, bouncing bouncing bouncing. 'Fun, right?'

I knew better than to expect a slick superspy as the hacker who traced my code back to me, but this guy? Really?

I shrugged. I didn't want him to know how much he'd shaken me with my own signature. 'Truth? They were a little too easy,' I said.

His face fell, and his bounce faltered. 'Oh.'

Seth stepped forward, clapping his hands together once. 'Thanks for coming. My name is—'

'I know who you are.'

Seth's lip quirked up ever so slightly. He was pleased. 'And this is Mouse.'

My eyes flicked back to my messenger, who waved.

'It's a nickname.'

Obviously.

'What am I doing here?' I asked, though my curiosity had waned now that I could see there was neither imminent danger nor gold at the end of this treasure hunt. At best, it looked like there might be an invitation to a LAN party. Behind the boys, a threadbare pool table was covered in laptops and wire tangles instead of balls and cues.

'First, we need a guarantee of confidentiality,' Seth said. 'Everything we're about to discuss is strictly secret.'

Seth's voice boomed with confidence, but it was hard to take a guy seriously when he was wearing a too-stiff T-shirt with Byte Me in neon lettering.

I leaned in and lowered my voice to a whisper. 'Secret, like, we all have decoder rings?'

He didn't flinch at my sarcasm. 'Secret, like, we could all get arrested.'

We, he said. *We* could *all* get arrested – not just me.

I relaxed a little. If anything, these guys were troublemakers who thought I was a kindred spirit. Whatever they might have on me, it didn't look like their goal was to rat me out.

'Or,' Seth continued, 'we could all have some fun – with the potential for fame and fortune on the side.'

My bullshit meter pinged at that. *Fame and fortune?* He sounded like a thousand other guys who all thought they had the next big idea. Maybe they'd overheard Zach and I talking about our app plans, and they wanted to pitch me something – likely something lame and already overdone.

'I'm listening,' I said, in my most bored voice.

Seth lifted his chin. 'You're familiar with the ACC?'

The question caught me off guard.

I nodded, surprised. Now I really was listening.

The American Cybersecurity Competition was an annual event hosted in a different city every summer. Teams of three competed to out-program and out-hack others for a cash prize. It was usually full of students from top colleges like MIT and Caltech, hoping to get noticed by big companies in need of cyberexperts. Rarely, a high school team got approved to compete. Zach and I had looked into it, but we couldn't think of another friend who could code.

Actually, we couldn't think of another friend at all.

'So, you can guess why you're here, right?' Mouse asked.

Yeah, I could count to three.

My heart hammered with anticipation. 'You need a third?'

They nodded.

'But . . .' So many questions swirled in my head. *Why me? How did you know? What's the catch?*

I settled on 'When is it?'

'June,' Seth said.

Mouse was more exact. 'Ten weeks.'

'Ten weeks?' I balked. 'But teams train together for months for that thing.'

'Years,' Seth corrected.

'Exactly. You don't just sign up on a whim.'

'It's not a whim,' he said. 'We were supposed to enter last year, but ... it didn't work out.'

A quiet fell over the basement, and even Mouse held still for a moment, his eyes on the floor.

Seth continued, 'We lost our third, and we've been looking for someone good enough to take his place.'

'And who was so great that they were almost irreplaceable?' I scoffed.

Seth met my eyes, his lips set in a grim line. 'Jordan Bishop.'

Oh.

Again with Jordan Bishop. This kid was more popular dead than he'd ever been alive.

Secretly, I couldn't help but be a little surprised that a guy from the trailer parks could code. Computers were kind of an expensive hobby.

I felt like an asshole the instant I thought it. Maybe I was no better than the kids who used to call him trash.

'Um ... sorry ... for your loss,' I muttered.

I shifted from foot to foot and suddenly couldn't figure

out what to do with my hands.

The boys let the awkward silence linger over the basement for a moment before Seth mustered up a rueful smile. 'Well, Jordan will still be a part of this, in a way.'

'Here comes the secret,' Mouse said, his bounce returning.

My curiosity dialed back up a notch.

'The competition is divided into sections,' Seth said. 'Most of it is done on-site – demonstration of coding skills, web system defences, hacking . . .'

'I know,' I said. 'It takes a whole weekend; teams are sequestered in a hotel; yada yada. What's the secret part?'

Seth huffed. I was spoiling his drumroll.

'Well, there is an off-site component every year – a challenge for teams to work on before the competition. This year, it's finding and exploiting flaws in the new cybermonitoring systems for schools.' He paused, letting that sink in.

School cybersnooping was a sore spot for all of us who lived online. Or hell, for anyone under eighteen, really. The monitoring systems were new and nationwide, but they could be traced right back here to Haver. To Jordan Bishop.

After Jordan's story went viral, the adults had gone and changed the laws, giving school districts the power to monitor students' online activity. They stripped away our privacy and freedom, and we didn't even get a vote.

'So . . . what? You're supposed to find holes in the system and patch them up? I'm not real interested in helping school spies.'

And by not interested I meant I would rather scoop out my own eyeballs with a spoon.

'Neither are we,' Mouse said quickly.

'The challenge doesn't say anything about fixing the flaws you find,' Seth pointed out.

I leaned back on my heels. My doubt was starting to take a back seat to my intrigue. For the first time, the two boys in front of me looked like real players. 'So instead of fixing the system . . . you want to tear it down.'

Mouse nodded, but Seth shook his head, his face serious.

'No. We want to blow it up.'

8

'What did you have in mind?' I asked Seth. 'You can't just hit the system with an exploit. There are too many pieces.'

The National Cyber Monitoring System was a complicated web of databases and reporting programs. I bitterly remembered being forced to register all my personal websites and social media accounts with Haver the first day of the school year. I had been so tempted to lie and say I had no online presence, but fear of getting busted had won out.

The self-reporting was just the jumping-off point. Low-level IT 'experts' spent hours trolling the web for school and mascot references, in hopes of catching kids acting out of line. When they found something, they would report it to the appropriate school district for punishment. Basically, they were paid tattletales – or, as most of us called them, cybersnoops.

'You're right, it's too complicated to hack,' Seth said. 'And if you want to try to crack any part of the system, the ACC is requiring teams to notify the cybermonitors first, to let them know it's for the competition.'

'Lame,' I scoffed.

'Totally,' Seth and Mouse agreed in unison.

'But how else can you do the real-world demonstration?'

Seth smiled. 'We have to get creative.'

'Creative how?'

'We're going to make the monitors come to *us*.'

Yep, intrigue was fully in the driver's seat now. Doubt was somewhere back in the trunk.

Seth nodded at Mouse to take over, and Mouse stepped forward, jittering.

'We're going to build a website,' he said. 'Something the snoops will want to bring down – a site that mocks the system – something very "*You can't catch me!*" y'know?'

He talked at such a rapid pace that his voice skittered a little, like a runaway train clattering too fast down the tracks.

'The site has to be unregistered, obviously,' Mouse went on. 'That's the whole point. If they can't track us down, we have a legit shot at winning the real-world portion, see? All we have to do is stay a step ahead of them until June and—'

I held up a hand to stop him. 'Two months is a long time to stay anonymous.'

'Ten weeks,' Seth corrected.

Mouse added, 'And they won't catch us – not with your help.'

I was flattered, but I tried not to let it show. I was still waiting for the other shoe. 'So, what kind of website are we talking?'

'Something to honor Jordan,' Seth said.

I wondered if the ACC gave out awards for irony.

See, the big deal about Jordan's death – at least, according to the rest of the world – hadn't been just that he lit himself up but that he'd done it because of things kids said to him online, the one place they could get away with it. That was even the slogan advocates used when they fought for the new cyberlaws: 'Internet bullies get away with MURDER.'

They'd called his suicide 'murder,' and while I wasn't sure I agreed with that, I definitely thought it was bullshit that no one had really been punished for what happened to him. I just didn't believe cybersnooping was the answer. It gave schools way too much access to us. If anyone was ever found to have an unlisted website or social media account, they could be expelled. Expulsion was mandatory if those accounts or websites included any material that could be interpreted as bullying. And on top of getting kicked out of school, the district legally had to report the whole mess to police for possible criminal charges. It was all a little too gestapo.

'How do you honor someone with a website?' I asked, wary.

Seth waved me over to the pool-table-turned-computer-terminal, Mouse bounding along behind him. 'It's easier to show you.'

We gathered around a tablet he had propped up at one end of the table. The screen glowed to life, revealing a mock-up of a website. A headline blazed across the top: 'Snoop This! A Safe Space to Sound Off.'

Below the headline, a cartoon image of Snoopy, from the Peanuts Gang, wore dark sunglasses and a Sherlock Holmes hat, while carrying a magnifying glass and a white cane.

'Get it?' Mouse pointed to the character. 'He's a blind snoop.'

I shook my head. There were so many things wrong with that, I didn't even know where to begin.

Farther down the page, a photo of Jordan Bishop filled the screen. He looked a lot like he had last year – blond hair buzzed close, skin spotted with acne, eyes squinted so you couldn't tell if he was smiling or cringing. The longer I stared at the photo, the more the background blurred, until an orange-gold glow seemed to frame his face like a fiery halo. I blinked a few times, and the screen returned to normal. Above his image, the title of the post was in bold: 'Their Laws Dishonor His Memory.'

'I don't understand,' I said. 'The cybermonitoring system—'

'He would have hated it,' Mouse interrupted.

'But it was set up in his name. Are you sure he wouldn't support – after what he – I mean, I heard some kids called him . . .'

'Welfare Rat?'

'Scum?'

'Beggar?'

'Troll?'

Seth answered with vehemence and Mouse with quiet disdain. They both sounded like the words on their tongues made them physically sick.

I spoke carefully, picking my way through this minefield. 'I just meant . . . the laws might have helped in his case.'

'Maybe,' Seth said. 'But he was an internet warrior first. He would *die* if he knew . . .'

He seemed to go mute as he realised what he'd said, and a little uncomfortable titter escaped Mouse's lips, before he slapped a hand to his mouth to stop it.

Awkward.

I swayed on the spot, unsure what to say.

Seth recovered first. 'Jordan didn't think it should be a crime to be smarter than the dipshit internet security guys working at most companies, and he didn't think it should be a crime to hack a website to prove it. More like applying for a job.'

'So ... he was for anarchy?' I asked.

Mouse shook his head. 'Nah, he thought it was wrong to share information he got from hacking.'

I bristled. Was that a reference to me publishing police emails? Was this some elaborate sting operation after all?

'But he said it wasn't up to us to draw the line,' Mouse said.

On that, Jordan Bishop and I agreed. I didn't like the morality police interfering with my freedom either, and up until the cyberlaws, the internet was the last place left where we could truly be free. Freedom still reigned in some dark corners of the web, but danger lurked there too, and by the sounds of it, so did Jordan.

Seth scratched absently at the pool table's worn felt. 'Anyway, he could handle a couple of ignorant online comments.'

The wall of flames seared into my memory begged to differ, but I kept the thought to myself.

What did I know? I wasn't winning any popularity contests at school, but until Malcolm Mahoney planted a punch on my face, I'd never really been pushed around – not in the halls of Haver and not online. I supposed Jordan's own buddies would understand him better than I could.

It suddenly occurred to me that neither of them had

been in the parade of people who stepped up to the mic at the afternoon assembly.

'Hey, if you were such good friends with the guy, why didn't you speak at his thing today?'

Mouse squirmed at the question, and Seth cast his eyes to the carpet.

'Oh my God,' I said. 'You're embarrassed. You don't want anybody to know you were friends.'

'It's not that simple,' Seth said, still not meeting my eyes. 'You don't know what it was like for him – what it could be like for us. The people who . . . There's always someone looking for the next Jordan to destroy.'

I looked back and forth between them, Mouse in constant motion and Seth in his Byte Me shirt. Yeah, these guys could probably relate to the Jordan Bishops of the world.

The question was, could they code? If their skills were half mine and Zach's, we could do some damage at this competition. Imagine Dad's face if I came home with a job offer from a top tech firm. I'd have to start practising my *I told you so* to make sure I got it exactly right.

Intrigue was about to pull out of the driveway when doubt popped the trunk.

My brain whirred. The website, while technically illegal, seemed innocent enough. But if we did get busted, it wasn't this small infraction I was worried about. What if we got in trouble, and police decided to dig a little deeper ... into my past internet activity?

Can of worms and all that.

I wanted to be on the ACC team – more than I'd wanted anything in a really long time – but I just wasn't sure it was worth the potential trouble.

'Look, I get what you're doing. I really do. But if this website is the only way onto the team ... sorry, I'm out.'

It was painful to say, and I needed to escape the basement before I changed my mind.

'Thanks anyway, guys. Good luck.' I pointed up at the narrow window behind me. 'Now should I just hop back out the way I came in or is there a door maybe ... '

'Oh, Eli.' Seth's grin reminded me of the way Zach looked when he spotted a checkmate. 'Who said we were giving you a choice?'

And now we've come to it.

They knew about me. Despite my best efforts to erase my online identity – to build up that bubble between Online Eli and the People of the Real World – I could feel my carefully crafted buffer deflating. My own personal air gap was about to collapse.

Up until this moment, they had made it sound like they were asking for my help. Now, I sensed, they were going to demand it . . . with blackmail.

I sighed. 'Okay, what do you know? And by the way, how do you know it?' As irritated as I was, I was also more than a little impressed that they'd tracked me down.

'Your signature,' Mouse said. 'I saw you scribble it on the cover of a notebook last semester. It looked so familiar, and I figured it was code, but I wasn't sure where I'd seen it, so I didn't know right away what you had done—'

'Allegedly done,' I interrupted.

'Right.' He nodded and bounced, then plowed forward, his words spilling out at top speed. 'I just knew we were the same, y'know? Like, the internet is this ocean, and we are the pirates, so when we needed someone, I had a feeling about you. I went looking for your signature online, but I couldn't find it, so I told myself, "*Think. Think.*'" He jabbed his temple hard with his finger as he said the words. '"*Think.*" And then I remembered.'

'Remembered what?' I managed to keep up my poker face, but inside, I was giving myself a mental beating. I thought I had covered my tracks so well, but if I could be stupid enough to ink clues onto my notebooks, who knows what other mistakes I had made.

'The signature was in a program I'd ripped,' Mouse said.

Here we go.

'It was the one used to crack the Game Zap network.'

Oh, that.

I couldn't help a sigh of relief. *The Game Zap crack? Kids' stuff.*

Literally. I was a kid when I did it – just a week shy of my thirteenth birthday.

Breaking into a gaming system seemed pretty small-time compared with the police department, although, yes, technically, it was also illegal.

My Game Zap code had been shared all over the web for two years before I ever hit Haver PD. After the shit show with the police department, I'd gone to great lengths to track down all my old codes and erase my signature on every website and forum where I found it, but there was nothing I could do about people who had already lifted my programs off the web and saved them to their own hard drives.

'I couldn't find it online, but I found it on my own computer,' Mouse confirmed.

So, they had something on me, but it wasn't *the* thing. I still felt cornered, but now I could see the exits.

'That was you, right?' Mouse looked awed.

I gave a noncommittal shrug.

'I knew it!' Mouse pumped his fists the air. 'So, I told Seth you were our guy, but he wasn't sure we could trust you, so I waited and watched you – not in a stalker way or anything, just, y'know, detectivelike – to see if you might be interested, and when I heard you and that guy Malcolm in the bathroom, I knew I was right about you.'

Mouse was panting by the time he finished, and I waited a beat to see if he would start again or possibly pass out.

'Uh-huh,' I said.

Because what else do you say to a guy who thinks you're *the one* because you got your face shoved in a urinal?

I spread my hands and said in my most unimpressed voice, 'Okay, you got me. I hacked a video game system. Big deal. You narc on me for that, and I'll turn you in for this. Your punishment will probably be worse with all the stupid new rules.'

'Care to test that theory?' Seth asked.

I started to respond, but Mouse stepped in – or more like stepped directly in front of me. 'Eli,' he said. 'If you want to go, you can go, but I think . . . no, I can *tell*. You want in.'

And I really did.

'Look, anything else but this site,' I said. Almost begged. 'There's a reason the ACC is asking you to tell the cybersnoops before you attempt a hack. They don't want you doing anything illegal. And an unregistered site is illegal.'

Seth frowned. 'Like you've never done anything illegal.'

'Right. So I probably know a little more about it than you,' I said. 'Guys, ask me to write you a program to get into the school district's databases, and I'm in. That's the kind of thing judges will be looking for. It's what every other team will be doing.'

'Exactly,' Seth said. 'It's what every other team will be doing. Which means it's not good enough.'

Not to mention that a panel of techno-judges who probably hated cybermonitoring with an equal passion would love to see a team subvert the system. Seth's plan was honestly kind of brilliant. But no way was I telling him that.

'You would need a lot of hits to catch the cybersnoops'
attention,' I said. 'Probably a thousand at least. Hard to get
that many clicks in just a few weeks.'

'Whatever.' Seth pretended to yawn. 'If you don't think
you can pull it off . . .'

That was low.

'You can't bait me, man. I'm not twelve years old.' Then
I couldn't help but add, 'But by the way, I could have pulled
this off when I was twelve too.'

I tried and failed to keep the *na-na na-na na* out of my
voice.

'But why would anyone click on this?' I stepped back to
the tablet propped up on the pool table among all the other
electronic debris. 'It's just a picture and a headline . . . a
headline that says . . .' I swiped to the top of the screen.
'"Sound Off": what does that even mean?'

'We were thinking of a forum.' Mouse was all optimism
and hyperactivity. 'Cyberlaws didn't just silence *bullies*.' He
threw up air quotes around the word. 'They silenced all of
us. No criticism allowed – not against schools, teachers,
other students – anything that could even be barely
defined as "bullying."'

Air quotes again. And this time he added an eye roll.

He wasn't alone in his frustration. I'd read about at
least a dozen free-speech lawsuits filed by student groups

across the country, from New York to L.A. But here in Haver, where it all started, we were more or less just taking the whole thing lying down. It wasn't that kids here had less to say, it was just ... I couldn't quite put my finger on it. Maybe since the laws could be traced back to Jordan, there was a level of guilt that kept us from speaking up. And now everyone was bursting with all of the unsaid things.

The rage and frustration and excitement we used to vomit onto the internet was just spinning around inside of us. Adults acted like the cyberlaws had somehow erased all that emotional anarchy, but it had only moved to a place they couldn't see. And that was the chaos of now.

I stared at the screen. This forum could be that spark. It wasn't healthy to keep things all bottled up. This site would offer a place to vent frustration, call out injustice, and maybe even tell a joke without fear of offending a cybermonitor. It could be a little oasis of free speech in a desert of internet oppression.

'A forum, though,' I said, failing to keep the skepticism out of my voice. 'Pretty boring.'

Mouse nodded. 'Yeah, but there's also a function for uploading videos—'

'Let's not get ahead of ourselves,' Seth interrupted. 'He hasn't agreed to join the team yet. And we still don't really know how he can help.'

I wanted to be offended, but instead of indignation I felt the tug of something primal to my hacker heart – the challenge of obscurity. Some people took to the internet hoping to get noticed; others hoped to be invisible. And it was that part of me – the part that liked to slink around in the cybershadows, all-seeing and all-knowing but never seen and never known – that spoke next.

'How are you keeping off the grid?' I asked.

'Thought you weren't interested,' Seth countered.

'Maybe I'm still undecided.'

Mouse answered, 'Tor networking.'

'That's not foolproof,' I said. 'A good snoop could still spot your server.'

Seth snorted. 'Yeah, if you're the National Security Agency – not the Haver High cyberpolice.'

He was right. This would be embarrassingly easy. But an extra layer of anonymity wouldn't hurt.

'It's still risky,' I said. 'But if you combine Tor with a VPN, then maybe—'

I stopped short as I realised both boys were leaning in, eager. They might as well have been taking notes.

'But hey,' I said, swinging my arms wide, 'like you said, I probably couldn't pull it off. Sounds like you've got it covered with your single layer of—'

'Fine!' Seth threw up his hands. 'Okay? Fine. We need you. We need you for the site, and we need you for our team. Do I have to get on my knees and beg?'

'It couldn't hurt,' I said, trying to keep a straight face.

Seth stayed standing and crossed his arms instead. 'Must be nice to have all the power.'

That caught me up short. *Me? Power?* What a joke. Power belonged to guys like Malcolm, who carried it around in their fists, or teachers like Señora Vega, who wielded the power that came with authority. What I wouldn't give for just an inch of that authority, but I was one of the decidedly powerless. Powerless to pass Spanish; powerless to send Misty back where she came from; powerless to impress girls like Isabel.

But I had somehow impressed these two guys in front of me, and that wasn't such a terrible feeling.

'Eli,' Seth said, his voice softer now, almost pleading. 'There will be a thousand guys just like us in this competition. We need to do something to stand out. It's the Wild Wild Web, and we are the cowboys of a new frontier. We have to be the fastest guns—'

'Okay,' I interrupted. 'So far tonight, I've been called a pirate, a cowboy, and a criminal. And as flattering as all that is, you don't actually know me or give a shit about me, which makes me the perfect fall guy if this goes off the rails.'

'We're bringing you in precisely so it *won't* go off the rails,' Seth said.

But that promise meant next to nothing from a guy who had tried to blackmail me within five minutes of meeting me. I worked my hands through my hair, as if I could massage the right answer into my brain.

The ACC was an incredible opportunity. If we won – which was a shoot-the-moon long shot – there were cash prizes and job offers that would allow me to bypass college altogether. I would be four years ahead of every other computer whiz who wasted time sitting in lecture halls listening to professors with a fraction of our coding skills. And even if we didn't win, recruiters from the biggest tech companies often handed out paid internships to worthy competitors.

That, at least, would get me away from my new faux family for an entire summer, if not forever. Better still, it would show Dad I was a rock star, not just a musician.

My eyes fell on Mouse's orange-and-blue shoes, the toes of each doing a complicated little tap dance. I felt the energy rolling off him and Seth – the kind of energy that came from being on the brink of something a little exciting, a little dangerous. And it was contagious. I felt myself becoming infected with it, felt myself leaning in rather than leaping back out the window.

I looked up from Mouse's shoes to meet his eyes. 'You think we can pull this off?'

Mouse paused his incessant toe-tapping. 'I think we have to try ... for Jordan.'

But not just for Jordan. For anyone who believed, as he did – despite the abuse he endured – in internet freedom.

Intrigue was flying down the highway ... doubt left behind on the side of the road.

The website was a chance to embarrass a system I loathed – a system designed to silence people in the one place I felt I had a voice. Maybe sometimes, to do right, you had to do a little bit of wrong.

It was enough to make me not say no right away, and by the time I crawled back out of the basement window at 2:00 a.m., the answer was yes.

10

My reasons for 'yes' went beyond my hatred of cybermonitoring, beyond my fear of having past transgressions exposed, even beyond the ACC and the chance to prove my dad wrong.

All of that paled in comparison to one thing.

The rush.

I hadn't felt it like this since I vowed to stay out of other people's computers. I never intended any harm with my hacks. I'd never even sold the IDs and credit card numbers I got from Game Zap. That wasn't the point. I was always just chasing the high that came with picking an internet lock. For me, it was the ultimate hack value – the 'because I can' feeling. It was my heroin.

I was still feeling that rush just before dawn the next morning, as I sat bleary-eyed in front of my computer, staring at the equally exhausted faces of Seth and Mouse on my screen.

'That's it,' Seth said, his speech slurred.

Mouse yawned. 'Are you sure?'

We'd all been too hyped after our meeting to sleep, but I don't remember which one of us was first to text the others.

I just remember we'd decided to get to work that same night. The adrenaline alone would have kept me up, even without the three Monster energy drinks, but hours later, with the sun starting to bleed red and orange through my bedroom window, I was regretting the caffeine binge.

'I'm sure.' Seth nodded. 'Torpedo all the evidence on your ends. From now on, all updates come from one computer.'

I was a little peeved that the computer was in Seth's basement, but I guess it made sense to operate from a single location.

For a second there was only the sound of keyboards clicking as Mouse and I worked to delete code from our hard drives.

Setting up the site to be invisible to snoops was easy. The hard part had been coming up with a name. We'd played verbal volleyball for an hour, with titles from Internet Avengers, which Seth said sounded too much like comic book heroes, to Snoop Shamers, which drew eye rolls all around. We'd finally settled on a suggestion by Mouse: FriendsofBishop.com.

'Clear,' Mouse said.

I nodded. 'Me too.'

Seth sucked in a deep breath. 'Okay, here we—'

'Wait!' Mouse sat up fast, looking over anxiously at something we couldn't see.

'What is it?' I felt a clench of panic in my gut, but finally, he sat back and motioned for us to be quieter.

'My mom just got up for work,' he whispered.

Seth shook his head, irritated. 'Anyway, here we—'

'Wait.' Me this time.

'What now?'

'Are you absolutely sure about the URL?' I still thought 'Friends of Bishop' was too big a bread crumb to put out there, even though Seth and Mouse insisted – with more than a little guilt – that no one would ever accuse them of being friends with Jordan Bishop.

'Yes, Eli,' Seth sighed. 'We're a thousand per cent sure.'

'One million per cent,' Mouse said. He'd been pretty adamant about the name once he'd come up with it, and for an otherwise jittery dude, his conviction carried a kind of command.

'Fine.' I gave in. 'Do it.'

Seth sat back, one corner of his mouth lifted in a smirk. 'I just did.'

The announcement gave me a jolt of energy, and I noticed Mouse, too, had started bouncing in his camera shot. We got right to work, opening the site from our own browsers, giving it the once-over. We each ran our own pen test – poking and prodding for weaknesses. After a few minutes, it was clear that FriendsofBishop.com was secure.

And then, because Seth apparently couldn't let any

moment go by without a cheesy line to ruin it, he said, 'That's a launch, boys! Let the games begin.'

He brought his hands together in one loud clap, prompting a *shush* from Mouse, while my heart hammered and a nervous grin touched my lips.

We were officially internet fugitives.

*

By the time school started, two hours later, I was a zombie. I floated through the first half of the day in a fog, and when I sat down next to Zach at lunch, I wasn't entirely sure how I'd even gotten to the cafeteria. Our table, butted up against the far wall, was populated with the usual people – a mix of introverts and sets of students whose groups weren't quite big enough to claim a table of their own. Zach and I were one of those sets.

'Wow. You get hit by a bus?' he greeted me.

'I wish,' I said. 'At least then I could sleep.'

'Coding?'

I hesitated. How would he react when he found out I was entering the ACC without him? It was something we were supposed to do together.

'Kind of.'

'Cool. What are you working on?'

The truth was right behind my teeth, but I couldn't quite spit it out. Even if Zach wasn't pissed about being left out of the competition, he still wouldn't approve of an unregistered website. Not that he was a fan of cybersnooping or anything; he just didn't get all riled up about it. Zach was a brilliant coder, but he would trade his keyboard for a chessboard in a heartbeat.

My passion, on the other hand, was singular.

And I wasn't sure Zach would understand. I decided to swallow my secret until I could figure out the right way to explain it. The truth was, I'd much rather be on a team with Zach. He could probably code circles around Seth and Mouse.

Next year, I vowed.

This year, I was stuck with the basement Goonies.

'Nothing specific. I had a huge blowout with my dad,' I said, deliberately changing subjects. 'I got – are you ready for this? – *grounded*.'

The turkey sandwich Zach had been about to devour now slipped from his hand to the table, his mouth still hanging open.

'You're joking. Does your dad even know what that means?'

'I doubt it.'

Zach and I shared a laugh and agreed that if I could still use the computer under the guise of doing homework, it was basically like not being grounded at all.

'Because where are you going to go anyway?' Zach chuckled.

I dug into my lunch to avoid answering with a lie.

*

'*Per favore*,' I pleaded with Señora Vega. I'd been begging her for extra credit, but she hadn't budged.

'*Por favor*,' she corrected me as she gathered up papers from her desk. '*Per favore* is Italian.'

'Are you sure?'

She paused her paper gathering long enough to raise her eyebrows at me.

'Right, you're sure.' I dragged a hand through my hair. 'Look, I know I've slacked off. I'm not asking for an A. Just a D – a measly little passing D – and I'll do A-quality extra credit to get it.'

She shoved her stack of papers into a colourful canvas bag and slung it over her shoulder. 'Eli, do you know what word is the same in both English and Spanish?'

'No,' I answered.

'Exactly. *No*.'

She pushed past me, but I followed her into the hallway like a little puppy – one of those annoying ones you can't get out from underfoot.

'*Por favor*, Señora. I'll do anything! I'm a desperate man.'

She deliberately ignored me, waving instead at someone behind me. '*¡Adiós, Isabela! Que tengas un buen fin de semana.*'

The voice that sang back caused me to look over my shoulder so fast, I cricked my neck.

'*¡Gracias! Y usted también.*' Isabel Ortega was smiling and waving at me.

Okay, not at me, but with Señora Vega standing so close, I could imagine it was me Isabel was beaming at.

As she drew up closer, passing us on her way down the hall, her eyes really did shift to me.

'Hi,' she said.

Simple. Polite. I could do that. Just a 'Hey' back would do.

So, of course, I did something else entirely.

I lifted my hand in an awkward wave that included an involuntary wiggle of my fingers, like a grandma might wave to a baby. '*Hola*,' I said. Except that I was so distracted by the betrayal of my fingers that I fumbled it, and it came out sounding more like '*Ooh la la.*'

Isabel's smile faded to a look of confusion, or maybe sympathy, as she walked away.

The humiliation of the moment was made exponentially worse by the fact that Señora Vega had witnessed the whole thing. She was watching me now with a smirk that hadn't been there a moment ago.

'*Mira*, Eli. There are fewer than two months left in the school year. I can't make you any promises. But if you keep – no, if you *start* working hard in class, I will consider an extra-credit project. Let's talk again in a couple of weeks.'

I managed to thank her in Spanish without butchering the word, and then scooted away before she could change her mind.

I exited the side door again, hoping for another Isabel sighting by the bike rack, but I couldn't get that lucky two days in a row. Instead of Isabel, I spotted Seth in the distance, tilted up on his toes and talking to a tall blonde. I had seen the girl strutting around school; she was the kind you couldn't miss – always with an entourage and a glittering smile that drew the eye even if she wasn't your type.

'Ashley Thorne.'

I jumped at the voice beside me. Mouse had snuck up so fast and stealthy I hadn't noticed him. His hands fiddled with the straps on his backpack as he balanced, as ever, on the balls of his feet.

'Who?' I said. The name sounded familiar.

Mouse pointed at Seth and the girl too pretty to be talking to Seth.

'Ashley Thorne. Senior. Likely prom queen. Varsity tennis champ. Evil incarnate.'

I blinked. 'Are she and Seth . . . ?'

84

Mouse laughed out loud, rocking back onto his heels. 'Yeah, right! Only in Seth's wet dreams. He just helps her out with school stuff sometimes.'

'Like tutoring?'

'If by "tutoring" you mean chasing her around school to give her quiz answers and offer up homework assignments for her to copy, then yeah, sure, he's her tutor.'

Now we were both laughing.

'Who knows?' I said. 'Maybe she's into guys who code.'

'Right!' Mouse's skinny shoulders shook. 'And maybe I'm secretly a sumo wrestler.'

'Oh yeah? What's your sumo name?'

Mouse didn't miss a beat. 'Small but mighty.'

'Mighty Mouse!'

'Nah, pretty sure that one's taken. Some old cartoon, I think.'

'That's Mickey Mouse,' I said.

'There's another one.'

I feigned shock. 'Two Mouses?!'

'Also two *mice*.' He grinned. 'Good thing we didn't recruit you for a grammar competition.'

I laughed at that, but when Mouse cast a glance back toward Seth and Ashley, a shadow crossed his face.

'What, you don't approve?' I asked.

'She was one of the ones,' he said.

It took me a minute to understand his meaning. 'Oh, she wasn't very nice to Jordan?'

Mouse laughed again, but this time there was no humour in it. 'That's one way to put it.'

I remembered now why Ashley's name sounded familiar. There had been an incident last year, right after school started, when she and some other junior girls had shredded a bunch of the incoming freshmen on social media. Maybe Jordan was one of them.

I had never connected that internet slaughter with the pretty girl talking to Seth.

'Guess she can be kind of vicious,' I said.

'She's something.' Mouse's voice bubbled over with a sudden darkness, but a second later it was gone, and sly sarcasm slipped back in. 'Seth is kind of a traitor for crushing on her, but now that he's her bitch, he's opened himself up to her abuse. And really, that's punishment enough.'

'Would he tell her about the website?' I asked.

'No.' Mouse shook his head. 'He wouldn't risk that.'

'If it's so risky, maybe we shouldn't be doing it.'

I sounded just like Zach. I supposed it was the guilt talking. That's what I got for going behind my best buddy's back and joining a team without him.

I scratched my cheek. 'The judges might even disqualify us if they consider the site illegal.'

'The ACC is more about standing out than winning. That's how you get internships – even job offers – by standing out. And Seth says this will get us noticed.'

There was something about the flat way he said it, almost as if he'd rehearsed this response, that made me push back. 'It could also get you blackballed. Companies don't want employees they can't trust.'

'No risk, no reward,' Mouse replied.

'Spoken like a true black hat.'

Mouse frowned at the implication that he was a bad-guy hacker. No doubt he believed a website subverting cyberlaws was a white-hat endeavor. 'You don't understand.'

'No, I get it,' I said. 'A real-world demonstration is more creative than just another program script, but maybe there's another way to fight the system.'

Mouse chewed his lip for a moment.

'We didn't stand up for him.' He spoke so softly I almost didn't hear him.

'What?'

He held still for a rare moment and looked up at me with huge eyes. In that same soft voice, he said, 'At the assembly yesterday. For Jordan. You were right. We didn't speak. There was a flyer – asking for "Friends of Bishop" to participate. No one volunteered, so they got some kids from Student Council.'

'Friends of Bishop, huh?'

Mouse's face was painted in guilt.

'I'm sorry,' I said, struggling for words. A second ago we were laughing and now this. Apparently Mouse's moods moved as fast as the rest of him, and I was thrown by the rapid shift.

'Don't be sorry,' Mouse said. 'Be *in*.'

'Okay,' I said, relieved to hear his voice go from whisper to resolve. 'I'm in.'

'Good.'

Mouse seemed to shrug off the moment and nodded toward the bike rack, where Seth was now alone, waving to them. 'Seth wanted me to let you know we're meeting at his house tomorrow to practise – and maybe Sunday too. We've never worked together, which puts us way behind the other teams.'

'Tell me about it.'

'I just did.' Mouse winked. 'See you tomorrow.'

'See you tomorrow,' I agreed as he bounded away to join Seth.

It wasn't until they had disappeared down the road that I remembered I was grounded.

11

Getting out of the house that weekend was going to take a special kind of personal sacrifice – the kind where I groveled to Misty. I waited until the morning, after Dad had already left for the day. It was typical for him to spend Saturdays in Iowa City on business and not return until late, which meant it fell to Misty to enforce my grounding.

'This is good,' I lied about the overcooked eggs and undercooked bacon on my breakfast plate. I forced myself to swallow and smile at her across the table.

I expected her to beam at the compliment, but instead she gave me a suspicious squint. 'What do you want?'

I pretended to be offended. 'Can't a guy just compliment the cook?'

'Not when the guy is you.'

I deserved that.

'No, really,' I said, forking another piece of limp bacon. 'It all tastes great.'

'It tastes like shit.' Misty let her own fork drop to the table. 'Come on, Eli, what's up?'

'Truth?'

'Truth.'

'I need to be un-grounded today so I can . . . study with Zach.'

Lie.

'Study what?'

'Spanish.'

'I can help you with that,' she said. *'Hablo español, ¿recuerdas?'*

Oh yeah, I'd forgotten. Or maybe I was just doubtful. Dad claimed she spoke Spanish, but he didn't know his *habla* from his *hola*.

'Did you study Spanish in college?' I asked, hoping to distract her while I thought of a better excuse to get out of the house.

'A little,' she said. 'But mostly I learned by just speaking it with people who are fluent. I had a lot of Cuban friends in Florida.'

I wondered if by 'friends' she meant 'customers,' and I wanted to jam my fists into my eye sockets to scrub away the mental image.

'So what is it, a vocab test? Verb conjugations?'

'Neither,' I said. 'Or both . . . kind of. It's like a project.'

Misty looked skeptical.

'I also need Zach's help with an English paper.'

Another lie. English wasn't my best subject, but like everything outside of Spanish, I had half-assed my way to an A anyway. Still, the fib had the intended effect on Misty. Or maybe I'd just worn her down. She agreed to let me off the hook for a few hours in the afternoon with the caveat that I be home before Dad. She looked as reluctant to give in as I had been to ask.

Guess that makes us even.

*

After four hours in Seth's basement, I wished Misty had said no.

I don't know what I'd been expecting, but it wasn't the virtual reality practise program Seth had downloaded from some cybercompetition tutorial website. Hour after hour, we looked for vulnerabilities in the fake security system of some fake company. Granted, it was a little harder than I thought it would be when Seth first described it, but it was also mind-numbingly dull. Pretend hacking just wasn't as much fun as real hacking.

It was a relief when Mouse slammed his laptop shut and declared, 'I'm done. I can't look at this anymore.'

Seth, the only one of us not bored, peeked around

the side of his own monitor. 'Let's just run one more scenario—'

'Done!' Mouse insisted.

'But—'

'Done!' This time we said it together.

Seth only pouted about being outvoted for a few seconds before he set his laptop aside and bounded over to the computer we'd designated for updating FriendsofBishop.com.

'Anything in the forum yet?' he asked.

'Don't even look,' I called over from where I was stretched out on the couch. 'It will just depress you.'

We had dropped the link to the site in all the right places online, and Haver kids had definitely noticed – the site had counted about a hundred unique hits in just 24 hours – but not a single post in the forum.

'Nothing,' Seth confirmed, slumping back in his chair. He used his feet to turn the spinning chair in a slow circle, head tipped back to stare at the ceiling for extra drama. 'We'll never get enough clicks at this rate. We've failed our friend.'

Mouse and I exchanged an eye roll. It was hard to tell if Seth's intensity was for show or for serious, but I was pretty certain he was more concerned about bombing the ACC at this point than leaving a legacy for Jordan.

'Give it half a second,' I said. 'People don't like to be the first to post on anything new. Once you get a few threads started, it will pick up.'

Mouse ticked his head to one side. 'Do you think it looks like a bait site?'

'Maybe,' I said. 'I hadn't thought of that.'

It was widely rumored that cybersnoops with nothing better to do would set up bait sites – online spaces like forums or private social spaces that seemed safe – to tempt kids into behaving badly online. Then they would bust them.

Seth stopped spinning and pounded a fist on the edge of the pool table. 'Shit. It does look like bait! People probably think the snoops slapped a Jordan picture up there to lure them in.'

Good. Maybe no one will use it, and we can dump the idea.

As much as I wanted to impress the ACC and embarrass the cybersystem, an equal part of me still feared the fallout.

'Bummer,' I said, trying to sound disappointed.

'How do we fix it?' Seth asked, his eyes drilling into the screen. 'How do we let people know it's legit?'

Mouse turned in his seat to face Seth. 'Maybe we should post more stuff.'

I shot laser beams into the back of his head, but he must not have felt them, because he kept babbling.

His fingers twirled a digital pen. 'We could start a few threads in the forum, let them know we're not snoops.'

'Yeah,' I said, drawing the word out. 'Because if you just *say* you're not a snoop, everyone will totally believe you.'

Mouse looked back long enough to stick out his tongue and show me his middle finger at the same time.

I laughed, and Mouse turned back to Seth. 'What if we posted a video of ourselves, explaining the site?'

'Um, yeah,' I said. 'Much better.'

Smart guys could be really stupid sometimes.

'Mouse,' Seth chimed in. 'I think you might be missing the point of what we're doing here.'

But Mouse was undeterred. 'Not our faces, dumb asses! We'd be in disguise – masks, voice modulation, the whole business.'

'And then people can still accuse you of being a snoop,' I pointed out.

'Oh.' He slipped down in his seat. 'Right. So no video.'

'Speaking of videos,' Seth said, snatching a tablet off the pool table and tossing it in our direction. 'Have you seen this one?'

Mouse and I, with all our athletic prowess, simultaneously ducked to avoid being hit by the flying tablet. When it landed safely on an empty armchair, I dove for it. The screen came to life as I lifted it, filled with a video freeze-frame. I knew right away from the angle that it was shot with a computer camera, and a second later, I realised I was looking at the inside of someone's bedroom. My heart hammered as I pressed play.

12

At first I could hear more than I could see. The sound of heavy grunting came through the tablet's speaker. The camera zoomed in, refocused. A guy was standing with his back to the room, lifting weights in front of a full-length mirror. His reflection revealed the face of a junior boy from school, Brett Carver. I only knew his name because half the time his face was plastered all over Haver High's social media for winning one sports championship or other. It took a second for me to realise his grunts were words.

'*There you go, baby. Yeah, big boy.*'

I cringed. 'Is he talking to—'

'His biceps, yes,' Seth said.

Mouse snickered. He'd obviously already seen the clip.

I glanced up and saw Seth was now sitting on the arm of Mouse's chair, both of them watching me watch . . .

'What is this?' I asked.

'What's it look like?' Seth said.

'It looks like some perv got control of that Carver kid's laptop cam.'

Seth smirked. 'Trust me, there's not much there worth seeing, even if we were interested.'

'*You're* the perverts?' I held the tablet away from me, feeling like a Peeping Tom by association.

From the speakers at my fingertips, Brett Carver huffed, 'Hey, sweet thing.'

Mouse and Seth burst into hysterics, practically rolling on the floor, and I had a hard time suppressing my own grin.

'How did you get in?' I asked.

Mouse, still laughing, raised his hand. 'It just took a couple emails.'

'He opened an attachment?'

'I promised hot naked girls. He went for it.'

'Boring when they make it that easy, huh?'

'Totally.'

We shared a smile before I could stop myself. I still wasn't sure why they were creeping on this guy. 'And why are we in Brett's bedroom? No offence, but he's not my type.'

'We keep an eye on our enemies,' Seth said, his voice breezy.

I paused the video to silence Brett's heavy breathing and let the tablet drop to my side. 'I'm sorry, your *enemies*?'

'Everyone who should have gone down for the Jordan thing,' Mouse said.

The Jordan thing.

Not his suicide or even his death, just … *the thing.* Maybe stripping away the detail stripped away some of the pain too.

'But what's the point of this?' I said, holding up the screen again. 'If you want to bust him trolling people online, you don't need his camera.'

'We need ammunition,' Seth answered.

I glanced down at the tablet, unimpressed. 'This is ammunition? So, he talks to his muscles. So what? I mean, it's embarrassing, I guess, but it's not that big of a—'

'There's more,' Seth promised.

Reluctantly, I played the rest of the video, eyes half-squinted shut in case I was about to see Brett's bare butt. We sniggered through a few more *Hey, good looking*s and *Yeah, baby*s before Brett finally dropped the weights and turned away from the mirror. The camera zoomed in again as he pulled something from the drawer of a nightstand – a syringe and a length of elastic. He sat down on his bed and tied the elastic tight around his upper arm. Then, closing one hand into a fist, he used the other hand to carefully guide the needle of the syringe to his inner elbow.

Holy shit.

'Steroids?' I asked.

'Or some other enhancer,' Seth said. 'He's a wrestler, you know.'

'I know.'

'And a runner and a football player. Varsity everything – but especially wrestling. It's his ticket to college.'

Mouse nodded in agreement. 'So if we ever catch him dragging anyone else the way he did Jordan—'

'If we ever even *hear* about it,' Seth cut in. 'His future? Over.'

'Poof,' Mouse said in a puff of air, then pantomimed popping a bubble.

I whistled appreciatively. 'Guess the guy better watch his back.'

Mouse and Seth nodded, proud, and I tossed the tablet onto the couch. 'That's what he gets for counting on college after high school, huh?'

Seth responded with a blank stare. 'What do you mean? What else is there after high school? College is everything.'

'It's not my everything.' I shrugged and dropped into an empty armchair, sinking into the worn leather. The more guys like Brett Carver got full rides to college, the more convinced I became that it wasn't for me. College increasingly seemed like a place for the Malcolm Mahoneys of the world to join a fraternity of other like-minded Neanderthals, so they could down beers and compare jockstraps.

Pass.

Seth was gaping at me, astounded and not even trying to hide it. 'And where exactly are you going, if not college?'

'I don't know *where*, but I know *what*. My buddy Zach and I are going to design apps—'

'Yeah, right.' Seth rolled his eyes. Hard. 'You and everybody else. Good luck with that.'

'Or I'll get a coding job,' I said. 'Who knows? But whatever I end up doing, I guarantee it will be the same thing you're doing after wasting four years and a billion dollars on Harvard or some shit.'

'I'm going to Stanford,' Seth sniffed.

'If you get in,' Mouse teased. Then he looked at me and screwed up his face, considering. 'I never thought of it that way. Most people *need* college to get a job. But if you can get the same job right out of high school . . .'

'You can't,' Seth said.

'Sure you can,' I argued. 'Coding jobs, anyway.'

Mouse tapped his chin. 'Interesting. Don't want to be a coder, though.'

'Oh yeah, what do you want to be?' I asked.

'A mahout,' he said without hesitation.

Mouse looked surprised by our blank stares and stopped

his rapid chin tap. 'A mahout,' he repeated. 'Y'know, like in Thailand? A mahout? A mahout!'

'You sound like a drunk owl,' Seth deadpanned.

I burst out laughing, and Mouse threw up his hands like we were the dumbest people he'd ever met.

'A mahout,' he said, 'is an elephant trainer.'

Then he sat back in his chair and pulled his computer into his lap, as if the matter was closed. And for a moment, it seemed like it was. Silence reigned in the basement as Seth and I each pictured gangly, fidgety Mouse riding atop the biggest beast in the animal kingdom.

A second later, we were rolling on the floor.

13

By the time I left Seth's house, I had five missed messages from Zach and three ignored calls from Misty. I knew what that meant without even listening to the voice mails. Dad usually didn't get home until after dinner on Saturdays, but occasionally he came back early, and it was already well past seven when I jumped on my bike to pedal home.

Halfway there, the sky opened up and dumped all over me – turning the road to river. My wheels cut a sharp line through the rising water as I sped toward my street. I was pumping so fast, I'd have been soaked with sweat if not with rain. I guess a part of me hoped Dad had called from Iowa City to say he was on his way and that I might still have a chance of beating him back. But that hope was dashed when I turned the corner and saw his car in the driveway.

I rolled right past it without stopping, all the way into the yard, where I ditched my bike in the mud and scaled the back porch to the little slope of roof outside my bedroom window. My sneakers slipped on the shingles, and my fingers struggled to get purchase on the ledge, but finally, I found a foothold and managed to wedge the window open.

My feet weren't even on the carpet yet when I saw Misty waiting with her arms crossed, long pink fingernails digging into the skin at her elbows, like she was physically holding something back. My first instinct was to tell her off for invading my privacy, but I was silenced by the look on her face.

'Your father is home,' she hissed.

'Does he—'

'No. He thinks you're up here studying Spanish.' Her cheeks went all blotchy red just then, and her voice broke in a way that made us both uncomfortable. 'He has no idea that you put me in a position to lie to him – no clue that you took advantage of me – that you have zero respect for—'

'Shh. Please.' I knew shushing her wasn't exactly the right response, but her voice was rising with every word, and neither of us wanted Dad to hear. I made a pleading face. 'I'm sorry, okay? You're right, and I'm sorry.'

Misty looked startled by my apology. And for every ounce of her surprise, I felt two ounces of disgust. The way she was just standing there, her arms all crossed and her face all full of worry, like she was a ... *parent* ...

made me want to puke. I vowed to never grovel to her again.

'It wasn't cool for me to cut it so close,' I said. The words were painful, scraping my throat on their way out.

'Or to ignore my phone calls,' she said.

'Or to ignore your phone calls.'

'Or to lie to me.'

'Or to lie to you – wait, what?'

'I called Zach. His mom picked up his cell. Apparently he was at a chess tournament all day.'

Your move, Eli.

I closed my eyes, wishing I had checked Zach's messages right away.

'I'm sorry for that too,' I said. But that was all I was giving her.

She stood in stony silence for a few more moments, waiting for an explanation, but the only sound was the squish of my water-soaked socks.

Finally, she took pity on me. She marched into the bathroom attached to my room to grab a towel, which she tossed at my face on her way out. Before closing the door, she turned back.

'Eli, I'm not trying to be your mom, but I can't really be your friend either. I have to be something in between, okay?'

If by 'in between,' you mean neither, then sure.

I nodded. The way she said it – all tired and sad – made me feel like a jerk, which made me rage at her for making me feel like a jerk. And round and round it went. Misty got my feelings all twisted up that way sometimes.

When she finally closed the door, I stood there in my room for another solid minute, dripping rainwater and guilt onto the carpet.

A buzz against my leg shook me out of my stupor. I squeezed my phone out of my wet pocket. Another text from Zach. I had muted him after the first few. This latest message was short.

I would have covered for you . . . whatever it is you're doing.

Shit. I was failing all over the place today. I hoped the ACC was worth it.

Sorry, I texted back, because telling him anything else would only make it worse.

No response.

He wanted an explanation, not an apology.

Normally, I would escape all this disappointment online, but right that minute, I needed a break from computers. Instead, I blew the dust off my Spanish workbooks and spent some time conjugating verbs. Ten minutes later, feeling lost in gibberish, I wished I'd gone to Zach's to study after all. I was tempted to ask Misty for help, but she'd done me too many favors already. It was hard enough to apologise to her without having to beg her to tutor me too.

I didn't remember falling asleep, but the next thing I knew, sunlight was streaming into my room, and I was peeling my face off a workbook page featuring colourful pictures of produce. My cell phone was vibrating along a small patch of my desk that wasn't covered in cords or hard drives. I slapped the phone until the vibrating stopped and flipped a switch on the side to turn the volume on. My head was drifting back toward my Spanish-workbook-turned-pillow when the phone went off again, this time blaring an irritating noise.

'Some snooze,' I muttered, stifling the alarm for a second time.

I shuffled into the bathroom and did a double take at my reflection over the sink. My cheek looked like it was covered in tattoos. Ink from where I had penned in the Spanish words for the various produce had transferred to my face while I slept. I grabbed a washcloth and started scrubbing the *manzanas* and *naranjas* off my jaw. Through the open door to my room, I heard my phone's alarm again. Except it wasn't as shrill as my alarm. Now that I'd had a few minutes to wake up, I realised it was Sunday.

I never set alarms for Sundays. Sundays were for sleeping in.

In my morning fog, I'd been silencing text

messages – probably from Zach. Man, I owed him such an apology. He wasn't a guy to hold a grudge, but I wouldn't blame him if the bitter taste lingered on this one. The thing is, Zach and I weren't just best friends; we were pretty much *exclusively* friends. Not inviting him was one thing. Forcing him to lie for me added insult to injury. I tried to imagine how I'd feel if our roles were reversed and shook my head at my still-ink-smudged reflection.

'You are a schmuck,' I told mirror-me.

I finished wiping the stains from my cheek and inspected my jawline to see if I was due for a shave, but even with a lot of squinting, I only found a few disappointing patches of barely-there stubble.

From the bedroom, my phone beeped once more.

I stripped off my clothes, now smelling a little mildewy after last night's ride in the rain, then grabbed my phone off the desk for the middle portion of my 'shower, shit, shave' routine. Once I was perched on the throne, I checked the messages.

Not one of them was from Zach.

It was a moment of déjà vu from the message bombs Mouse had sent me earlier in the week. But these messages weren't from Mouse either. They were from the anonymous account we'd set up to monitor the website. I scrolled down the list – a dozen new comments.

Comments on what?

We'd been waiting for forum activity, but comments were for pages and posts, and the only post we had up was Jordan's mug. Why would people suddenly have something to say about that?

After the list of alerts, I had a single message each from Seth and Mouse, both simple and short. Mouse had sent a smiley rat-face emoticon with devil horns, and Seth's message was just two words: 'Phase 2.'

With a tightening sensation in my throat, I closed my messages and opened my browser, my thumbs shaking as they tapped out FriendsofBishop.com. When the page loaded, it wasn't Jordan's mug I was staring at but Brett Carver's. The junkie jock and his syringe full of steroids were the new front-page stars, and above the video a headline screamed:

Haver High Hero Exposed.
Who will be next?

14

'You lied to me!'

The words were flying out of my mouth before I'd even finished sliding through the little window into Seth's basement. When my shoes hit the carpet, more words spilled out.

'This was the plan all along, wasn't it? This – this – *video vengeance*.'

They didn't deny it, but Mouse at least had the good grace to look guilty. He was shifting from foot to foot in front of me, like one of those guys who hangs out on the fringe of the dance floor, moving to the music without doing anything that could actually be confused with dancing.

'We hadn't decided for sure, when we recruited you,' he said.

'Bullshit.'

I'd had all morning to let my rage build up. Seth had refused to discuss it over the phone, insisting we meet in his basement and bypass his parents by coming through the window. I'd had to wait around for hours until Dad and Misty left to hit the riverboat casino. They liked to go to the Sunday buffet and then stay to gamble for a couple of hours. Or more accurately, Misty liked to go and dragged Dad with her. It gave me just enough time to speed over to Seth's for the ass-ripping I had planned.

'That is why you've been watching people, right? To get something juicy enough to post online?' I remembered what they'd said about keeping tabs on their enemies – Jordan's enemies. My hands were in my hair, pulling so hard it hurt my scalp. These guys weren't just coders. They were con artists. 'You knew I wouldn't sign on for that, so you tricked me.'

'You're the one who said a forum was a boring idea,' Seth pointed out.

He was leaning against the pool table, arms crossed, screens on either side of him glowing with the new entry on FriendsofBishop.com. His hair was a mess and his eyes bloodshot, like he'd been up all night waiting for us. Maybe he had been.

'Better boring than busted.' I was spitting and nearly shouting. 'It's one thing to make a site staying ahead of the snoops. But to put up a video that was obviously hacked? I mean, were you guys born this stupid or did it take special training?'

They both flinched at the insult, but I didn't give them time to protest.

I thrust a hand toward the monitors behind Seth. 'I'm not even sure we can submit this to the ACC now.'

'Why not?' Mouse asked.

'Who cares?' Seth said, almost simultaneously.

'Why not?' I echoed. 'Who cares?!'

'Polly want a cracker?' Seth parroted.

'This isn't funny.'

'It's a little bit funny,' Mouse said.

Seth uncrossed his arms. 'You laughed at the video yesterday.'

'Yesterday I didn't know you were going to show it to the whole world!'

'Neither did we,' Mouse said. 'Not for sure. Not until last night.'

'What happened last night?' I asked.

Seth glowered. 'Brett was on social media telling people our site was a fake – set up by cybermonitors.'

'So?'

Seth didn't answer, and I looked to Mouse, who stilled.

'So, he said it couldn't possibly be real, because no one liked Jordan enough to set up a website in his memory.'

I faltered. Tiny cracks spread across the surface of my rage. The hands that had been pulling my hair now laced together at the back of my neck.

'Shit,' I said. 'That's … that really sucks. I'm sorry.'

'You get it, then.' Mouse said. He turned to Seth. 'Told you he'd understand.'

I sighed. 'I don't *not* get it. But you just took this to a whole new level.'

'And it worked,' Seth said. 'We got the clicks.'

'Of course you got the clicks. I saw the bait you left.'

They had dropped the link anonymously all over social media with lines like 'Have you seen Brett Carver shooting up?' and 'Haver football hero: champ or cheat?'

'But who cares about clicks if the site goes too far to enter into the competition?'

Personally, I didn't give a shit about Brett Carver, but this video could trigger an investigation that exposed my past. Destroying Brett could destroy me too, and I wasn't interested in being collateral damage.

Seth shook his head. 'You still don't get it. This isn't just about the ACC. It's about justice. For Jordan.'

'Adrestia,' I muttered, the code word floating to the surface of my thoughts.

'Goddess of revenge,' Mouse confirmed.

The truth was there all along.

They didn't just want to honor Jordan. They wanted to avenge him.

'*Who will be next?*' I quoted the web post. 'Who's after

Brett? You going to take out everyone who ever said anything mean to Jordan?'

I imagined that was a long list.

'You make it sound like they called him a dweeb and gave him a wedgie.' Seth's voice crackled with heat. 'They *killed* Jordan. Their words obliterated him.'

He undocked one of the laptop monitors and strode across the room to me, jabbing a finger at the freeze-frame of Brett Carver with a needle in his arm. 'This guy you feel so sorry for? He spread a rumor online that Jordan was screwing a teacher.'

'Who?' I couldn't help but ask.

'Mr. Fogerty,' Mouse said. 'We think Brett was flunking chemistry, and Mr. Fogerty wouldn't give him a pass. It would have cost him his spot on all his teams.'

Seth barreled on. 'Whatever the reason – Brett and his buddies had it out for Mr. Fogerty *and* Jordan. They even did some really nasty photoshops of the two of them – fake, obviously fake, but still embarrassing. And when Jordan tried to fight back, it just got worse. The things they said ...'

Mouse supplied the word Seth couldn't bring himself to say. '*Queen Jordan, Fogerty's faggot friend—*'

I held up a hand to make him stop. It was true what I'd heard – the very worst things done to Jordan had been done online.

'Was Jordan gay?' I asked.

'Does it matter?' Seth snapped. 'That's not the point, Eli!'

'Shit, sorry. I just – I didn't mean—'

'The point is, it could have been me. It could have been you. We're all Jordan Bishop.'

Beside Seth, Mouse was nodding fervently, in time with his own manic bouncing.

'Eli,' Seth said – quietly now. 'They told him he'd be better off dead.'

Mouse stopped bouncing.

The whole room went still, and I felt like an intruder on a private, painful memory.

I still wasn't sure I fell in with the Jordan Bishops, but I did feel the tug of indignation on their behalf. Maybe Seth and Mouse were justified in their revenge, but they'd risked doing as much damage to themselves – and *me* – as they hoped to do to Brett. An unregistered website was a minor infraction. An unregistered website full of illegally obtained videos was a plea to be expelled and possibly even arrested.

'Look,' I said. 'I don't know if this whole thing is noble or stupid or both, but either way, it's a shit show.'

I pointed to the screen in Seth's hand. 'That is clearly shot from a computer cam you shouldn't have access to.

Even if you manage to keep ahead of the cybersnoops, you still have to expose yourself at the competition to get credit for the website. You want to break the law and then confess on a national stage? Just because the ACC issued the challenge doesn't mean we won't end up with our asses in orange.'

Mouse looked to Seth. 'I guess we hadn't thought about that.'

But clearly Seth *had* thought about it. He didn't even blink as I laid it all out for them.

'Forget the ACC,' he said. 'This is bigger than that now.'

Mouse chewed his lower lip for a minute, thinking, but soon he was nodding. 'He's right. This is more important.'

'For you guys, maybe,' I said. 'But I'm only in this for the competition. If you still plan on submitting this for the real-world portion ... then, I'm sorry, I'm out.'

I hated giving up the chance to compete, and I was surprised to realise it also bummed me out that I'd be giving up the next few Saturdays in Seth's basement. After yesterday's session, I was kind of looking forward to spending my weekends with this new crew.

'Is this really any worse than the Game Zap crack?' Seth asked in earnest. 'I'll bet that's not even the half of it. Come on, Eli. What else have you done?'

He said it in awe, but it somehow still sounded like a threat. He had no idea how right he was.

'You can't be out,' Mouse said. 'We need three to compete!'

'Fine, then take down the video and put up something else,' I begged.

'I have this other video,' Mouse started. 'Of a guy—'

'That's not what I meant.'

Seth ticked his head to one side. 'I'll make you a deal.'

'What's that?'

'You stick with us, and we'll take the video down.'

'Fine. Great! That's all I—'

'*Waaaait.*' He dragged out the word, annoyed by my interruption. 'I still think videos are the key to getting clicks. And clicks are what will make the website a worthy entry for the ACC.'

He paused as if expecting me to concur. When I stayed stubbornly silent, he went on. 'So we'll agree not to hack any more computer cameras, if you agree to help us find videos another way.'

'And how am I supposed to do that?'

Seth smirked. 'Aren't you supposed to be some sort of genius? I'm sure you'll figure it out.'

I stared at him for a long moment. I had no idea what kind of videos he had in mind or how I was supposed to get them, but maybe if I stayed on the team, eventually I could change their minds. I just had to stall them for a bit.

'Fine,' I said.

'Yes!' Mouse pumped a fist in the air.

'But if *one more* video goes up that I think could get us in trouble, we burn the site down and think of another entry for the ACC.'

'Sure, whatever.' Seth waved a dismissive hand. 'Go ahead and write a backup entry – some generic program for hacking school cyberdatabases or whatever boring thing you suggested the other day. We don't need it, and you'll help us with the site no matter what.'

'Why do you say that?'

'Because,' Mouse said. 'You're our accomplice now.'

His face broke open in a grin, and he gripped my shoulder in such a buddy way that 'accomplice' managed to sound a lot like 'friend.'

15

'I knew this name was going to come back to haunt us,' I said, pointing to the URL at the top of the screen.

I was in a swivel chair at the end of the pool table, in front of our designated computer for FriendsofBishop. com, flanked by Seth and Mouse. They peered over my shoulders at the website, looking unconcerned.

'We can't be totally anonymous,' Mouse said. 'We want the people who hurt Jordan to know: We're watching.'

The words would have been powerful if Mouse hadn't punctuated them by pointing two splayed fingers first at his own eyeballs and then at the computer.

'We're putting assholes on alert,' Seth agreed. 'The people you're pushing around have friends. Jordan Bishop had friends. And they're coming for you.'

Brett Carver had friends too, and they had made that clear on the website. Most of the comments under his video were from 'Friends of Brett,' calling 'Friends of Bishop' cowards and assholes. One message, which I suspected was from Brett himself, even questioned the size of our anatomy.

But there were other comments too. 'I am Jordan 2' called Brett a cheat who deserved to be taken down; 'Anon11' hoped we didn't get busted; and 'Victim of Brett' gave a detailed account of how Carver and his cronies had humiliated him during a wrestling weigh-in.

So much for anonymity.

Even though I hadn't posted the video, I felt a small swell of pride that the post had given silenced kids a place to speak up.

'This is the one I wanted you to see,' Mouse said, pointing out a comment at the very bottom of the screen. 'It came in just before you got here.'

I leaned in to read what 'Friend of a Friend' had to say. The comment was a simple question: *How do I submit my video?*

'What video?' I asked.

'We don't know,' Seth said. 'But we want to find out. What if it's something good on one of the other douchebags who hated on Jordan?'

'And what if it's a video of someone you're not even after?' I countered.

'That's fine too,' Seth said.

I craned my neck to frown at him. 'What do you mean? I thought this was all about your great revenge.'

'Justice,' Seth corrected. 'Not revenge.'

'Whatever. It's some vigilante shit.'

'Well, what if it was more than that?' Seth took a long breath and shared a side glance with Mouse. 'What if we could save the next Jordan? Everybody's got a Brett. Even you, Eli.'

I scrolled back up to the video. 'I don't have a Brett.'

'He's got a Malcolm Mahoney,' Mouse said.

I cringed, remembering how Mouse had witnessed my bathroom humiliation. But this wasn't Malcolm. This was some guy I didn't know. And maybe he was an even worse guy than Malcolm, but his crimes had nothing to do with me.

'I don't know if I'm into playing judge and jury for everyone at Haver,' I said. 'But I don't hate the idea of sourcing video from other people. Let them do the dirty work . . . instead of lurking inside people's bedrooms.'

'Why you gotta make it sound so creepy?' Mouse complained.

I raised my eyebrows in response, and he shrugged. 'Okay, yeah, you're right.'

'So, how do we contact this person?' Seth asked.

I tapped the keyboard, thinking.

Space, backspace. Space, backspace.

It was possible to hunt down the IP associated with the comment, but it was risky too. The comment could be bait left by a cybersnoop who *wanted* us to come looking. And even if we tracked them down, it was just one person – one video. Hardly enough material to keep the website going.

I sat upright, shot through with the energy of a new idea, and perched on the edge of my seat. My fingers hovered over the keyboard – humming with anticipation.

'We don't contact them. They contact us.'

I started keying in code as I thought out loud.

'We'll need an untraceable email ...'

Space, backspace. Space, backspace.

'... and an extra layer of anonymity ...'

My fingers and brain raced to see which could stay ahead of the other.

'... and a response form.'

Seth and Mouse leaned in, watching me work, and Mouse read over my shoulder as I typed up a new page for our site.

'Tired of being a victim? Need a little justice? Friends of Bishop are friends of yours!

Send us your story and the video clip you want us to share. All entries are anonymous.'

He paused. 'Um ... Eli, I thought you said ...'

'You want more videos, right? Let's see what's out there without worming into people's computers. This saves us from breaking any laws ... or, any *more* laws.'

I didn't take my eyes off the screen, but in the reflective surface, I saw Seth and Mouse exchange a small smile. They thought this meant I was on board. In truth, they just didn't know how good their dirt on me really was. If I wasn't there to help cover their asses, they were much more likely to get busted ... which meant *I* was more likely to get busted too. It was a chain reaction that could lead from Friends of Bishop to Game Zap and all the way to the police department job, no matter how well I covered my tracks. I was their accomplice now, after all. I had to stay involved, for my own security.

That's what I told myself as my lines of code filled the screen.

I sank into the familiarity of it – my fingers, the keys beneath them, the letters and numbers blending together. It was a dance, and I knew all the steps by heart. When I coded, the outside world went just a little bit quiet. Voices muted, colours faded. Seth and Mouse disappeared from my peripheral vision, and even the computer seemed to blur into nonexistence. It was just me and the code.

I vaguely heard the guys whispering as they watched me work, their voices hushed with awe. I may or may not have added a little flourish for their benefit, but I resisted the urge to build my signature into the code. It was enough to show off for my audience of two.

The more I worked, the more I realised it wasn't just the coding I was enjoying. The deeper truth was that I liked the idea of putting people like Malcolm Mahoney on alert and watching cybersnoops chase their tails. There was poetry in it – taking down the Haver High slime by subverting the very system that was created, and had yet failed, to keep them in check. And I could be a part of it.

All I had to do was ruin a few lives and break a few laws ... *again*.

My phone beeped at some point, and I was so caught up in my code, I half expected it to be someone contributing a video already. Instead, it was a text message from Zach – a simple question mark. He was waiting for an explanation for last night, and I still hadn't figured out what to tell him. With a little bit of guilt, I ignored the text and pocketed my phone. I could always find him later. He spent his Sundays watching the old guys play chess in the park – a spectator sport only Zach could truly appreciate. The image of the stone chessboards built into the park gave me an idea.

On the front page of the website, I spent a couple of minutes tinkering with the headline. Instead of 'Friends of Bishop,' I replaced the name with a picture of a bishop chess piece. Then I returned to the response form and added three lines.

The kings and queens of Haver High took out our Bishop.

But this game's not over yet.

Your move.

16

'Eli, you did not do that.'

'I swear, I did.'

Zach buried his face in his hands. 'What were you thinking?'

'I wasn't thinking at all, obviously!'

'You really wiggled your fingers at her?'

'And said, "*Ooh la la*."'

Zach groaned, and I sank down in my chair. 'I know!'

As humiliating as it was to recap my Isabel encounter, I was grateful that Zach was still speaking to me, and that we had the din of the cafeteria to drown out our conversation, so no one else could overhear.

Part of me had been surprised to find him at our lunch table on Monday, across from an empty seat that I hoped was still mine. I had paused behind the blue plastic chair, eyes on Zach, whose eyes were on his lunch. But I could tell by the way he broke his chips into tiny pieces instead of eating them that he sensed my presence without looking up. The conversation that followed had gone something like this:

'Hey,' I said.

A pause.

'Hey.'

'Look, I'm sorry. I shouldn't have put you in that position. I had no idea she'd call you. She's so lame.'

No response. Two more potato chips turned to dust.

'And I should have answered your texts or called or just come over or . . .'

The words spilling out of my mouth weren't the ones Zach wanted to hear, and I knew it, but I couldn't tell him about my new extracurricular activities.

'I was on my bike all day,' I said. 'Being grounded blows. I needed to get out of the house – away from Misty and all her bubbly bullshit.'

The best lies were half-truths.

'And I turned the ringer down on my phone in case she called—'

Zach kicked the chair out with his foot, and I sat down, grateful.

When he finally looked up, I stared him right in the eye and told the absolute truth.

'I'm sorry.'

He forgave me with a shrug and brushed the potato chip crumbles from his hands. 'I won my tournament.'

'Naturally.'

'The last game took less than twenty moves. The guy totally forgot to castle. His king was just hanging out there committing suicide ...'

I smiled as Zach rattled off his play-by-play, and soon I was recapping my Isabel encounter for his amusement.

'You realise you're going to die a virgin, right?' he said.

I flung a french fry at him. 'Say it a little louder. The guys in the kitchen didn't hear you.'

'The guys in the kitchen can't hear anything through their hairnets.'

We laughed, and for a moment it almost felt like the weekend had never happened ... *almost*.

Zach didn't know it, but everything I hadn't told him – about Seth and Mouse and the website and the ACC – had created a bubble between us. Like a computer never connected to the internet or Malcolm's fist not quite reaching my face, the bubble was another air gap, isolating me from the rest of the world in order to protect my secrets.

*

The first video came in that afternoon. Less than five seconds after the alert hit my phone, I had a message from Seth summoning us to a basement meeting after school. For security, we'd agreed to only view site submissions from a designated Friends of Bishop computer, so if I wanted to see it, I had to show up. And since this whole grounding thing still wasn't very clear, Misty said it was fine to go as long as I was home in time for dinner. I was pretty sure I'd heard a sigh of relief in her voice. One less hour spent with awful Eli.

Well, right back at ya.

By the time Mouse and I dumped our backpacks on the ratty basement couch, there were more videos ... and even more emails.

'Anything good?' I asked.

Seth was positioned at the end of the pool table, face lit up by the screen glowing in front of him. His mouth turned up in a hint of a smile. 'Oh yeah.'

Most of the messages were from people claiming *boy X* cheated on *girl Y* or *so-and-so* stole liquids from the chem lab to get high, with no evidence to back it up. But two or three people had managed to provide some video support for their claims, and at least one of them was usable.

Seth opened that video as Mouse and I crowded around to watch. It looked like it had been covertly shot with a cell phone in the halls of Haver. A redheaded girl I didn't recognise could clearly be heard calling her Calculus teacher a bitch and her Advanced Biology teacher something even worse.

I waited for more, but the video stopped a few seconds later.

Mouse clapped his hands together once and did a little dance. 'Jackpot!'

I shrugged. 'What's the big deal?'

'*Who* is the big deal,' Seth corrected.

'Yeah, still not getting it.'

Mouse stopped dancing around and aimed a finger at the redhead on the screen like a gun. 'That lying wench got Jordan banned from three different social sites. Claimed he was stalking her. Then she spread that rumour all over the sites he was banned from, so he couldn't even defend himself. I mean, she *wishes* someone would stalk her, the ugly troll.'

He fired his imaginary gun, and I sensed it again – the darkness below the surface. Maybe it was why Mouse moved around so much. If he held still too long, the darkness might just seep out and swallow him up.

I crossed my arms. '*Was* he stalking . . .'

'No!' Seth said. 'She just made it up to get attention. Damn, Eli. You're the reason rumors like that spread in the first place – people believing the bullshit they read online.'

'Okay, fine. She's a liar who deserves a spot on our wall of shame. But I don't see what's so bad about this video. Everyone talks shit about their teachers.'

'Not her,' Seth said. 'At least no one *thinks* she does. You probably don't know her, because she's a senior like me, but she's the biggest kiss-ass in my grade. She practically genuflects before teachers.'

'So?' I said.

'So she asked those teachers to write her recommendations for Yale. I wonder what kind of letters they'll write after they see this.'

There was a gleeful tone to Seth's voice, and I got the feeling his joy was about more than justice for Jordan.

But I had no love for anyone who made up stories to get people blackballed online. I didn't like seeing people abuse the internet that way – making it a place of exclusion instead of inclusion. There was enough of that garbage going on at school.

'No objections here,' I said.

'Post it,' Mouse agreed.

A few keystrokes later, the redhead had taken over the top spot on Friends of Bishop under the headline 'Haver High's Vicious Valedictorian.'

'It's good,' Seth said. 'But it's not Brett-Carver-shooting-steroids good. It won't get us to our user goal. What if we don't get any more videos?'

'I have more,' Mouse said.

But the clip he had in mind was another one from Brett's

bedroom, and Seth and I vetoed it almost immediately. Besides the fact that I wanted to avoid any more hacked videos, this one in particular seemed like a bad idea. It featured Brett and one of his buddies bragging about all the girls they'd 'banged.'

'That would be way more embarrassing for the girls they're talking about than the dudes,' Seth said.

I agreed. 'If we ever get busted for this, I don't want a bunch of pissed-off chicks after us. I don't know about you guys, but I'm not looking to give girls more reasons to turn me down.'

'Preach,' Mouse said, throwing up a fist. 'We leave the ladies alone.'

I pointed to the video. 'Except this one?'

'She's no lady,' Mouse said.

'So, what are the criteria?' I asked. 'Who gets a post, and who gets a pass?'

'Anyone who tortured Jordan, for starters,' Seth said.

'And anyone *like* them,' Mouse added.

Seth rocked his swivel chair from side to side. 'Plus, it just depends on how good the video is. It has to be click-worthy.'

'Whatever,' I said. 'As long as the videos keep coming from somewhere else. We can defend the site as free speech, but we'll have a hard time explaining why we're hanging out in people's bedrooms.'

I looked pointedly at Mouse. 'It's not just illegal. It's also way pervy.'

His hands flew up. 'Fine. I'll kill the connection. I'm not trying to spend my summer behind bars. But you better hope we get some legit submissions.'

As if in response, a small *ding* from the computer speakers alerted us to yet another email.

I smirked. 'I don't think it will be a problem.'

17

We had created a monster. An itty-bitty, baby monster – mostly harmless – but a monster nonetheless. And the thing about monsters is they grow into something with teeth and rage, something too big to control. I had a sense of it in the beginning, the smallest notion that this could become too big for us, but like the mother of any monster, I loved it despite the danger.

That danger was palpable the next day at school. The video of Brett had been one thing – the work of a hacker with an agenda – but a cell phone recording from inside our own walls? That was something else entirely.

I could hardly believe my ears when I stepped onto campus and heard kids talking about Friends of Bishop ... or more like whispering. The halls of Haver High had gone oddly quiet, with students speaking in hushed voices whenever they discussed the site, as if they could get in trouble just for watching it. Or maybe they were afraid to be heard talking about anything at all – in case someone was recording them. Every cell phone pulled from a pocket got a suspicious glance, every private conversation required a check around for eavesdroppers.

And still the emails were streaming in. Practically overnight, our website had become a portal to internet freedom – a place for people to unload, to tell their truths, to get their revenge. Granted, most of that truth and revenge was bottled up in our email account and would never make it onto the site, but kids were reaching out anyway – desperate for an oasis in this desert of strict new rules that silenced students.

This guy has a clip of kids smoking a bong on the baseball field. That guy has a blurry video of two teachers making out in the staff break room. Sometimes the motivation for payback was clear, like a girl wanting to out her boyfriend for giving her crabs. Sometimes it just seemed like straight-up mean shit.

The latter reinforced my lack of faith in mankind ... or Haver-kind, at least. I had to wonder if school cybermonitoring laws really did keep a lot of evil stuff off the internet.

On the other hand, I could sense the desperation in some of the messages ... from kids who would always be targets, with or without the internet – kids pushed around in locker rooms or tortured when teachers weren't paying attention, kids ignored until they went silent or mistreated until they turned bitter and angry.

The truth was there in the emails and in the whispers around school – Seth had been right. What we were doing was bigger than the ACC – maybe even bigger than showing up the cybersnoops. We'd turned on a little light in the darkness. The Jordan Bishops of the world were still out there, and we had just given them a voice.

The thought had me walking taller, holding my head higher, instead of shuffling around with my eyes on my feet . . . which is probably why I noticed Isabel at her locker as I rounded a corner into the South Wing. Most kids had already scooted off to their first period, so the hallway was practically empty.

This was my chance for a 'hello' do-over. I didn't even have to speak. I could just lift my hand in a quick wave – no finger wiggling this time – and mosey on by. More mysterious that way.

Isabel's body turned ever so slightly in my direction.

I veered hard to the left and buried my face in a drinking fountain.

Smooth.

The fountain was on a corner at the junction of two hallways, and while Isabel dug for something in her locker to my right, a trio of girls gathered outside a classroom to my left – Ashley Thorne at their centre. Her voice carried in the now deserted hallway.

'I mean, I'm not saying any of them are copycats or anything, but I just think it's a little coincidental that two years after I started Pretty Pouty, suddenly five other girls from Haver have their own beauty vlogs.'

Ashley's friends droned their assent, and she continued. 'Not that any of them have as many followers as me, so we're not in competition or anything, but still.'

'Isabel Ortega has a lot of followers,' one of the other girls spoke up.

I choked on the water, some of it dribbling down my chin. I released the button to stop the flow, but I stayed hunched over the fountain, afraid to move. In my peripheral vision, I could see Isabel had gone still, listening. Around the corner, in the other hallway, Ashley went on, oblivious.

'She is definitely not competition. No offence, but the palettes she uses are all clown colours. No subtlety.'

'She's good at contouring,' the other girl said, then rushed to add, 'I mean, if you're into that.'

'Oh, totally!' Ashley said, her voice all patronizing generosity now. 'She's awesome with a brush. I just mean the make-up she uses is limited. It's not her fault. It's that dark complexion.'

I heard a soft huff to my right and dared to turn my head. Isabel was looking right at me. We locked eyes in a silent conversation. She knew that I knew that she knew they were talking about her. And the only thing more awkward than that was the fact that I was still bent over a now dry water fountain. I moved to turn it on again – anything was better than standing up and drawing attention to myself just then – but Isabel shook her head at me. She wanted to hear, and the fountain would be too loud.

My hand froze over the button; my back ached. I vowed to never walk this particular hallway ever again. Girls were scary.

'I'm not racist or anything,' Ashley explained to her friends, who jumped to reassure her she wasn't. 'But you can only use so many colours on brown skin. It's very limiting for the audience.'

A teacher called from inside the classroom next to Ashley, and she and her friends disappeared through the doorway. I stood up finally, stretching my spine. Isabel's eyes were still locked on me, as if daring me to agree with Ashley and company.

All I'd wanted to do was wave, but now I found myself easing over to Isabel's locker and saying, 'Wow. Jealous much?'

It made my whole world to see her face break open in a smile.

'Thanks.'

'Seriously, she's obviously really insecure.' I was on a roll. 'Nobody cares what she thinks.'

Isabel's eyes were watery, but she kept smiling as she closed her locker. 'A lot of people care, actually. She has a ton of followers. Her opinion matters.'

'Not to me.'

Knocked it out of the park.

'Then you're not paying attention,' Isabel said.

Foul ball.

'You might not like her,' Isabel said, backing away down the hall. 'But her popularity here at school is totally irrelevant. All that counts is who you are online.'

I couldn't disagree with that, but when I opened my mouth to tell her so, she had already turned to walk away.

I raised my hand in a wave she couldn't see.

18

Hours later, I realised I should have whipped out my cell phone to record Ashley's 'not racist' rant. While everyone else was looking over their shoulder, she was oblivious to the threat of being caught on camera. Or maybe she just thought nobody would dare. The idea irritated me. What good was it raising a monster if it couldn't sharpen its fangs on people like Ashley Thorne, who shit all over people like Isabel Ortega?

I had Isabel and Ashley on the brain the whole bike ride home, and since thinking about girls tends to take up all my available gray matter, I almost didn't notice when I rolled up to the house that Dad's car was in the driveway. And I definitely didn't notice him standing in the front yard under our giant maple tree – bigger than all the ones out back.

'Eli!'

I dragged a foot to stop but stayed perched on my bike, blinking at him like he was just a mirage – which wasn't that far off. It was so rare to see Dad home this early, he might very well have been an illusion or trick of the mind.

When he called my name again and waved me over, I

decided he was real and let my bike fall to the concrete. He was hovering between the thick trunk of the maple and the bench parked beneath it – the one we treated like a gravestone.

Dad claimed my mom liked to sit there for hours, just thinking, but I always thought that sounded like a phony memory, because who likes to sit under a tree doing nothing? If that was true, my mom had been pretty boring. I wouldn't know. I couldn't remember her.

'Have a seat,' Dad said.

I stayed standing. Sitting on the 'mom' bench always made me feel uncomfortable, especially when Dad was watching. His eyes would get sort of sad, and he'd look at me as if he expected something – I don't know what – to happen.

When I didn't sit, he dropped onto the bench himself. He was in his jogging shorts and one of those tight nylon-looking shirts that cyclists always wore. It was bright orange and black and not Dad's style at all. It looked like something Misty had picked out on one of her 'we all need to be exercising' kicks.

'No suit today?' I asked.

'Took the day off.'

'You never take a day off.'

'Misty asked me to.'

Unless Misty asks you to.

'She's been feeling a little down,' Dad said. 'It's what I wanted to talk to you about.'

He gave me a sharp look that silenced my groan before I even got it out.

'You really let her down, Eli.'

So, she had narced on me after all.

What a snake. A guy comes home late one time . . .

'She's so disappointed you don't want her help with Spanish.'

Oh, is that all?

I sat on the bench, finally, so that Dad wouldn't notice the relief on my face. 'Zach can help me,' I said. 'With Misty it's just too . . . too much, I guess.'

'She does have a strong personality.' Dad pulled at the front of his black-and-orange shirt.

'You look like a jack-o'-lantern,' I told him.

He laughed for the briefest moment, then rubbed a hand down his face, wiping the smile away. 'The thing is, she's trying. And that's all I'm asking you to do with her. Try. Make an effort, okay?'

I hated it when adults said things like that. What did it even mean?

'An effort to do what?'

'Just be kinder. Make her feel more welcome – more – more—'

'More like my mom?'

'I didn't say that.'

'Because that's a pretty messed-up thing to ask,' I said.

'I didn't—'

'Especially on *this* bench.'

'That's enough!'

And it was. Enough. The bench thing had been a low blow. We both knew it meant more to Dad than to me. But if he missed my mom so much, maybe he shouldn't be trying to shove a new one down my throat.

He sighed. 'Eli, remember when we were buds?'

'Yeah,' I huffed. 'I remember. Back when you took days off for *me* instead of *her*.'

I waited for him to contradict me or promise to take another day off or just argue in some way. Instead, a cold silence filled the space under the sugar-maple branches. I swallowed the lump forming in my throat. A reassuring lie would have been better than this – this quiet confirmation that Misty came first. For Dad, she hadn't just replaced Mom. She'd replaced me.

I gave him one more second to tell me I was wrong, and then I left him sitting there on the bench that apparently didn't mean anything anymore.

*

I managed to avoid Dad and Misty for the rest of the night with homework excuses while holed up in my room, video-chatting with Seth and Mouse and marveling at the activity on Friends of Bishop.

'Twenty-three new comments,' Seth said, reading from his own screen.

'Just today?' I asked.

'Just in the last two hours.'

I whistled.

'Did you post it yet?' Mouse asked Seth.

'It's still uploading.'

My stomach tightened in anticipation. If the cybersnoops weren't paying attention to us already, they would be after this. It was one thing to set our sights on students, but tonight we were taking on a teacher. Our latest video featured Mrs. Windemere, Freshman Biology, loading up a shopping cart full of booze. No big deal, if she was planning a party or something. But the grocery store's security footage showed her taking a big swig from one of those bottles and stashing it in her bag.

'Who sent us this one?' I checked our emails and answered my own question. 'Anonymous. I wonder how they got it.'

Mouse waved a hand. 'Easy. I know like six kids from school who work there.'

'And I can name a hundred who hate Mrs. Windemere,' Seth said.

'A hundred and one,' I agreed.

I'd never met a meaner teacher and always wondered why someone like Windemere went into education when she clearly hated kids.

'Okay, it's done,' Seth said. He smiled into the camera. 'And so is she.'

Mouse yawned. 'Let's do the rest tomorrow.'

We decided to finish filtering through our emails later and signed off.

Only a few of those emails were actual video submissions, but we had plenty of requests from people hoping we would hack their enemies. Everyone at Haver had a story to tell about someone who had pushed them around, beat them down, or generally pissed them off. And even though we'd sworn not to hack anyone else, I was sorely tempted after reading some of the stories.

But most of the claims couldn't be confirmed. Some kids wanted revenge for cruelty that stretched all the way back to first grade. Others were still holding grudges about rumors spread online that had long been erased.

It was funny how the internet worked. When you wanted a rumour to go away, it was everywhere; when you went looking for it, it was impossible to find, if you didn't know exactly where to search. It's why parents were so clueless and why cyberlaws had been their only solution.

Even a guy like me, who knew his way around the web, had a hard time finding things. I couldn't even track down evidence of what had happened to Jordan online. His cyberfeud with the redhead now starring on our site had faded into internet oblivion, and the rumors about him and Mr. Fogerty must have spread through Chat Mob – one of those mobile group chat rooms that disappeared as soon as people closed the app.

Chat Mob had been shut down, along with Snapchat and a bunch of other apps, during the first phase of the cybermonitoring setup. And now it looked like Friends of Bishop had become the new spot for group chat. Except ours didn't disappear, which meant these kids were counting on us staying ahead of the cybersnoops.

And they must have trusted us, because the comments were getting bolder.

That girl is a snatch. Subscribing.
I knew Carver was a cheat! Hope he gets busted.
Keep the vids coming. So many Haver-holes need to be knocked off their thrones.

Our little monster was growing up right before our eyes.

19

A different kind of monster crossed my path in the halls between Chemistry and Advanced Lit the next day, and it seemed determined to get my attention.

I averted my gaze, but Malcolm had already seen me and was making a beeline in my direction. Of course, he couldn't go five steps without causing mayhem, so on his way down the hall, he managed to kick his foot a little to the left – just enough to catch the ankle of a boy passing the other direction, so the poor kid went down in a shower of loose papers and heavy textbooks. Malcolm's eyes were on me the whole time.

I shook my head. The cruelty was almost like an afterthought with Malcolm – a reflex. He had impulse-control issues, and the impulse was to cause suffering.

'You got a problem, Bennett?' he asked, stopping in front of me.

I looked at the boy now scraping himself off the floor.

Malcolm glanced back, a grin on his face. 'It's not polite to stare at clumsy people. Not everyone is as graceful as you, Tinker Bell.'

I started to push past him without responding, but his hand caught my chest. 'Hold on a second. I've been looking for you.'

I gritted my teeth. 'Oh yeah?'

Why was this guy suddenly so interested in me? The way he pressed his fingers into my shirt, the way his face purpled until his freckles blended into one another – you'd think I was the one who knocked up his girlfriend. But that was his own mistake. I was just the unfortunate bystander.

'Yeah,' he growled, voice low, so the kids around us couldn't hear. 'I want to remind you of our deal.'

'Deal?'

'Yeah, nutsack. The deal where you keep your mouth shut about what you saw in the bathroom in exchange for me not pounding your face in.'

As if I even cared about his personal drama. I had better things to do than worry about Malcolm Mahoney and his girl becoming tragic high school statistics. The thought sent a laugh bubbling up to my lips that surprised me as much as Malcolm.

His hand on my chest turned to a fist. 'You laughing at me, Bennett? You been running your mouth off? Because if you have—'

'I haven't,' I said, choking back my chuckles.

'Uh-huh.' He squinted his eyes, deciding whether to believe me; then his fist relaxed as he leaned back. 'Good. I better not see a video of the boys' bathroom pop up on that Bishop's Buddies or whatever it's called.'

I froze. Looked around. Did Malcolm know? Did everyone? How did they figure me out?

I stammered, 'I – I – I don't know what you mean.'

Malcolm snorted. 'Figures. It's the only thing anyone's talking about, and you don't even know about it. It's a website, moron. Look it up.'

I relaxed so much then that I could have made a puddle on the floor. He didn't know I was behind the site. He was just worried I might be a creeper with a camera. Friends of Bishop had made Malcolm Mahoney scared – of *me* – of anyone willing to hit record.

And there it was again. The rush. Malcolm had the fists, but I had a bigger weapon – one that could keep guys like him from causing mayhem. Too often, hackers got painted as the villains, but maybe it was possible to be a hero too. It was just a matter of perspective.

Eli Bennett. Vigilante.

I could get used to that.

'Oh, that website.' A grin stretched across my face, and I leaned in to Malcolm to whisper. 'Hope nobody was recording what you just did to that kid.'

He looked over his shoulder at the boy picking his books up off the floor. 'Who cares?'

I held up my hands in an innocent gesture. 'Maybe no one. Just, y'know . . . assault charges and all that. Wouldn't want to get arrested with a little one on the way.'

Malcolm's head whipped back around to me, a threatening look in his eyes, but I also noticed his face had gone pale.

'Just be careful,' I said, before sauntering away.

I wished I *had* recorded him, but it was hard to catch people's bad behavior on camera without cracking into their computers.

As I passed the boy cleaning up the last of Malcolm's mess, I tried to give him a reassuring smile, but he only shuffled off, head hanging low. There was something painfully familiar about it, and I felt a heat rising in my chest. Between guys like Malcolm Mahoney and girls like Ashley Thorne, maybe some people deserved to be hacked.

*

It was all I could do to not recount the moment with Malcolm to Zach when I caught up to him in the cafeteria at lunch. There was just no way to tell the story without telling him about Friends of Bishop too. I hated keeping this from him, but the more the website grew, the more I believed in it, and the more I knew Zach wouldn't.

Until last night, I might have had a hope of making him understand, but that window had closed when we went after a teacher. No matter how unfair she was to students, no matter what irresponsible or possibly illegal things she did outside of school, Zach would disapprove. He still believed teachers were infallible and justice was something only carried out by cops and lawyers.

So I swallowed my excitement about besting Malcolm and stuck to our favourite topic – the app that would make us rich someday. As usual, our ideas were all derivative, and something that seemed like a good idea one day seemed tired the next.

'What about an augmented reality game?' Zach asked. 'Like that one that had people walking into walls a couple years ago.'

He snagged a french fry off my plate, and I stabbed one of his chicken nuggets with my plastic fork.

'I still think we should just go basic,' I said. 'A simple matching game, *Candy Crush*-style, with lots of in-app purchases.' I was all about the profit.

'Crowded market,' Zach argued.

'True but . . .' I drifted off as a cluster of girls walked past our table. On the edge of the group, Isabel caught my eye and waved. I waved back, without embarrassing myself this time, and we both said, 'Hi.' It all went really smoothly when I didn't have time to overthink it.

Zach gaped at me. 'What was that about?'

'We talked a little yesterday. It's no big deal.' I tried to shrug it off, but the grin on my face just wouldn't lie down.

'You should get her to tutor you in Spanish,' Zach said.

'In exchange for what?' I laughed. 'A lesson in computer programming?'

'Oh, you'd love that,' Zach teased. 'I'll bet you're just dying to give her a *penetration test*.'

I rolled my eyes at his hacker humour. 'Weak.'

'You want to *inject her with your code*.'

'Stop!' I punched his shoulder, but we were both laughing.

Talking girls and games made me almost feel normal, and for a second, in my usual seat across from Zach at the most invisible table in the Haver High cafeteria . . . I wasn't a hacker hero or any kind of vigilante at all. My world was simple and small, and the air gap that protected me from the rest of the world was still in place.

20

Within a week, the number of messages on the site had doubled, and a lot of them now had videos attached. I imagined people walking the halls of Haver with their cell phones constantly out and recording video, burning up their batteries ... just in case.

'These videos are shit,' Seth complained. 'They're all shaky.'

We were sprawled over the old couches in Seth's basement on Saturday, laptops balanced on knees, practising for the ACC. Well, Mouse and I were practising. Seth was obsessing.

'Dude, put the website away.' I tapped the screen in front of me. 'We're almost done with this unit.'

Seth was the one who'd insisted we run the attack simulations in his practise program, and now we were failing the last drill, because he was too distracted to do his part.

He ignored me, scrolling through more video submissions. 'And most of them are just people talking behind other people's backs.'

Mouse and I exchanged a look and gave in together, tossing our laptops aside.

'We're in the business of justice,' Seth said, 'not gossip. This is just petty.'

'Remember when we were in the business of winning the ACC?' I reminded him.

'We can kill two birds with one website,' Seth countered.

'Speaking of petty.' Mouse jumped in. 'I heard people talking about our Vicious Valedictorian post this week.'

Seth looked up from the computer propped on his lap. 'And?'

'And they said she might get that title stripped.' Mouse continued in a voice full of mock curiosity, 'Hey, Seth, who's next in line to become valedictorian again? Oh wait – it's you, right?'

Seth didn't answer, but his mouth turned up in the tiniest smile.

'I knew it!' Mouse hooted. 'Tell the truth. You sent that video, didn't you?'

Seth slapped his laptop shut and spluttered, 'Did not – never be so stupid – don't need to—'

'Whoa, touchy!' I laughed.

Mouse shook his head, grinning. 'As my pal Shakespeare would say, "The lady doth protest too much."'

Seth answered with a middle finger and a huff, while Mouse and I cracked up.

It didn't matter that so many videos were 'petty' or poor quality, because we had enough now that we could pick and choose, which was exactly how we spent the rest of the afternoon – separating the worthy videos from the unworthy.

'This is definitely the one,' Mouse said a couple of hours later, turning his screen around.

Our new headline stretched across the top of the screen. 'Who Run the World?'

Below it, a video starring a freshman homophobe who got a kick out of calling kids 'tranny.' Apparently one of those 'trannies' used to be his friend, and said friend just happened to hold on to a video of our little homophobe around age ten – all dressed up in booty shorts and his mom's heels, dancing to Beyoncé's 'Run the World (Girls).'

A worthy video, indeed. It had nothing to do with Jordan and everything to do with him at the same time. The guy in the video hadn't done anything directly to Jordan, but he had victims of his own. The way we saw it . . . whoever submitted this video was just another Jordan waiting to burn a hole in our cafeteria floor.

'Nice title,' I said.

Mouse grinned in response, and his face reminded me of an expression my aunt always used – the one about a cat and the cream.

'Hey, Mouse, what's your real name?'

'I'll never tell.'

'It's William,' Seth said from behind his laptop.

Mouse's eyebrows gathered together, and his feet – always tapping – worked overtime, so the computer in his lap bounced.

'Why "Mouse"?' I asked. 'Is it because you can deliver a RAT?'

A Remote Access Trojan was what he'd used to get inside Brett's computer and take over the camera.

'What?'

'You know, *mouse . . . rat.*'

'Oh. No.' He shook his head. 'Like the dormouse in *Alice in Wonderland.*'

'I don't get it.'

'Because that mouse is always so sleepy, and this mouse' – he pointed to himself and smiled wide – 'is always so awake!'

I nodded appreciatively. 'I dig it. Maybe I can be the caterpillar – he's all wise and shit, right?'

'You need a hookah,' Mouse said. 'Who should Seth be?'

I didn't hesitate. 'Tweedle Dum.'

'Or the rabbit,' Mouse offered. 'He's pretty uptight.'

Seth groaned but didn't engage.

'Or one of those talking cards.' I grinned.

'Or the Mad Hatter!'

'Yes!'

We were both snickering now, and Seth finally put his tablet aside with a sigh. 'I would be the Cheshire Cat . . . clearly.'

I squinted one eye and looked him over. 'Nah, you're more of a Queen of Hearts.'

I dodged the pillow Seth hurled in my direction and hit the floor laughing. When I looked up, Mouse was tapping the screen, a freeze-frame of the homophobe in heels.

'Excuse me, but I think *this* is the queen.'

Even Seth laughed at that, and we both gave Mouse our approval for the post.

I felt a surge of adrenaline as he published the page. How would people react to this new video? Would our submissions double again? I had laughed when Seth called me powerful that first day, but he was right. There was power in what we knew how to do online, power in our ability to stay anonymous. We were the puppet masters, and no one at Haver had a clue. I wondered what they would say if they knew who was pulling their strings.

*

The next day was a typical lazy Sunday playing video games in the living room with Zach. Normally, we'd be gaming at his house, but he'd come to my place since technically, I was still grounded – though that punishment seemed to be wearing off by the day. Misty had let me go to Seth's yesterday with an übergeneric explanation about my new study group, and I was pretty sure Dad had forgotten he ever grounded me in the first place.

I had just taken aim at some enemy troops, when Misty leaned into my vision, blocking the screen. I ducked my head, trying to see around her big hair and her big – *ugh, I wish she'd just put them away already.*

'These are the low-sodium pretzels, but I have regular if you boys want them,' she said, dropping a bowl on the coffee table.

'Thanks,' Zach said, stuffing a fistful in his mouth.

'Thanks,' I echoed, waving her out of the way.

She moved a second too late, and blood splattered my side of the screen – my soldier dead.

'Thanks *a lot*,' I muttered as she walked away.

'Relax,' Zach said.

'She got me killed.'

'So what? You'll regen.' He dropped his controller. 'This game sucks anyway.'

'We'll come up with better,' I agreed.

'Hey, what about a shooting game that interacts with the real world?'

'You're still on that augmented reality stuff?'

'It's the next big thing.'

'Maybe, but a shooting game?' I twisted my lips. 'Possibly not in the best taste.'

Zach half ignored me, his imagination taking over. 'So we keep it clean. Nothing too gory or too real. Like paintball without all the pain. Or laser tag without the black-light arena, because the *whole world* is your arena.'

I tried to see what Zach was seeing. 'You mean, you'd point your phone to shoot another player, and if you aim just right and hit *their* phone—'

'—you'd get points,' Zach finished. 'And maybe you can steal whatever weapons they've collected.'

'So we'd drop weapons, like *Pokémon*, all over the place.'

'Right. But how do you know who's the enemy? Do people have to join teams, maybe?'

Now, *that* sounded original. The challenge of it set something clicking and whirring inside me. Numbers streamed past my vision, then lines of code. My fingers suddenly itched for a keyboard.

But before I could get to a computer, my phone interrupted. I checked the screen – lit up with a message from Seth.

First Haver 'hero' bites the dust.

Over the top of my phone, I saw Zach tip his chin at me. 'Is it Isabel?' he teased.

'Who's Isabel?' Misty called from the kitchen.

I ignored them both and opened a link attached to Seth's message. It was an article in the sports section of the *Haver Herald* website. The headline read 'Steroid Scandal' above a photo montage of Brett in his various team uniforms. But only the first few lines of the story were about Brett – how he was caught on camera, how he was banned from all sports, how his scholarships were being revoked.

Basically, this kid's life is over. Next paragraph.

My stomach tightened and my breath caught in my chest. It was one thing to feel a sense of power; it was another to see that power played out. We had made this happen. Seth was pretty much claiming it as a victory. But if Brett was the bad guy, why did I suddenly feel sick to my stomach?

The article went on to say some of Brett's teammates were under investigation for steroid use and that all Haver athletes might have to submit to testing. And the last bit ... was about us.

The scandal appears to have been exposed by anonymous hackers calling themselves Friends of Bishop. Investigators with Haver school district's cybersurveillance team say there's no evidence yet that the hackers are students, though their moniker may be a reference to Jordan Bishop, a Haver High freshman who made national headlines last year when he committed suicide by fire in the school cafeteria.

The story wrapped up with the obligatory paragraph about how Jordan's death changed national laws involving students' cyberactivity, yada yada. I let out a long breath before I remembered that Zach was sitting right next to me.

'Not Isabel?' he said, his forehead scrunched up in a concerned way. 'You all right?'

My heart was racing, my stomach churning – definitely not all right.

'I'm fine,' I said. I held up my phone with the article. 'Have you seen this? Some kids at school got busted for steroids because of a video that ... well, because of a website ...'

God, I was so close to telling him the truth.

'Oh, that revenge site?' Zach said.

'It's more like a *justice* – um, yeah, yeah that one.'

I was a little surprised he'd even heard of it. For two guys who never unplugged, Zach and I were generally disconnected from the rest of Haver High.

'They got people busted?' Zach let out a low whistle. 'Crazy.'

'Crazy,' I echoed.

'Who sent that to you?' he asked.

'No one.' I fumbled for an answer. 'I ... have a Google Alert for stories about school.'

Zach seemed satisfied with that. He picked up his controller and started to reset our game.

'So ... what do you think of that site?' I tried to sound casual.

Zach's eyes stayed on the screen. 'I haven't really looked at it, but whoever's behind it seem like white hats instead of black hats, so that's good, I guess.'

Relief washed over me. Maybe I *could* tell Zach—

'Really stupid white hats, though,' Zach added.

I bristled. 'What? Why?'

'Well, they're breaking some big-time laws, busting into people's computers and stuff.'

'They're vigilantes,' I said, trying hard not to sound defensive.

'They're idiots.'

I was glad Zach was watching the game, so he couldn't see me glaring at him. 'Only if they get caught.'

'*When* they get caught. They're going to end up hurting themselves worse than anyone else.'

The confession that had been on my lips just a moment ago now slid back down my throat and sat there in a hard lump. It stung to have your best friend disapprove, even if he didn't know it was you he disapproved of.

'Guys!' Misty stomped into the living room and parked in front of the TV, hands on hips. '*Who* is *Isabel*?'

21

I spent the final few hours of the weekend hammering our website from my home computer – attempting to crack it from the outside. I tried all methods of tracing associated IP addresses or domain ownership, and sometime around midnight, I was finally satisfied that we were still anonymous.

All clear, I texted Seth and Mouse.

Told you, Seth shot back.

Mouse sent a smiley face with whiskers and pointy ears.

Earlier, in a frantic group phone call, Mouse had panicked that 'investigators' were looking for us, but Seth had assured him school district cyberinvestigators were just a step above hall monitors. I agreed, but I was more concerned about other people like us. Sometimes, when a hack got a little attention in the news, other hackers made a game of trying to track the newsmakers down, and if our cover got blown too soon, we wouldn't be able to submit the site to the ACC.

I could only hope we stayed two steps ahead of everyone on our tail.

Zach's words were still rattling around in my head, keeping me awake as much as the two Monsters and a Red Bull I had burned through while testing the site.

I distracted myself by watching Isabel's video channel. I didn't understand all the contouring and shading she was talking about as she covered her face with different creams and powders, but I loved that she did it in two different languages. This counted as studying Spanish, right?

Still, a guy can only watch make-up videos for so long, and I ended up cruising the web for nothing in particular and falling down that internet rabbit hole where a search for a new backpack leads to hiking leads to Appalachian Trail, and suddenly you're spending the next two hours reading some guy's travel blog about the three months he spent hiking the AT.

This sort of web trap happened to me a lot, but it wasn't a complete waste of time. I liked to catalog all my internet trivia for future use impressing girls. Maybe someday a girl would want to know whether it's more common to hike the Appalachian Trail from the north end or the south, and I would be ready with the answer.

*

If I had any lingering doubts about whether the school

cybersnoops had tracked us down, they disintegrated Monday morning. Flyers posted in every hallway had the distinct whiff of desperation. Seth ripped down one that had been taped to a no-bullying sign and read aloud:

'Stand up to cyberbullies.
Anyone with information about websites targeting or belittling students or posting videos without their knowledge should report those sites and their users to the administration. Emails and phone calls will be anonymous. Further, any student found to be contributing to such a site could face penalties including suspension, expulsion, or even criminal charges.'

He crumpled the flyer into a ball and tossed it into his open locker. 'Well, that's going to hurt our submissions.'

'Cyberbullies?' Mouse said, his usual bounce shifting to more of a slow rock from foot to foot. 'Is that what we are?'

'No.' Seth said. 'We're the ones *stopping* them. The school's just embarrassed that we're doing their job for them.'

I shushed them both. The morning chatter of hundreds of students, combined with Haver's shitty hallway acoustics, made it impossible to overhear anyone else's conversation, but cell phones could still pick up voices, and thanks to our trend-setting, camera phones were constantly recording. Wouldn't it be laughable if we got caught confessing on camera ... the architects of our own undoing?

Seth lowered his voice to a whisper, so Mouse and I had to lean in to hear. 'I'm just saying, that article embarrassed the shit out of the school. The site is already demonstrating that cybermonitoring doesn't work. The ACC judges are going to eat it up.'

Mouse fished the ball of paper from Seth's locker and spread it open, reading it over as if the message might change.

'But we're not the bullies, right?' He asked again, his face folded in a frown.

'Would you stop using that word?' Seth growled.

They shared a look that I didn't understand, and a second later, the staring contest was broken by an arm swinging down between them.

'Here's one!'

A hand connected to the swinging arm plucked the flyer out of Mouse's grasp.

Seth spun to snatch it back but retreated when he saw the boy who had grabbed it. He was a senior, like Seth, but packing an extra fifty pounds of muscle and standing at least a foot taller.

'Check it out.' The boy held the flyer out to two of his friends, and they all crowded around to read it. 'It's got to be because of the Carver video, right?'

'Or Windemere,' one friend said. He looked up at us, as if we were part of their hallway huddle. 'I heard she got fired.'

'No way,' Mouse said, real awe in his voice.

The boy nodded. 'Yeah, she hasn't been here for like a week.'

'Nah,' the other friend jumped in. 'She's not fired ... yet. My mom says she's going to stay home and get paid for it while they investigate.'

'She's probably home getting her booze on,' the flyer snatcher quipped. His friends laughed, and we joined in, awkwardly. Then they moved on down the hall, smashing the paper back into a ball.

Our group fell silent in their wake. It was one thing to wish bad things for Mrs. Windemere. It was another thing to make that wish come true.

'Eli!' A sharp voice sliced through the quiet, and we broke apart in a guilty way.

Zach stopped in his tracks, doing a double take as he saw the two strangers I was standing with. He adjusted his pack on his shoulder. 'You weren't at your locker.'

'Yeah, I was at Seth's locker.' I made a lame gesture at Seth, as if this somehow explained anything.

An uncomfortable silence grew as Zach waited for me to say more. I glanced at Seth and Mouse, who stared back as if to say, *He's your friend. Deal with it.*

'Spanish!' I blurted out. 'Seth's helping me out. He's in Senior Spanish, so . . .'

'I take French,' Seth said. Then, at my death glare, he added, 'And Spanish. I also take Spanish. Languages are so easy. I would take German, but why take something you already speak fluently, right?'

If it had been anybody but Seth, it would have sounded like backpedaling, but his effortless arrogance really sold it.

The eye roll I shared with Zach was genuine.

'I should have just asked Misty,' I said.

I expected Zach to laugh, but instead he squinted a little, the way he does in chess when he doesn't understand the move his opponent just made. His narrowed eyes travelled from me to Seth to Mouse and then lingered, as if waiting for the small jumpy kid to explain his presence.

But all he got was, 'Hi. I'm Mouse.'

'Hi,' Zach replied. He adjusted the pack slung over his shoulder and shifted his weight from one foot to the other. Finally, he looked back at me, and his squint had smoothed out – replaced by a blank look better fitting a poker player than a chess master. 'Guess I'll catch you at lunch then.'

I slumped against the wall of lockers as Zach shuffled off.

'Who is that chode?' Seth asked.

'He's my friend, and he's not a chode. He's a wicked coder, actually. I would have asked him to join us if the ACC allowed teams of four.'

And if I didn't think he would narc on all of us before we had a chance to compete.

'He could be an alternate,' Mouse suggested.

I shook my head. 'I don't think he'd go for the website.'

'Oh. In that case . . .' Mouse pressed his lips into a cross between a smile and a frown that somehow passed for an apology.

'You haven't told him anything, have you?' Seth demanded.

'No, not at all—'

'Because if we get busted before the competition, we'll fail the off-site section.'

'I know, I didn't—'

'It won't be a successful exploit unless we get all the way to the ACC without getting caught.'

'Relax,' I said. 'I'm not trying to blow our cover.'

The ACC was my chance to escape Haver and Misty and college and to live a life less . . . *expected*. That alone was worth a few more weeks of white lies.

Mouse twisted back and forth, bumping my arm with his elbow every other swing. 'Your friend should come hang with us sometime, though . . . when we're not practising.

Or working on the website. Or in Seth's basement.'

'When are we ever not doing those things?' I asked.

Seth slammed his locker shut. 'Never. So tell your chode friend you're sorry, and maybe next year he can take my spot on the team.'

My thoughts exactly.

I watched Seth walk away, shaking my head. 'What's his problem today?'

'The flyers freaked him out,' Mouse said. 'Plus, he's got senior stress. All the graduating kids are cranky right now. Also, you know, he's just kind of a dick sometimes.'

I laughed. 'Truth.'

We started down the hall together in silence until Mouse hopped ahead and turned to walk backward in front of me. He tilted his head to one side, a serious look on his face. 'What is a chode, anyway?'

22

I took a deliberately circuitous route to first period, through the South Wing, hoping to run into Isabel.

And when I did, I wished I hadn't.

She was at her locker, but so was someone else ... and they were standing a little too close. I couldn't see Isabel's expression, only the back of her head as she looked up at a brick wall with a red mop on top – Malcolm. I was too far away to hear what they were talking about, but whatever it was, it made me want to punch his freckled face. I hung back a little bit, dawdling at the drinking fountain, until he finally walked away. When he was gone, I moved extra slow down the hall to give Isabel time to notice me.

'Hey!' she said, with a big, bright smile. She had on a pale pink lipstick that made her teeth look really white. I suddenly wondered about the colour of my own teeth and vowed to steal some of Misty's whitening toothpaste.

'So you hang out with Malcolm Mahoney?'

I couldn't help myself. And it was all I could do not to blurt out that he'd gotten a girl knocked up.

'Ugh, no.' She pulled a face. 'I don't hang out with that

pinche pelirrojo. He just offered to pay me to write a history paper. *¡Que la chingada!*'

I had no idea what she'd just said, but I was 99 per cent sure she was cursing and 100 per cent sure it was sexy.

'I didn't catch all that,' I confessed. 'I'm pretty terrible at Spanish.'

'Aren't you in Señora Vega's class?'

'Yes, and failing it ... sorry,' I added, because it seemed like I owed her an apology.

Isabel wrapped her arms around a stack of notebooks and looked at the floor. 'Well, I could help you with that – if you wanted.'

It felt like my feet left the ground a little bit.

'Really? That'd be – yes, you, please – great!'

That was a sentence, right?

Isabel looked up, her smile even bigger than before. 'What's your number? I'll text you mine, and we'll figure out a day you can come over ...'

I floated higher as Isabel tapped her number into my phone and laughed at something I wasn't even quite aware I was saying. By the time she flashed a final smile and waved goodbye, I was on the ceiling.

Of course, when I told this story to Zach later, I would come off much cooler, and there would be absolutely zero floating.

But I didn't get the chance to tell him the story at all, because he never showed in the cafeteria for lunch, and in Spanish he sat on the opposite side of the room and was the first out the door when the bell rang.

Sorry, gotta jet to 5th period! and Taking a library lunch today, his texts claimed.

I didn't buy it. He was pouting about the fact that he'd found me hanging out with Seth and Mouse. Part of me felt guilty, but another part was indignant. Can't a guy have more than one friend? Maybe when the competition was over, I could get everyone together, and Zach would eventually like Seth and Mouse. Well ... maybe just Mouse.

My last shot to catch Zach was after school. He had chess club on Mondays, and he wouldn't skip it – even if he knew I could find him there.

After my last period, I pushed through a set of doors on the third floor into one of Haver's tall echoing stairwells. Most kids used the two open-air staircases at either end of the main building, but this stair led straight down to the classroom where Zach and the other chess nerds gathered. It was a favourite spot for smokers to sneak a cigarette, since it was usually empty, and I gagged a little on the stale aroma of old Marlboros. Voices rose up from somewhere below me – whispers magnified to shouts in this concrete tunnel.

'Notre Dame is out. That's all of them now.'

'Even Iowa State?'

A bark of a laugh held zero humour. 'State didn't just rescind my scholarship. They revoked my admission.'

I froze on the landing just above the second floor. I recognised the voices now. Brett and one of his teammates – the one whose life we *didn't* ruin – were leaning over a railing, looking down into the bowels of the school. I tiptoed backward, pressing myself against the wall. If I went up, they might notice my footsteps, but if I went down, they'd definitely know I'd overheard them. I was stuck, just as I'd been when I'd heard Ashley talking about Isabel. I was starting to feel like a professional creeper.

'I bet they'll all revoke my admissions now.'

'So you'll go to community college for a year first . . .'

And then something awful happened. Just ten feet below me, Brett started to cry.

'Oh, hey, man – don't – it's okay.' His friend struggled to say something comforting, and I tried, in vain, to teleport myself out of the stairwell and into another dimension. I needed to be anywhere but here, overhearing this.

'Even if they don't,' Brett sobbed, 'I can't afford to go – not without a scholarship. That was my only shot.'

'I know. I'm sor—'

'I didn't even want to take that shit. You know I didn't.'

His friend went on the defence. 'Hey, nobody forced you—'

'Like I had a choice, though, right?' Brett sniffed back his tears. 'Everyone's on the same junk. It's the only way to compete. You can't stand out to recruiters if everyone else on the mat is juiced up.'

Don't feel sorry for him, I lectured myself. I tried to remember the awful things Seth had told me about Brett – how he'd tortured Jordan online, calling him 'faggot' and encouraging him to *die*. He was scum, and he did not deserve my sympathy.

Brett's whimpering gave way to a growl. 'What did I even do to deserve this? Who do these shits think they are to screw with me?'

'You have any online enemies besides that trailer trash Bishop?' his friend asked.

My hands clenched into fists.

Even now.

So much for respecting the dead.

'Not that I know of,' Brett said. 'It's like he's still trolling me from beyond the grave.'

Jordan trolling Brett? Sounded to me like it was the other way around.

'Wouldn't be surprised.' Brett's friend laughed. 'He always was a creep.'

'At least I don't have to take that junk anymore,' Brett said. 'So sick of feeling wired all the time.'

'Guess you owe Friends of Bishop a big thanks, then.'

I could hear the sarcasm in his friend's voice.

'Yeah,' Brett snorted. 'I'll be sure to thank them while I'm stomping their faces into the floor.'

Huh. Guess those 'roids haven't totally worn off yet.

'Did the police find anything on your laptop?'

Brett huffed. 'Nothing to find. The hard drive is completely fried.'

I felt a small stab of guilt. I couldn't relate to losing sports scholarships, but a trashed computer? That was painful. And possibly my fault.

I'd told Mouse to cover his tracks. It sounded like he'd set them on fire.

'Maybe I deserve it,' Brett said, his emotional pendulum swinging from rage back to remorse.

This kid would really benefit from getting off the sauce.

'What are you talking about?'

'For taking that junk – for dragging Bishop – maybe it's karma or whatever.'

I closed my eyes and leaned my head back against the cool concrete. *Why can't he just be an asshole?*

'It's not karma,' Brett's friend said. 'It's a bunch of jack-holes with no dicks. Okay?'

'Okay.' Brett sniffed.

I heard the muffled clap of hands patting backs and pictured the bro hug happening below me.

'Now, dry out and meet me at my locker,' his friend ordered.

Shoes squeaked on the floor. A heavy door opened with a *whoosh*; then it slammed, the sound reverberating up and down the stairwell. There were only two of us left to listen to the echoes . . . and one of us was a complete douchebag. I just wasn't sure which one.

23

I never made it to chess club. I just couldn't face Zach after what I'd overheard on the stairs. Instead, I put on my headphones, blasted the loudest, most mind-erasing music I could find, and shuffled home.

Not that home was any great escape. Before I even opened the front door, movement through the kitchen window caught my eye. I paused with my hand on the doorknob, peeking through the glass, and though I couldn't hear them over my music, I could tell by Dad's tightly crossed arms and Misty's wild gesturing that they were having a fight. Well, far be it for me to interrupt a good fight. I tiptoed around the house to the side entrance, slipped off my headphones, and headed up toward my room.

'. . . doesn't need a friend. He needs discipline. He needs to understand consequences.'

I paused with one foot on the bottom step. The fight was about me?

'Don't do that. Don't accuse me of trying to be his friend. I'm not. But you can't expect me to be his parent either—'

'I do expect that.'

'*You* are his parent, Paul.'

I inched toward the kitchen, leaning against the wall next to the open doorway.

Misty's voice was pleading. 'You are never here, and he needs you. He needs his dad.'

'He needs a mom!'

'His mom is *dead*!'

I flinched at that, and as I did, my shoulder hit the corner of a picture frame, knocking it off the wall. It landed with a clatter, and the silence that followed was total.

The house settled around us, creaking and humming, trying desperately to drown out our terrible quiet.

Finally, from the kitchen, Dad offered up a weak 'Eli?'

I cleared my throat. 'Um, yeah.'

Misty's husky voice dropped to a whisper. 'Shit.'

Shit, indeed.

More annoying than Misty mentioning my mom, was the fact that I'd overheard it. And they'd overheard me overhearing. Now we were going to have to have some big 'family moment' about it.

Misty appeared in the doorway, one hand holding the frame, as if for support.

'Eli, I am so, so, sorry. I shouldn't have said that so cas—'

'You shouldn't talk about my mom at all.'

If I had to endure this awkwardness, she should at least suffer alongside me.

The truth was, I wasn't as sensitive to comments about my mom as everyone expected me to be. I was just a tiny baby when the cancer got her. I guess it made me sad sometimes, in a distant sort of way, but it was hard to miss someone you never really knew. I think I mostly missed the *idea* of a mom ... at least, I had until Dad brought Misty home.

Dad appeared in the doorway behind Misty, his hands squeezing her shoulders, because she was the one who needed comforting, apparently.

'Eli, you have to understand the position I've put Misty in. This new family dynamic is difficult for all of us.'

'Family?' I couldn't keep the disgust out of my voice.

The muscles in Dad's face tightened. 'Yes, family, and I expect you to show some respect—'

'Respect?' I asked. 'Or kindness? Because last week, it was kindness.'

Dad's face purpled. 'It's both, Eli. And if I hear that tone—'

'Paul, stop.' Misty pushed Dad's hand off her shoulder and stepped toward me. 'I'm sorry, okay? It wasn't a cool thing to blurt out like that – whether you were listening or not.'

I usually didn't miss an opportunity to punish Misty, but the guilt on her face was so intense, I felt compelled, as a human, to say something to make her feel better.

'Fine,' I said.

It was all she was getting, and it was enough. She let out a breath and shrank back into the kitchen. Dad stayed in the doorway, watching me.

'What about the stuff *you* said?' I asked.

'Which stuff?' Dad was smart enough to realise I probably hadn't heard the entire conversation.

'That junk about discipline and consequences. You think I'm still a little kid.'

'I don't think you're a little kid. I think you can be ... irresponsible.'

'So, you're saying you don't trust me.'

'No, that's not what I'm saying. That's what you're hearing.'

I hated when he said things like that – like I was incapable of reading between the lines of his parental bullshit.

'Well, trust this,' I said. 'I found a Spanish tutor, and she's going to help me convince Señora Vega to give me extra credit.'

Dad's eyes widened a little. 'That's great, Eli. That's—'

'Yeah, but I have to go to her house to study sometimes, so . . . is the grounding over now or what?'

Dad watched me for a long moment, his face giving away none of the calculations I knew were happening in his brain. He didn't trust me. Or at the very least, he didn't trust my judgment.

A clattering sound came from the kitchen as Misty pulled plates down from the cabinet.

I guess that was fair. I didn't trust his either.

I don't know if the next words out of his mouth were because he believed me about the Spanish tutor or because he just felt guilty about what I'd overheard.

'Yes, the grounding is over.'

*

I celebrated my new freedom by immediately texting Isabel to set up our study session. We messaged back and forth for a few minutes – long enough to be more than friendly but not so long that I wound up texting something embarrassing just to fill space on the screen. She gave me the link to her vlog, and I didn't tell her that I had already found it.

I expected the only thing on Isabel's vlog that would interest me would be Isabel herself, but there was more to it than just beauty tips. In October, she had posted a whole string of videos about Halloween make-up, and last summer, some of her first vlogs had been ideas for people going to Comic-Con. Her Incredible Hulk make-up was amazing.

I scrolled through the comments on one of her Halloween videos, in which she expertly transformed her face into that of the ultimate vampire, Nosferatu. The final result gave me chills, and I wasn't surprised that more people responded to this clip than any other she'd posted. Most had praise for Isabel's work, encouraging her to become a professional make-up artist, but not all the praise was genuine. One comment in particular dripped with false flattery.

Wow, great job. It's so impressive how pale you can make your face. Did you get that base from a beauty supply store or a costume shop? Just curious. Thanks for the video. If you want to see how to do a SEXY vampire for Halloween, visit my vlog, Pretty Pouty.

I clicked the link, and Ashley Thorne filled my screen, looking more herself than ever with long fangs and red eyes. Other than the teeth and contacts, her face was more prom-perfect than Halloween-horror. I was irritated to see her video had twice as many comments as Isabel's, even though it was only half as good.

I should have shut the computer down right then – just closed both video pages and moved on with my life – but as I watched Ashley run about thirty different brushes along her cheek, smiling and primping for the camera, I thought of the things she'd said and the way Isabel had absorbed her words.

There wasn't enough blush in the world to cover up all that ugly.

Almost against my will, I found myself looking for ways to worm into Ashley's computer. Her passwords were too strong for my botnet to crack right away, so I took a simpler approach. I shot her an email and masked it to look like it was from the video host – another glowing comment for her to moderate on her latest post. She opened it almost immediately and clicked the link inside. To make sure she didn't get suspicious, I directed the link to her vlog, and while she was busy looking for that new comment, a payload was spreading through her computer, allowing me access to everything from her keystrokes to her camera.

Too easy.

I made a note of her passwords as she logged on to various social media, and checked her camera every so often.

It was an hour before anything interesting happened, and it was more than I'd expected to get. I was working on a paper when Ashley's voice came through my speakers, low and flirty.

'Hey, baby.'

I opened her camera, surprised to see her looking right at it – at me.

'Uh, hi?' I said.

'Are you alone?'

I looked behind me. 'Yes?'

'Perfect,' she purred. She rolled her shoulders under tiny black straps connected to a slinky nightgown.

'I don't understand,' I said. This defied logic. 'How can you see me?'

'Nope, just me,' she said, giggling.

It took a second for me to realise that response didn't make sense ... and then another second to realise she wasn't talking to me at all.

Yep, computer genius here, forgetting how all of this works the second he sees a girl in lingerie.

I leaned back in my desk chair. *Holy shit. She's in a video chat.*

I watched with a sick fascination. What did the Ashley Thornes of the world talk about in private video chats? The answer to that became clear in a matter of minutes. Ashley wasn't just chatting. She was doing a striptease for the guy on the other end of the line – probably her boyfriend.

Or not. Who knows how this stuff works.

I squirmed. I didn't know what I'd hoped to catch by accessing her computer, but it wasn't this. I was no pervert. Still, it was hard to look away. Ashley couldn't compare to Isabel Ortega, but she was a female and a pretty spectacularly shaped one.

She hid all her warts on the inside.

I knew I should cut the feed, but instinct told me this might be the best dirt I'd ever get on Ashley Thorne, so with a little reluctance and a lot of self-loathing, I took a few screenshots and recorded a short video before turning off the computer. I saved the video to a flash drive, erased all traces of it from my PC, and then took a long hot shower to wash off the guilt.

24

But it turns out, guilt doesn't slide off so easy. It sticks to you like a film you can't rinse away. It was still there at lunch the next day, where I ate alone, because Zach didn't show again. It was there in Spanish, as I struggled to concentrate, because every time Señora Vega adjusted her scarf, I saw Ashley lifting her hands to lower her bra straps.

The guilt even followed me home and sat at my kitchen table, along with Mouse and Seth.

'You really don't have another outlet?' Mouse asked, hopping up to circle the island counter for the tenth time.

'It's a kitchen, not an electronics store,' I grumbled.

I was a little irritated at the surprise company. I'd tried to say no when Seth called this emergency midweek practise session. But we'd spent so much time working on the website, we'd slacked off on prepping for the other sections of the competition.

'I can grab you guys one more power strip,' Misty said. She stepped over a web of cords already snaking across the floor and did the limbo under one pulled taut between a wall outlet and the table.

'Where are you finding all these strips?' I asked.

I thought I was the computer nerd around here.

'I'm running a black-market hardware shop out of the basement.'

She winked on her way out of the kitchen, and Seth laughed hysterically until I kicked him under the table.

This was exactly why I didn't invite dudes over to the house.

Unfortunately, Seth's parents had kicked us out, so they could treat their basement for termites.

'Mouse, you're up,' I said.

He abandoned his search for the outlet and scooted back to his chair, typing before he even sat down. 'Piece of cake,' he bragged, fingers flying. 'You guys are making it too easy.'

I *hmph*ed in response.

We were using Seth's practise program to build our own security system, defending an imaginary corporation, and Mouse was playing the part of the hacker, trying to bust through our walls. Mostly, he was kicking our ass. It was harder to play defence.

After a while, I sank into the work and forgot to be annoyed. We took turns writing code and picking apart each other's work, with the occasional interruption from Misty.

Seth raised his voice whenever she walked by, trying to impress her with fancy phrases like 'hierarchical file structure' and 'terminal emulation' . . . except he stumbled over it a bit and said something closer to 'terminal ejaculation.'

Mouse just stared at her, slack-jawed and, for once, holding perfectly still.

'What are you boys working on again?' Misty asked after a couple of hours. She tried to sound casual and pulled a water bottle from the fridge.

The same thing we were working on the last three times you asked.

'Just practising for a coding contest,' I told her. Again.

Either that wasn't enough, or she didn't believe me, because she kept peeping over our shoulders like she expected to understand anything on the screen. This time, when she tried to look at my laptop, I slapped it shut.

'We were about to take a break,' I announced.

Seth's head popped up over his own laptop. 'We were?'

'Yeah, let's break,' Mouse said. 'I'm starving.'

'I'll order pizza!' Misty clapped her hands like this was the best idea ever, and Seth and Mouse nodded in agreement.

I stifled a groan.

When she left the room to call in the order, I looked around the table.

'So ... have any of you seen Brett lately?'

Mouse shook his head. 'No, but I overheard Principal Givens talking about Friends of—'

'*Shh!*' I whipped my head around, sure I would see Misty's big blond hair at the edge of a doorframe as she snooped on us.

'About the website,' Mouse amended. 'He was telling a couple of the teachers that he didn't know what they were going to do.'

'They can't find us.' Seth grinned, smug. 'The ACC is going to love this.'

As if he needed any more convincing of his own genius, he made us grudgingly agree that the website was the perfect way to demonstrate failures in the cybersnooping system, and he gloated once more over the fact that we'd brought down Brett.

'Yeah ... about that,' I said.

'What?'

'Nothing. It's just ... I ran into – or I accidentally overheard Brett talking and ... I don't know. Something about not wanting to take steroids and feeling pressured.'

'And?' Seth's stare was a challenge, and I met it.

'And maybe we don't have the whole story. I'm not saying he didn't deserve it, but ...'

Seth's face turned a blotchy red, and he rose up a little in his seat. 'You think what happened to Brett is worse than what happened to Jordan?'

'Not even close,' Mouse snarled.

'No, I'm not saying that, but—' I hesitated, shifting around in my seat. Seth and Mouse had more invested than I did. I was in this to impress ACC judges and embarrass a system I detested. But Seth and Mouse were on a personal mission to avenge their friend. No mercy. When it came to Jordan's enemies, I would always be outvoted.

'Look, maybe you don't care about Brett, but care about this.' I leaned in and lowered my voice. 'That was a huge takedown. Cybermonitors are already looking for us; the news is already talking about us.'

Seth and Mouse exchanged a smile, proud. They weren't getting it.

'Guys, if people hear Brett's side of the story, some of them – a lot of them – are going to feel sorry for him. And that other girl too. Not sure how well that will play at the ACC.'

As I talked, my hand reached absently for a nearby keyboard, my fingers doing their favourite dance.

Space, backspace. Space, backspace.

This was just another problem to solve – a difficult line of code.

In truth, the twinge of guilt I felt about Brett was just that – a twinge. My bigger concern was for my own ass. Brett had promised to pound our faces into the floor, and he wouldn't be the last. The more kids we took down, the more people would be looking for us with torches and pitchforks. We were damn lucky not to have been caught already, and it might be better to quit while we were ahead.

'We need to be careful, or people will think *we're* the bad guys.'

'And what are *you*? Innocent?' Seth challenged. 'Your white hat has a smudge on it too, Eli.'

'I didn't post that video of Brett,' I reminded him.

Mouse shushed us both as Misty came back into the kitchen to announce pizza was on its way. She danced out again, and we lowered our voices to whispers.

'Not the video,' Seth said. 'Game Zap. You're not so perfect.'

'Exactly.' I hissed. 'Take it from me, you don't want to know what it feels like always looking over your shoulder. I'm trying to help you out here.'

Mouse stretched a hand out toward each of us in a placating gesture. 'Hey, hey. You're *both* the prettiest.'

We laughed, the tension broken.

'None of this is going to matter if we don't get more videos, anyway,' I said. 'Submissions are drying up.'

That was putting it mildly. In the 24 hours since the school had threatened to expel anyone who contributed to the site, not only had people stopped sending us videos but we'd also had an avalanche of emails from kids asking to take theirs back.

'We still have a few left,' Seth said. 'Mouse, how many?'

'Four.'

Five.

But I had no intention of sharing the Ashley clip with Seth or Mouse. I still wasn't sure why I'd even recorded it. Wasn't I the one who made a rule against hacking for videos?

Seth shook his head. 'No, that can't be it.'

'Four that we agreed to post,' Mouse said. 'The rest are junk.'

'What about the one with Tony getting his ass kicked?'

Mouse's fingers raced over his keyboard as he brought up the site. 'Posted this morning.' He grinned. 'My personal favourite.'

The Tony in question had not only been part of the Jordan Bishop online torture team, but he'd also apparently spent the majority of his grade school years beating the shit out of Mouse. It was no surprise Mouse had done a happy dance when someone had sent us a video of Tony getting knocked out by some thugs from a rival school after a football game last fall. We'd gotten a lot of videos of fights caught on camera, but this was the only one featuring someone who really deserved a smackdown. As an extra-special gift to Mouse, Tony even cried a little at the end.

'Not a bad video to go out on,' I said. 'Honestly, even if we never posted another clip, I bet we still scared the crap out of everyone. You've seen the way people are acting at school.'

But Seth was a man obsessed. 'Oh, we're not even close to the curtain call yet.'

'Why not?' I asked. 'If this is about the ACC, we've already demonstrated the use of fragmented networking and masked IPs and about fifty other methods to find flaws in the—'

'We've only been online for two weeks. The competition isn't for two *months*. It's not enough.'

'And if no one sends us any more videos?' I asked.

'Then we get them ourselves,' Seth said.

Ashley's striptease danced in my vision, and I pressed my fingers to my eyes to make it go away.

'No. We agreed no hacking. We still have to out ourselves in June. Who cares if we win if they take us all away in handcuffs?' I gestured left and then right. 'Here's your trophy. Here's your jail cell.'

Mouse laughed, but Seth shook his head. 'It's not just about the ACC. We're not done until we have a video of everyone who shit on Jordan.'

'Everyone?' I asked.

'Everyone.'

'Even Ashley?' The question came fast and sharp from Mouse and left a quiet turbulence in its wake.

From laughter to darkness again in the space of a second. Mouse was giving me whiplash.

Seth tried to shrug it off, but I could tell he was uneasy under Mouse's gaze. 'We don't know for sure that Ashley did anything to—'

'We know,' Mouse said. 'That vlog—'

'Got taken down. And we never even saw it.' Seth shrugged.

I wasn't sure what they were talking about, but I wasn't surprised to hear Ashley had used her vlog for evil.

Mouse looked at me to explain. 'Last year, Ashley posted this video on Pretty Pouty – it's this vid channel—'

'I'm familiar,' I said.

'Well, she called the video "Pretty Pervy." It was like a warning video for freshman girls to stay away from certain guys.'

'Let me guess,' I said. 'Jordan was one of them?'

'Jordan and anyone he hung out with,' Mouse said quietly.

Ouch.

'Guess that didn't help you guys get dates, huh?' I gave a weak smile, but Seth and Mouse weren't even looking at me.

They were locked in a staring contest, a battle that had everything to do with the friend they lost and nothing to do with me. I felt an unexpected surge of jealousy. I was in my own kitchen but sitting in someone else's seat.

Finally, Seth held up his hands. 'Hey, you get something on Ashley Thorne, I'm happy to add her to the site. It would generate a ton of traffic.'

'Too bad no one would ever dare take a video of her,' Mouse said.

Space, backspace. Space, backspace.

'Yeah, too bad,' I echoed.

The guilt I felt over creeping into Ashley's bedroom through her laptop camera was more than a twinge. Seth was wrong. My white hat wasn't just smudged. It was downright dirty.

25

The next night, I upgraded my company from Seth and Mouse to Isabel. I stood outside her front door for three whole minutes before working up the courage to ring the bell, and when I finally reached for it, the door swung open.

'Why are you just standing there?' a woman demanded. The look in her eye was part teasing and part suspicious of the creeper loitering on her porch.

Awesome first impression.

I started to stammer out a response, but Isabel rescued me by pushing around the woman and dragging me into the house by the wrist.

'No interrogations, Mom!' she barked.

I managed to call a 'nice to meet you' over my shoulder as Isabel ushered me down a long hall to a room half-full of exercise equipment and half-full of cameras and lights on tall stands.

'This used to be our gym,' she explained, gesturing to the workout gear shoved up against one wall. 'But my mom was hanging clothes on the exercise bike more than she was riding it, so she said I could turn it into my studio.'

She flipped a couple of switches, and the lights illuminated a large white desk buried under make-up and mirrors. Behind the desk, two high-backed chairs were covered with leopard- and zebra-print fabric.

'Wow,' I said, letting my backpack fall to the floor.

'Pretty cool, huh?' Isabel dropped into the zebra chair.

I sat on the leopard pattern, instantly warm under the heat of the lights. 'It's really professional.'

'Thanks. I got a lot of equipment for Christmas and my birthday. I have a couple advertisers on my vlog, but not enough to pay for all this.' She gestured around at the cameras and piles of make-up. Then she hesitated and began rearranging things on the desk. 'I guess it looks a little messy.'

'No, it reminds me of my own desk,' I said. 'Except instead of make-up, it's wires and computer chips. Probably looks like chaos to everyone else, but it makes sense to me.'

'Yes!' Isabel said. 'Exactly.'

But she was still organizing jars and tubes into slightly neater piles. As she worked, a sheet of paper emerged from under the mess. It was a sketch of a lion, his face and mane painted entirely with make-up.

I lifted it off the desk. 'Cool. Is this for a video demo? It looks kind of like the ones you did for Halloween last – I mean, it could be for Halloween, if you ever – if you wanted—'

'You watched my videos?' Isabel's smile was shrewd.

I'd just given her the upper hand.

'I might have checked you out,' I said. 'I mean, them – checked them out – the videos.'

I suck at this.

She smiled wider and plucked the paper from my hand. 'This is for school. I'm doing make-up for the musical.'

'Oh yeah. *The Wizard of Oz*, right?'

I'd seen the Emerald City posters up around school.

'Yep. I love doing stage make-up.'

I scanned the desk for more evidence of her work and caught a glimpse of myself in one of the mirrors. I pulled a face. A zit I hadn't thought was a big deal at home was suddenly an oozing red dome of disgusting. I cupped a hand around my chin.

'Harsh lighting.'

'Accurate lighting,' Isabel corrected. She smiled, pointing her chin at mine. 'I can help you with that.'

'With what? This? No.' I didn't move my hand.

Isabel laughed out loud and reached for my face. 'It's probably an ingrown hair from shaving. It happens to a lot of men.'

Men, she said. *Not boys.*

Her fingers wrapped around mine, and I let her tug my hand away to expose my ugly new friend. 'Oh yeah, no problem,' she said.

She let go of my hand to dip her fingers in a tiny pot of beige mud – at least, that's what it looked like. This time, when she reached for me, I pulled back.

'I don't think so,' I said. 'I don't wear make-up.'

'Why not?'

'Uh ... 'cause I'm a guy?'

Isabel rolled her eyes. 'A lot of guys wear make-up. Hollywood actors wear make-up – on- *and* offscreen. Are you so much more manly than them?'

She raised one dark eyebrow in a sharply defined arch, and the answer to her question was clear.

'No,' I said. Then I gave in and let her go to work.

Within thirty seconds I had forgotten all about my make-up phobia. I was too focused on the way Isabel leaned in close, her face just inches from mine. I could feel the tickle of her hair and smell her gum. Spearmint.

She chattered as she dabbed my face with this and that, quizzing me on Spanish vocab and laughing at my mispronunciations. It felt easy, talking to her – even if I didn't understand all the words. Finally, after what seemed like a ridiculous amount of time to spend covering up one zit, she declared she was finished and held up a mirror.

'Whoa, it's like you erased it,' I said, turning my head side to side. The zit was invisible from every angle.

Isabel set down the mirror, and suddenly – without

the make-up and brushes to buffer – the too-small space between us was uncomfortably close.

I cleared my throat but didn't move. 'Did you know only twenty per cent of hikers who attempt the Appalachian Trail finish it?'

'Oh,' Isabel said quietly. She stayed as still as I was. 'That's ... interesting?'

And then we were both moving, slowly, and not away from each other. We were closing the distance between us, making the too-small space even smaller. It was about to disappear completely when someone knocked on the door.

We broke apart so fast, my chair rocked back on two legs, and Isabel had to stifle a laugh.

'Dinner's in twenty minutes,' Isabel's mom said, poking her head in the door. 'Eli, do you want to stay?'

'Sure. Or no, I mean. No, I have to go home for dinner. But thanks.'

She smiled and backed out of the room, pushing the door open all the way as she went. As soon as she was gone, I dropped my head into my hands.

'Oh my God, I thought that only happened in movies.'

Isabel couldn't contain her laugh anymore. 'Seriously! Her timing was perfect.'

I looked up with a smile. 'Actually, I thought it was pretty terrible.'

Isabel didn't need any blush for the pink her cheeks turned just then.

'If we only have twenty minutes, we should probably open a book,' she said.

I tried to hide my disappointment at this change in activity and pulled a Spanish workbook from my backpack.

'Why did you offer to help me?' I asked.

Isabel grinned. 'I took pity on you after that *Ooh la la*.'

I hung my head in exaggerated embarrassment, and Isabel laughed out loud.

'No, no!' she cried. 'It was so cute!'

I looked up. 'Cute?'

She met my eyes for only a second before glancing away. 'Also, I owe you for not outing me to Ashley in the hallway. That must have been . . . awkward.'

'Nah,' I lied. 'It wasn't so bad. Besides, I had a good view.'

Isabel busied herself with clearing us a study space on the desk, but I could see the smile spreading across her face. Zach would never believe I could be this confident around a girl. Maybe it was Isabel calling me a man that made me really feel like one.

We spent the rest of the time genuinely studying, practising conjugations and grammar, and despite my best efforts, I couldn't quite re-create the moment that had been spoiled. Still, spending the afternoon with a girl who made my stomach do this strange swooping thing? I didn't want it to end.

I was reluctantly packing up my workbooks when Isabel got a text that made her groan.

'What's wrong?' I asked.

'I'm supposed to go to the Ravens concert this weekend, but I just lost my ride.'

'That sucks. Where are they playing?'

'It's in a field outside Iowa City, so like an hour away. Damn!' She wrapped a fist around her phone and pounded it on her leg. 'All my friends are going up Friday to camp out, but I have dress rehearsal – full make-up. I can't get out of it. This other girl was supposed to go up Saturday with me, but she bailed.'

'I'm sorry,' I said. And I really was. I liked smiling Isabel much more than scowling Isabel.

She thought a moment. 'Unless . . .'

She looked up at me, and I could almost see the light bulb turn on over her head. 'I have this extra ticket now. I don't suppose you like the Ravens?'

The Ravens were one of those bands kids followed around all summer, from state to state, selling bean burritos out of the backs of their trucks for gas money and getting high and swaying to the same songs every other night. I didn't really see the appeal . . . until now.

'I *love* the Ravens,' I said. 'Or, well – I love concerts – or music, *love* music.'

Well, that last bit was true, anyway.

I yanked my headphones out of my backpack and wrapped them around my neck to prove it.

'Do you want to go?' Isabel asked, balancing on her toes in a way that reminded me of Mouse. 'Please say yes.'

I didn't hesitate. 'Yes.'

'Yay!'

'Except . . .'

'Oh no.'

'No, it's just, I don't have a car, and I kind of doubt my dad or his girlfriend will let me borrow theirs for an out-of-town trip.'

Isabel's excitement disintegrated.

'My friend Mouse has a car, though,' I spit out. 'We'd have to get him a ticket, and inviting him might mean inviting a few other people, but . . .'

'Okay,' Isabel agreed, smiling again. 'That's fine. Invite anyone you want. Tickets are super cheap online – practically free, because the Ravens are amazing like that.'

'Yeah,' I agreed. 'Amazing.'

In fact, they were pretty much my new favourite band.

26

I called Mouse before I even pulled out of Isabel's driveway and threatened his life if he didn't agree to drive us all to the concert Saturday. I had to promise to buy his ticket and pay for gas, but that was a small price for an entire day of music, a girl, and glorious freedom.

Then I drove straight to Zach's house and pounded on his front door.

'Where's the fire?' Zach's dad threw the door open, a broad smile on his face and a dish towel draped over one shoulder. 'Hey, Eli. Come on in. Zach's in the kitchen.'

Zach wasn't the only one. His mom was zooming around, as always, cleaning up their dinner mess, while his little sister bounced a soccer ball on her knee – one hand spotting the ball, the other wrapped around a grilled cheese sandwich. Zach was the calm at the centre of the storm, sitting cross-legged on top of the kitchen counter, his computer in his lap. Zach frowned when he saw me, but he hopped off the counter and motioned for me to follow him down a hall to his room. I started talking as soon as he closed the door.

'Look, I know you're annoyed with me right now, and I probably owe you an apology, but can we just skip past all of that and fast-forward to the part where I tell you I just spent the last two hours at Isabel Ortega's house?!'

Zach's eyes, which had narrowed as I talked, now flew open wide. 'What?'

'Yeah.'

'Isabel.'

'Yep.'

'Ortega.'

'The one and only.'

'Did you—'

'No, Zach, I did not *inject her with my code.*'

He laughed, and I collapsed onto his bed, overwhelmed by my good fortune.

'What were you doing at her house?'

I told him all about the Ashley–Isabel encounter and how it had given me the guts to talk to Isabel, how she had offered to help me with Spanish, and how we'd almost kissed. I didn't even try to sound cool in the retelling, because this was Zach, and he knew exactly how big a deal an almost-kiss with Isabel Ortega was.

'And hey,' I said, sitting up, 'she invited me to a concert this weekend and said I could invite anyone I want. You *have* to come.'

'What concert?'

'The Ravens.'

He scrunched up his face. 'Are we Ravens fans?'

'We are now.'

He nodded. He understood.

And I realised my good fortune wasn't limited to Isabel.

I made myself a promise right then that I wouldn't blow Zach off again – not for ACC practise or Friends of Bishop or even a girl.

'The concert is up north at some fairgrounds outside of Iowa City,' I said.

'Okay.'

'And Isabel needed a ride.'

'But we don't have cars.'

'Right.' I held my breath, not looking forward to this next part. 'That's why I had to invite Mouse. You met him the other day – sort of.'

'Oh.' Zach's face went dark.

'And Seth. He'll probably go too—'

'Why are you hanging out with Seth March?' Zach exploded. 'He's such a d-bag, and he's not even in our grade. And don't say he's helping you with Spanish, because I'm not that stupid.'

I tugged at a loose thread on Zach's comforter. The seconds ticked by as I pulled the string, watching it slowly unravel back and forth along the comforter's edge.

'I wanted to tell you,' I said without looking up.

Zach's desk chair squeaked as he dropped into it and rolled it forward to sit square in front of me.

'Tell me what?'

Everything.

But *everything* was still too dangerous. We had two months to go before the reveal, and I honestly didn't know if I could trust Zach to keep our secret that long. It was a shitty thing to ask of him – maybe even shittier than not telling him at all.

I decided a half-truth was better than a lie.

'We're entering the American Cybersecurity Competition. Seth and Mouse and I.'

Zach stared at me. 'That's … not what I was expecting,' he finally said.

'They invited me onto their team,' I rushed to explain. 'I didn't tell you because I felt guilty, like it was a … a … I don't know, *betrayal*. I thought you might get—'

'Wow. The ACC,' Zach breathed, and I heard the jealousy in his exhale. 'Lucky you.'

'I know. I know. It should be me and you going, not me and them, but—'

'How long have you known?'

I covered my face with my hands. Keeping the website a secret was one thing, but not telling Zach about the competition seemed really silly now.

'Two weeks,' I said.

Zach crossed his arms and let out a little grunt of disgust. 'Well, that explains a lot.'

'I'm sorry.'

'For what?'

'For . . . I don't know. Entering without you?'

'Well, that's stupid,' he said.

It was my turn to be speechless.

'Why would you be sorry about that?' Zach asked. 'If they'd asked me, I'd have said yes too.'

When I finally found my voice, I said, 'You would? I mean . . . you're not mad?'

'About you joining their team? No.'

I sensed a 'but' coming.

'But . . .'

There it is.

'You lying about it? Yeah, that part kind of pisses me off. Like I'm so sensitive I couldn't handle it if you told me.'

'No, that's not what—'

'Or I'm such a dick I'd be mad at you for doing it.'

'No, I – shit, I'm sorry. I don't know what I was worried about.'

'I mean, I'm totally jealous,' Zach assured me. 'But I don't blame you.'

'Well, next year, we're entering together, you and me . . . and maybe Mouse. He's a Java genius. I think you'll like him.'

'Where is the competition?' Zach asked. 'Don't they hold it in a different city every year?'

'Chicago,' I said. 'In June. Seth said his parents are going to drive us and pay for our hotel.'

Zach looked doubtful. 'Uh-huh. And what's your dad say about that?'

'I haven't exactly mentioned it yet.'

He laughed. 'Good luck with that. Maybe I can take your spot on the team when he says no.'

We talked a little more about the ACC and a lot more about Isabel, and then we worked on our augmented reality app for the rest of the night. By the time I left Zach's house, we were so back to normal that I almost forgot to feel guilty for not telling him about the website.

*

Persuading my friends to go to the concert had been easy. Persuading Dad to let *me* go was another story.

'But it's not even overnight,' I said, my voice dangerously close to a whine. 'It's just up and back on Saturday.'

'You mentioned camping,' Dad said.

'Other people will be camping. Not me.'

We were squared off across the kitchen island. Dad had only half listened to my request before shooting it down, and I'd had to remind him twice that he had already ungrounded me.

'But you'll be at some campsite?' he said.

'No, Dad, forget the camping. No one is camping, okay?'

'I think camping would be a good experience for you. Spend some time outdoors, away from your computer. Unplug a little.'

'Dad—'

'I did Outward Bound around your age. It was the best—'

'Dad!'

'What?'

'It's just a concert. It's just one Saturday.'

Dad squinted at me. 'You sure this isn't some computer convention you're sneaking off to?'

I paused. Was there an insult in there? I had to be a pretty major loser if my own dad found it so unbelievable that I would go to a concert.

'First of all,' I said, 'there's really no such thing as a "computer convention." Second of all, you can Google it. The Ravens. Saturday. Outside of Iowa City.'

'I'm still not—'

'Look, you're always saying I need to expand my horizons ... find more interests, right? Well, that's what I'm doing. I bet they don't even have Wi-Fi.'

'Hmm.' Dad twisted his lips in calculation. 'And your driver is a boy named ... Mouse?'

'It's a nickname.'

'It's disturbing.'

'Oh for the love!' Misty's voice exploded from the doorway. 'I can't listen to you two bicker back and forth anymore. Let the kid go to the concert already.'

Kid? Me? She was one to talk.

But she was taking my side, in her own way, so I kept my trap shut for the moment.

It took about ten seconds for Misty to do what I'd been trying to do for ten minutes, but she persuaded Dad to let me go. When he left the kitchen, I shoved my hands in my pockets and said a grudging 'Thanks.'

'Have you ever been to a concert?' Misty asked.

I shook my head, a little embarrassed. Misty had probably been to a hundred concerts.

'It's a rite of passage,' she said.

'It's just a concert.'

She smiled in this knowing way, like she was so much older and wiser. *Gag.*

'You're going with Zach?' she asked. She circled the island to dig for something in the fridge. She'd been doing that a lot lately – as if she was searching for just the right food for us to bond over.

'Yeah, Zach . . . and some other people.'

Misty emerged from the fridge with a slice of this store-bought chocolate cake she was obsessed with. It was kind of hypocritical the way she sugar-binged in between the healthy meals she made us choke down. She pulled two forks from a drawer and handed me one. 'What other people? Your friends who were here the other day?'

'Them and also . . . this girl.'

'Isabel?'

Nosy.

'Yeah.'

'You don't have to talk about her if you don't want to,' she said.

Not falling for that reverse psychology.

But talking about Isabel had quickly become my favourite thing, so I forked a chunk of cake and spoke through a mouthful of chocolate. 'She's just this girl helping me with Spanish. Her family's from Mexico, so she grew up speaking both.'

Misty nodded and said, extra-casual, 'You know, if you wanted to impress a girl who speaks Spanish, you might say something like, "*Veo la luz de las estrellas en tus ojos*" . . . if you wanted to.'

'If I wanted to,' I repeated, looking away.

We both took a bite of cake and chewed quietly for a minute.

Then I tried out the words. '*Vea la loose duh—*'

'*Veo la luz de las estrellas en tus ojos.*'

'Sounds a little flowery.'

Misty waved her fork around. 'So maybe something more like, "*Me haces sonreîr*".'

I attempted to translate. 'You make me . . .'

'Smile.'

'Right.' I pulled out my phone. 'Can you spell that?'

Misty dictated a few more compliments in Spanish, and I saved them all on my cell, trying not to seem too grateful. Two thank-yous in one day felt excessive, so when we finished, I just gave her a sharp nod as I put away my phone.

'Cool.'

'Cool,' she echoed, the ghost of a smile on her lips.

27

I got up extra early Saturday to spend some time covering up my chin zit with the little tub of make-up Misty had left in my room after my black eye. I must have absorbed some of Isabel's skill, because I didn't do a half-bad job.

'*Me haces sonreír*,' I said to my reflection. '*Me gustas mucho.*'

'Not bad.'

The voice startled me so much I dropped the make-up jar in the sink with a clatter.

'Dad, don't sneak up on me like that.'

'Your room but my house,' Dad said. He peered into the sink. 'Is that Misty's make—'

'It's nothing.' I snatched up the jar and hid it in my fist.

'I am heading up to Iowa City for work today. I thought maybe, since we were going the same direction, you might want a ride to your concert – you and your friends.'

'You want to drive us?' I choked out. 'Am I being punished for something?'

Dad leaned on the doorframe and winked. 'Just yanking your chain, bud. I was sixteen once too, y'know.'

'You sure about that?'

He rubbed his bald dome. 'Had a full head of hair and everything.'

'Impossible.'

'Hey, you missed a spot.' He tapped his chin to indicate my zit and then laughed as I checked my work in the mirror.

'Drive safe,' he said, closing the door as he ducked out.

It had been like that for a few days now – ever since I told him I'd finally scored an extra-credit assignment for Spanish. Isabel had helped with that. I'd dragged her to Señora Vega's room to swear she was my tutor. The two had talked crazy fast in Spanish, then looked at me and cracked up laughing – whatever that was about – and by the end of the conversation, Vega had offered me extra credit for a series of reports written in Spanish.

Dad had been impressed, and the feeling I got from this new proud dad was a lot like the feeling I got after we launched the website, and I'd started walking with my head up instead of pointed at the floor.

And my head just kept tilting higher. Every day we didn't get busted by a cybersnoop my confidence grew. The two videos we posted that week were a little embarrassing for a couple of deserving people, but we managed not to ruin any lives, so I chalked that up as a win. Even Malcolm had stayed out of my eyesight the rest of the week, so I was flying pretty high as I got dressed and bounded down the stairs to the kitchen.

'What are you smiling about?' Misty said, startling me out of my thoughts.

'Uh, nothing. Just – excited to get out of the house today.'

'Me too.' She leaned against the counter, waiting for me to ask her what her plans were. Lucky for her, I was in an extra great mood, so I obliged.

'I'm just headed to the farmers market for some seeds,' she said. 'I'm going to start a garden in the backyard, I think.'

'Sounds like a party.'

'Well, it's no concert with my friends,' she laughed. 'But I like working with my hands.'

And all your other parts.

I held my breath for a second, afraid I'd said it out loud. Then I frowned. Something must be wrong. Usually I was proud of zingers like that, but this one tasted a little … bitter, maybe? Even though Misty couldn't hear my thoughts, I felt the sudden urge to apologise – or at least change the subject.

'Hey, Misty, is this outfit okay? For an outdoor concert? Or any concert?'

She motioned for me to turn in a circle, so she could inspect my jeans and faded gray T-shirt.

'Not bad for a guy who's never been to a concert. You didn't break the cardinal rule, at least.'

'What's that?'

'Wearing a shirt of the band you're going to see.'

'Guess I'd have to be a fan of the band to have their shirt to begin with,' I said.

I checked to make sure I had my wallet and started gathering up gum and snacks and other items I'd need for the day.

Misty handed me something that looked like a mini deodorant stick.

'Sunscreen,' she said, when I sniffed at it.

I stuck it in my back pocket. 'Thanks.'

'It doesn't matter if you're a fan of the band,' she said. 'It's not really about that.'

'What do you mean?' I could sense her getting deep on me, and I fidgeted a little.

Her voice was wistful – or as wistful as it could be with its gravel texture. 'These moments go by really fast. Make sure you stop and appreciate them while they're happening instead of looking back and wishing you could relive them.'

Definitely too deep. She was trying to force some 'moment' on me.

'Um. I'll do that,' I said.

A horn honked outside. Mouse.

I checked my pockets one more time – cell phone, sunglasses, wallet, gum, sunscreen, granola bars, Chapstick (coconut-flavored, just in case), and two small flash drives that I had taken to carrying around with me everywhere. They were mostly full of website files, that I was afraid to leave on my computer in case Misty snooped.

Not that she could get through my firewalls, but hey, I didn't know she spoke Spanish either, so I guess you can't be too careful.

Mouse honked again, more insistently.

'Go, already!' Misty said, shoving me toward the door.

I glanced back after I stepped off the porch at Misty standing in the doorway, looking every inch a mom. It was the kind of pose that normally made me retch, but today – I don't know, maybe it was the good mood again, but it didn't bother me so much.

I said an awkward goodbye and bailed.

*

'See this?' Mouse shoved a phone in my face before I'd even closed the car door.

'Hello to you t—'

'Look!' He slapped the phone into my hand and rapped the screen fast with his finger. His other hand was on the wheel as he navigated his way backward down the drive.

'All right, all right!' I took the phone out from under his finger hammer.

On the screen, Mrs. Windemere looked out with sad eyes from an unflattering mugshot. 'Haver High Teacher Arrested for Shoplifting,' the headline blazed.

So much for not ruining any lives this week.

'You can go to jail for that?' I asked.

'Of course. Read the rest of it.'

'I'm not sure I want to.'

This was putting a serious kink in my happy day.

'It calls us "digital detectives"!' Mouse reached over to tap the screen again, but I held the phone out of his reach.

'Just drive.'

He put both hands back on the wheel but rattled on. 'It says Friends of Bishop has helped solve two crimes already, busting a drug ring—'

'It wasn't a drug ring.'

'—and now a teacher. It says instead of looking for us, maybe cybermonitors should be asking for our help. Our *help*! Can you believe that?'

I really couldn't.

All along, I'd been worried about the site getting us in

too much trouble to take it to the competition, but here we were – at least one news site's definition of internet heroes.

*

Seth was our first stop on the way out of town. At first I was relieved to see he hadn't worn his Byte Me T-shirt, until I realised he was wearing one that read Khaleesi is My Queen. I almost asked him to change it, but I was afraid of what else was in his closet.

'Shotgun!' he cried, opening the passenger door and practically dragging me out of the front seat.

I didn't mind getting in back. That would just mean I had to spend the next hour squished up next to Isabel. No problem.

'Did you see?' Mouse said, passing his phone to Seth.

I tuned out while they made fun of the mugshot and congratulated themselves. They could only talk about it for so long anyway, because soon we were pulling up to Zach's house.

He climbed in back with me, and the reception from the front seat was only mildly chilly.

'It's going to get crowded in here,' Seth complained under his breath.

'Well, feel free to get out, then,' Zach said.

Mouse flipped around in his seat and gave Zach a jittery fist bump. 'Hey, we met the other day. Hi again! Sorry we have to keep Seth around, but we need him to split the snacks. Road food is expensive. Do you know the actual production cost of turkey jerky?'

Zach's icy front thawed a little. 'Next to nothing, I bet.'

'Exactly!' Mouse spun back around and put the car in gear. 'The markup is insane. I'm going to study economics when I get to Caltech ...'

'I thought you were going to be an elephant herder,' I said.

Mouse rolled his eyes as he put the car in gear. 'Trainer, not herder. But that obviously won't pay the bills.'

'Duh, Eli!' Seth said with mock seriousness. 'Clearly, Mouse is also going to do all the other elephant herders' taxes to make ends meet.'

Seth and I laughed, but next to me, Zach was serious and leaned forward to say to Mouse, 'You want to be a mahout?'

Because of course, Zach would know what that is.

'I read there's a camp you can go to in Thailand for that,' Zach said.

'I know!' Mouse bobbed up and down in the driver's seat. 'But you have to be eighteen, so I'm thinking summer after graduation ...'

I smiled to myself as Zach and Mouse chattered on. I knew those two would hit it off.

But my smile faded as we neared our next destination, and I frantically ordered everyone to 'be cool' and not embarrass me in front of Isabel. In turn, they all laughed their asses off and promised to do their best to utterly humiliate me. By the time we pulled up outside her house, I had broken out into a sweat.

I dried my palms on my jeans and shoved over to give her maximum space as she slid into the seat next to me.

'Eli,' Zach said from my other side. 'A little room?'

'Oh, sorry.' I had squished him right up against the door. I coughed to clear my throat and spoke to the rest of the car. 'Guys, this is Isabel. Isabel, these are the guys.'

'Hi, guys,' she said, a wink in her voice.

And then, by some miracle, we managed to get out of town without any of them doing a single thing to embarrass me.

*

Halfway down the road, Mouse and Seth got into a pretty entertaining argument over the radio. Seth had been up all night crafting what he declared 'the ultimate road-trip playlist,' but Mouse insisted on full control of his audio system – 'no exceptions.'

From the back seat, Zach and Isabel and I placed bets on who would crack first. It turned out to be Mouse.

'Fine! Play your stupid songs,' he snapped at Seth.

'I knew it!' Isabel laughed.

Zach clucked his tongue. 'Mouse, you let me down, man. I placed money on you.'

'Speaking of . . .' I said, holding out my hand. Zach dug in his pocket and dropped two quarters in my palm.

'You cost me half a Mountain Dew,' he complained to Mouse.

'I'm sorry,' Mouse said. 'He wore me down!'

'He usually does,' I drawled.

'Quiet.' Seth shushed us all and loaded up his playlist. 'Prepare to be amazed.'

And then all chatter stopped as we were drowned out by a relentless drumbeat. No one complained about the song choice, and even Mouse grudgingly turned up the volume, until the car felt like one giant pounding speaker. The percussion hit a crescendo near the end of the song, and we all drummed along, hands pounding seats, feet pounding the floor, until I couldn't tell whether the car was shaking from the bass or from our stomping.

My body vibrated with energy, alive in a way I'd never quite felt before. Misty's words crept into my head, about appreciating these moments while they're happening, and

I smiled around the car ... at everyone lost in the beat, at this moment of total freedom ... and deliberately soaked it in. My eyes fell on Isabel, her dark hair whipped into a wild, beautiful mess by the wind rushing through our open windows.

This is the greatest day of my life.

She caught me staring and smiled, bumping her shoulder into mine.

So far.

28

I could have stayed in Mouse's car, flying down the highway, all day, but too soon we were in a long line of cars snaking down a dirt road between two fields that stank of fresh manure.

'I hope it doesn't smell like this during the show,' Seth complained, covering his nose.

Mouse laughed. 'Trust me, all we'll be able to smell during the show is marijuana.'

'Hey, how do you say "marijuana" in Spanish?' I asked Isabel.

When she answered, I could tell she was holding back a laugh. 'Uh ... "*marijuana*."'

'Oh yeah,' I stuttered, feeling stupid. 'It does sound Spanish.'

And here I'd been worried about the guys embarrassing me. Turned out, I could do that all by myself.

'It's Mexican, specifically,' Isabel said. 'We just learned about it in World Hist – Oh! Eli!' She squeezed my arm, and the squeeze went all the way to my chest. 'That's what we should do for your first extra-credit report – the Mexican Revolution.'

'Which was about pot?'

Isabel laughed out loud and put her hands to her face. '*¡Ay, Dios mío!* You need a history tutor too.'

The crawling line of cars finally dumped out into a giant swath of dirt serving as a parking lot. All around us, people were sporting fringe and tie-dye, apparently confused about whether they were here to see the Ravens or the Grateful Dead.

'Did we make a left turn into Coachella?' Seth asked as we spilled out of the car.

'Totally,' Zach agreed. 'What a bunch of posers.'

They looked at each other sideways for a second, unsure of how they felt about sharing an opinion.

I was about to join their chorus of derision when I noticed the black bag resting on Isabel's hip had a layer of fringe on the flap.

'Give it a chance,' I said. 'Nothing wrong with a little dress-up.'

Zach snorted and started to mock me, but I shot him a look that only a best friend would understand, and he clammed up. Fortunately, Isabel didn't see because she was texting furiously. She looked up and announced her friends were waiting for us by the entrance.

Us?

I had half expected, once we got to the concert, that Isabel would ditch us. It was a pleasant surprise that she was willing to introduce us to her friends … her *girl* friends. The guys would all owe me so big after today.

Isabel's friends weren't the only kids from school at the show. Guys from chess club chatted up Zach while we stood in line to get through the gates, a group of laughing freshman girls swirled around us as we entered the outdoor arena, and kids from almost every one of my classes were lazing on the grassy hill that looked down on a massive stage. It was strange seeing all these familiar faces in an unfamiliar setting. Somehow with green fields and blue sky as the backdrop instead of hallways and classrooms, everyone looked a little bit different … a little bit more the same.

We found a patch of grass, and Isabel and her friends started unloading their giant purses. Isabel pulled a blanket from hers and spread it on the ground. One of her friends, a tall girl with long wavy hair, had managed to get two large flasks past the bag check, and she held them up now, one in each hand.

'Whiskey?'

Zach and Seth practically knocked each other down trying to be the first to take a sip, and I had to stifle a laugh. I knew for a fact that they were more interested in the girl than the booze.

Seth got there first. 'Nice flask,' he said. 'Pewter?'

'What?' She wrinkled her forehead.

'The metal.' He tapped it with a finger. 'It's pewter instead of stainless steel, right? More traditional – helps preserve the flavor.'

He looked pretty proud of himself, but Isabel's friend only shrugged.

'Oh. I have no idea.' She took a swig from the other flask and laughed. 'I just stole these from my dad.'

Zach watched the entire exchange and then took a different approach.

'Cool boots,' he said, pointing past the girl's long legs to her fringe-covered footwear.

I caught his eye and flashed a thumbs-up when she wasn't looking. Much better to compliment the boots than the barware.

Soon the sun was setting and the music starting, and everything was electric. I didn't have to be a Ravens fan to appreciate musicians going wild onstage while the sky exploded into a kaleidoscope of orange and red behind them.

And that spectacle was nothing compared with the one happening right in front of me. Mouse was a tornado of terrible dance moves. His elbows were akimbo in a crazy chicken stance while his feet kicked out an Irish jig and his head banged off beat. And somehow he managed to do all of this while also spinning around in a circle. At first I was embarrassed for him – and for myself, for bringing him – but Isabel and her friends were disarmed by his whacky moves, and soon they were imitating the steps.

I marveled at the skinny little weirdo, the way he just threw himself out there with zero self-consciousness, the complete lack of surprise he showed when others started to copy him. It was more than confidence. It was complete abandon. He danced like it was his last chance.

Isabel hung back while her friends skipped around Mouse.

'You don't dance?' I asked her.

She laughed. 'Contrary to popular belief, not all Latinas have moves.'

'Well, me neither,' I said. 'I'm really not good at anything besides computers.'

'Nah, there's more to you than that,' Isabel said, looking up at me through thick lashes. 'I can tell when people are keeping secrets, and you, Eli Bennett, have secrets.'

Truth.

'You can tell, huh?' I said, trying to keep my voice light.

'Yep. My *abuela* says I have "the sight".'

'The sight? Sounds like a superpower.'

She grinned. 'Watch out. My real power is that people always end up giving up their secrets to me.'

I shivered then, and I wasn't sure if it was because of Isabel's 'sight' or the fact that she had just moved to stand closer to me.

Most of us couldn't keep up with Mouse and just set to swaying back and forth to the music. Isabel and I swayed side by side, bumping shoulders a lot ... accidentally at first, then on purpose.

I barely heard the songs being played, but as the sun sank behind the stage and the crowd moved and pulsed like a giant beating heart, I already knew this would go down in my own personal history as one of the greatest concerts of all time.

29

The energy from the show followed us into the parking lot. No one seemed eager to leave, and so the crowd stayed, lingering in the dirt lot, forming clusters around trucks and tents – a postshow tailgate party.

Our group swelled to include other kids from school, and I was annoyed to see Ashley Thorne at the centre of the crowd. She had some ridiculous scarf tied around her head like the one Misty had worn last Halloween when she dressed up as a hippie chick, and she was talking at the top of her lungs, so it was impossible for anyone else to have a conversation. I leaned against the front grill of a pickup, wedged between Isabel and Mouse, and tried to ignore her. A little apart from the crowd, Isabel's friends were in the shadows, passing a joint back and forth, while Seth wandered in circles, trying to get a phone signal.

And Dad thought *I* couldn't unplug.

'I haven't submitted any videos,' I heard Ashley say from a few feet away. 'But I know people who have.'

My ears, trying so hard to tune Ashley out, now tuned back in.

'Maybe,' she said, in answer to a question I couldn't hear. 'If they really deserved it. But you have to be careful, you know?' She lowered her voice for drama, but somehow it still carried. 'Wherever you are, whatever you're doing, Friends of Bishop could be listening, watching.'

You have no idea.

I patted my pocket subconsciously, checking to see that my flash drives were still there – including one with a file marked 'Ashley Thorne.' It burned like a red letter *A* in my pocket. I wasn't actually sure what that meant, because I hadn't bothered to read *The Scarlet Letter* for Lit, but I got the gist that it was something to feel guilty about.

The group around Ashley rumbled with conversation, and it struck me that if the Chat Mob app still existed, most of these people would be standing around texting each other instead of talking to each other. It was just one more way life was different after Jordan. I could pick out other voices now, kids all talking about the website but no one copping to submitting any videos.

'What does that even mean?' someone asked. '"Friends of Bishop"?'

'Jordan Bishop,' someone else answered.

'Are you sure?'

People were talking on top of each other now.

'It's so obvious!'

'Everyone knows that!'

'The website started the same week as his . . . anniversary, or whatever.'

Then Ashley's voice cut through the rest. 'Guys, not to be mean, but . . . did Jordan Bishop even *have* friends?'

On my right, Mouse went uncharacteristically still. I felt it where his shoulder touched my arm – a cord pulled taut and vibrating with tension. I tried to read his expression, but with the truck's headlights blazing behind him, his face was all shadow. I was grateful he didn't know I once asked the same question about Jordan.

One person suggested Friends of Bishop were students from a rival school. Another thought maybe we were the district's cybersnoops, setting a trap to catch people behaving badly online. And a few people called us cowards, but if anyone else agreed, they were too afraid to vocalise it. I just couldn't tell whether they were afraid of us . . . or afraid of disagreeing with Ashley, who seemed to be our biggest fan.

The irony.

A girl next to Ashley sighed. 'Whoever they are, they're scary. And awesome,' she rushed to add, looking around as though a camera might be recording her. 'Awesome-scary.'

'I totally know what you mean,' a guy near the centre of

the group said. 'Hackers are like today's mobsters – scary but kind of awesome at the same time.'

I ducked my head so no one would see me smile. Not that I wanted to be called a mobster, but the comparison made me feel a strange mix of pride and shame.

'What do you think?' I asked Isabel quietly.

'About Friends of Bishop?' She screwed up her lips. '*No lo sé.* They're smart. Really smart. They'd have to be, to not get caught.'

I nodded, smiling.

Isabel continued, 'But I don't think they're Jordan Bishop's friends. I think maybe they're just anarchists.'

'Why's that?'

'Because if they were really his friends, where were they last year?'

On my other side, Mouse pushed off the truck. I turned to say something – anything – to soften Isabel's words, but he was already walking away, his usually light feet dragging. His abrupt exit was covered by the rest of the crowd starting to break up. Kids were calling out good nights, and car engines were revving. All across the parking lot, headlights came on, and tires spun softly on the dirt.

Isabel planned to ride home with her friends, but she waved them away.

'Two minutes,' she promised them, with a head tilt in my direction.

I pretended not to notice.

But whatever Isabel thought we could accomplish in those two minutes was ruined by the fact that Ashley and her pals were among the few people left loitering. The circle tightened, bringing them close enough for Ashley to notice us in her orbit.

'Hi, Isabel,' she said.

'Hey.'

The girls exchanged uneasy smiles.

'I love that sweater!' Ashley's voice was overly sweet, as she reached out to feel the fabric of Isabel's sleeve. 'I used to have the same one, but I donated it. Now I wish I'd kept it.'

Isabel's response was a stony silence I didn't understand. She narrowed her eyes and hunched her shoulders, as if bracing for a blow.

And then the blow came.

'I gave mine to Fashion with Passion,' Ashley said. 'Is that where you got it?'

Fashion with Passion was a program for underprivileged families in Haver. Rich people donated stuff to feel good about themselves, and poor people begrudgingly took their worn-out hand-me-downs so they could spend money on things like food instead. And so the world went 'round.

I didn't think Isabel's family needed any handouts, based on the size of their house and all of that expensive camera equipment they'd bought for her, but what did facts matter to people like Ashley?

'I get a lot of vintage pieces there,' Isabel said, crossing her arms over the sweater.

'Oh, totally. Vintage, retro . . . and last year's designs at a discount.' Ashley flashed a bleached-white smile. 'Well, it looks *so much better* on you.'

Isabel's face finally cracked in a one-sided smirk.

'Yeah,' she said. 'It does.'

Then she stood up straight, leaned over to kiss my cheek, and walked away . . . Ashley gaping at her back.

'God,' Ashley said. 'You try to be nice to someone . . .'

She looked at me for confirmation, but I just rolled my eyes and trotted off after Isabel. My cheek was sticky with her lip gloss, and I felt cheated out of learning what that gloss tasted like. I caught up to her, grinning and ready to scoop her up in a victory hug, but I stopped short when I saw her face.

She hurried to brush them away, but I'd already seen the tears.

'I'm sorry,' she said.

I fell into step beside her. 'Sorry for what? She's the jerk. You were – you were amazing. You totally shut her down—'

'Eli, stop,' Isabel said. 'Don't pity me, *por favor*. It only makes it worse.'

'I'm not – I swear, I'm not—'

'I'll call you tomorrow, okay?' Then she left me again, this time without a kiss, and jogged across the lot to her waiting friends.

I watched her go, feeling the cold and dark of the night suddenly rush around me. And in that cold dark – a spark. It flickered somewhere deep inside and quickly caught – spreading heat through my veins, until I was absolutely on fire.

I spun on my heel and stormed back to where Seth was standing alone, his arm high, phone to the sky – still trying to get a signal. I grabbed his other arm and forced open his hand. He tried to pull back, startled by this sudden human interaction, but I held him tight. Then I reached into my back pocket, closed my hand over the right flash drive, and pressed it into his palm.

'The Ashley Thorne file,' I told him. 'It'll be our best post yet.'

30

I woke up the next day with the dry taste of regret in my mouth and a sick feeling in my stomach. I hadn't even touched the whiskey, but I was hungover all the same. I knew I'd had a blast, but the end of the night was a little fuzzy and the feeling this morning was awful. That was a hangover, right?

I called Seth before I got out of bed.

'Don't post the video of Ashley,' I said, by way of hello.

'Okay.'

I paused. That was too easy. 'Okay?'

'Yeah, okay. It was a little . . .'

'Too much?'

'Yeah.' He let the word out in a breath, sounding relieved that I'd called. 'I felt kind of gross watching it.'

I shared his relief. 'Me too.'

'So you must have . . .'

'Yeah, I did. But I already erased the RAT from her computer.'

'Was there anything else?'

'Nothing.' Aside from her striptease, Ashley Thorne was

surprisingly boring to spy on, like a robot that shut down when no one else was around. 'Forget about Ashley. Just delete that video, and we'll never speak of it again.'

Silence on the other end of the line.

'Seth? You still there?'

'I'm here.'

'Dude, you have to delete it.'

'I will, I will,' he promised. 'I'm just thinking about other ways to get videos. We've bottomed out on submissions.'

He was right about that. With every new article or TV clip, our video entries shrank. The bigger the headline, the smaller our inbox. The site was still getting a ton of traffic and a slew of emails – a combination of kudos and screw-yous, and here and there, even a few victims in need of vengeance – but no videos. A lot of people seemed to hope we would do the dirty work for them, and I had just shown Seth proof that I wasn't above the dirty work.

'Look,' I said. 'I've been thinking of digging something up on Malcolm Mahoney. If I can get into his computer and catch *him* doing a striptease ... now that, I'm happy to put on the site.'

Seth laughed. 'I'd like to see that.'

'Seriously, though, I think we've already proved our point enough to impress the ACC judges with the real-world challenge. Maybe we need to start focusing more on the other sections of the competition.'

'We do need to practise protecting email infrastructure during a live attack,' Seth agreed.

I took that as a yes and got off the phone before he could change his mind.

Then I stayed in bed for a few more minutes, staring at the ceiling. I'd managed to distract Seth for the moment, but the Ashley video was still a live grenade in his hands. And I had put it there.

And I'm supposed to be a genius.

*

'New high score!'

'No way! You cheated.'

Isabel nudged me to the side to see the score for herself.

We were at the arcade on Friday after school, celebrating the wrap-up of my Mexican Revolution report. Isabel had made me write it all myself, which took three whole days, before she would even look at it. Then she had shredded it with a red pen and passed it back. Brutal, but this reward at the end of the week was worth it.

'You have to hit the left button really fast, right when the ball appears on the ramp,' a voice carried over from a few feet away.

It was a freshman from Haver leaning over a pinball machine, trying to tell Malcolm how to beat the game. The downtown arcade was always packed with kids on Fridays, backpacks and purses covering the floor, lines in front of all the games. It drew every grade and every group at Haver

'Don't smudge the glass.' Malcolm shoved the kid to the side, knocking him down. That'd teach him to give pinball pointers to an ape.

I shook my head at the scene. 'Sometimes I wish I could use ones and zeros to reprogram that guy's brain.'

Isabel rolled her eyes and pulled me to the next machine. 'Okay, nerd, let's just keep moving. Best two out of three.'

But I couldn't stop watching Malcolm – watching and wondering why Friends of Bishop hadn't scared him off being a bully. The website was supposed to protect people like that little pinball wizard from guys like Malcom.

One by one, cash cards dried up, and kids moved on from the video games to the corner of the arcade that sold pizza and pop – also the only corner where the free Wi-Fi worked. Outside the pizza window, tables were full of kids on their laptops and phones, all tapped into the same network, all oblivious to the digital threads tying them together. They thought they were sitting apart – this group at a separate table from that group – but I could sense the spiderweb of energy that connected them. I could practically see it.

Isabel and I dropped our backpacks at a table not far from where Malcom sat alone, draining a Coke and texting furiously. I wished he would just get out of my eyesight already.

'Want to split a pizza?' I asked Isabel. 'My treat.'

'No, thanks. I have a family dinner thing at ...' She checked the time on her phone. 'Oh no! I'm already late.'

'Come on,' I said. 'I'll let you have all my pepperoni.'

'Tempting. But I can't.'

She kissed my cheek – *can't a guy get some lip action?* – and promised to call me later.

I was debating whether to follow her out, when Malcom pulled something from his backpack that made me stay. It was a tablet and a keyboard, and I said a silent thank-you to the cybergods for this golden opportunity. Not only was Malcolm dumb enough to log on to public Wi-Fi, he was also clueless about the equipment he was using. I couldn't pass this up.

I tugged my laptop out of my bag and fired up my key-sniffing software. It was one of those dangerous programs absolutely anyone could download for free off the internet. And all I needed to make it work was a tiny antenna that I always kept in my backpack ... just in case. I plugged the antenna into a USB port and set the software spinning.

Seconds later, it had sniffed out a vulnerability ... one wireless keyboard in use nearby.

Two mouse clicks later, my screen disappeared and was replaced with a blank slate. Now all I had to do was sit back and watch whatever Malcolm typed appear on my screen. I would know every key he touched. Unlike when I'd spied on Ashley, this one didn't give me any guilt at all. In fact, I found myself hoping to see something I could use against him. After witnessing the kind of trouble Malcolm was willing to get into right out in public, I could only imagine what he did when people weren't looking.

All I needed were a couple of usernames and passwords, and I would control his accounts. Even if I didn't find anything juicy, at the very least, I could hold his social media for ransom until he agreed to stop pushing people around.

But he didn't visit any of the usual social sites or even check his email. And after a few minutes of spying, I lost my appetite for justice. Malcolm was a surprisingly fast typer, and his keystrokes flowed across my screen.

Teenage dads
Joint custody
Paternal rights
Prenatal care

Best baby doctors Haver Iowa

Well, this was no fun.

I wanted dirt, and Malcom was giving me doting dad-to-be. It made it kind of hard to hate the guy, and as the web searches went on, I started feeling downright sorry for him.

Cost of raising a baby
Jobs that don't require college
How to apply for food stamps
What is welfare?

Finally, I closed my laptop and slipped out of the arcade, feeling like I'd seen even more of Malcolm than I had of Ashley.

*

I was due at Seth's house for ACC practise, and I took a winding route there, barely conscious of where I was going, letting my feet drag me forward by sheer muscle memory. I was too wrapped up in my own thoughts – teeter-tottering between pity and pissed off. Of course, Malcom would have to go and suddenly become father of the year after all the shitty things he'd done. It didn't excuse the way he treated everyone. He still deserved a spot on our website's wall of shame ... didn't he?

I slammed my headphones over my ears and cranked the volume on a Ravens song I'd downloaded after the concert. It was supposed to remind me of brushing shoulders with Isabel, but instead, I just kept picturing Malcolm's words on my laptop and the way he had hunched over the tablet in the coffee shop, making sure nobody else could see the screen – embarrassed, even as he sat there trying to do the right thing.

Maybe it was possible for a bad guy to be a good dad. And maybe ... just maybe ... Malcolm Mahoney was already being punished enough.

31

Halfway to Seth's house, I realised it would have been faster to go home and get my bike ... and drier too. I was dripping with sweat when I turned onto his street. They say 'April showers bring May flowers' or whatever, but here it was – almost May now, and the only showers I'd seen were from my pits, and I doubted they were going to sprout anything as nice as a flower.

I was about to walk up to Seth's front door, when I heard a noise at the side of the house. I detoured around the corner and saw Mouse facedown on the ground, with his legs half through the basement window.

'Hey,' I said.

He waved in response, shimmying further inside, feetfirst.

'What are you doing?'

'Seth's late,' Mouse said. 'He's tutoring, and the lesson ran long.'

'No one else is home?'

Mouse paused, waist-deep in the basement. 'No, they're here. I just prefer this way.'

I raised an eyebrow.

'To avoid parents,' he explained. 'Less small talk.'

The kid had a point.

I waited for him to drop out of sight, then followed him through the window.

The basement was dark and still half-plastered in sheets of plastic from the debugging, but Seth had returned all our computer equipment to the pool table. It was the only area of the rec room not covered in a film.

'I thought when you had termites, they wrapped your whole house in a big circus tent,' I said.

Mouse hopped around the pool table, turning on laptops and other equipment piece by piece. 'That's a full fumigation. This was some spot treatment Seth's dad did. He's kind of a do-it-yourselfer.'

I reached a finger toward the filmy coating on the coffee table, but Mouse stopped me.

'I wouldn't touch that!'

'Why not?'

'I said his dad's a do-it-yourselfer. I didn't say he knew what he was doing when he did it himself.'

I pulled my finger back and tucked both hands in my pockets. 'Thanks for the warning.'

'Seth's just like him,' Mouse said, firing up another computer. 'Thinks he knows everything and can do everything better than everyone else.'

Couldn't have said it better myself.

'Who is Seth tutoring?'

Mouse shook his head in distaste. 'Ashley.'

I felt a tightening in my chest. Seth had promised he'd delete the video of Ashley, but what if he'd kept it just to perv on her? It had been hard enough for me to look away from that striptease, and I didn't even like the girl.

I sat down at our computer dedicated to Friends of Bishop just as Mouse flipped the last switch at the other end of the pool table. From end to end, the table hummed with energy. Blue and white lights glowed where cables connected modems to routers to laptops to hard drives. All of it linked, all of it feeding a single system – every component essential to keeping that system alive. And that's what it was to me ... alive.

I touched my fingers to the keyboard and closed my eyes for a second, imagining I could feel the hum, that I was part of it – this virtual circle of life.

'Eli?' Mouse asked. 'You okay?'

'I'm fine. I'm just checking something.'

My eyes opened, and my fingers moved, searching the computer for Ashley's file. He had already given me back the flash drive, with the file wiped, as promised. But I had to see for myself that he hadn't saved a backup version. I did a root search for all videos but found nothing new since I'd shared the Ashley video with Seth. I tried a couple more scans, in case he'd hidden it somehow, but everything came up clean.

'What are you looking for?' Mouse asked, standing behind me now.

I jumped at his voice, not sure how he'd gone from the far end of the table to looking over my shoulder without me noticing.

'Nothing. Just a video I shouldn't have—'

'The one of Ashley?' Mouse interrupted.

I spun in my chair. 'He showed you?'

Mouse pulled up a second swivel chair and straddled it backward, using his feet on the legs to rock it side to side. 'I didn't see it. He just told me about it. Sounds pretty kinky.'

'Yeah, but not in a good way.'

'She's not a good person, you know,' Mouse said after a moment. 'She probably deserves—'

'Mouse, trust me. If you saw the video, you would feel gross about posting it.'

'You heard what she said – at the concert – about Jordan not having any friends—'

'I heard her.' I ran a hand over my face. 'Look, she's an asshole, for sure. But even if she deserved to have that video out there, we could get in so much trouble, and not just for hacking. We'd probably be breaking all kinds of laws we don't even know about.'

Mouse nodded, defeated, and pressed his forehead to the back of the chair. 'That would suck.'

He spun the seat all the way around twice, then stuck his leg out like a kickstand to stop and lifted his face. 'Hey, Eli.'

'Yeah?'

'You know that freshman caught wearing his mom's clothes?'

'The one who made his own music video?' I laughed, but Mouse didn't join me.

His face creased into a frown. 'Yeah, him.'

'What about him?'

'He missed a couple days of school last week, and when he came back, his face was all messed up.' Mouse raised his hands to his own face, demonstrating. 'Like, eyes all swollen and purple, and his jaw kind of sitting off to the side a little.'

'So?' I said. 'What, did he get hit by a bus or something?'

'He got hit by his dad.'

Mouse said it in one quick breath, and it seemed to suck the air out of the room. I wasn't sure I wanted to hear the rest of this story.

'Or maybe his mom,' Mouse said, his words spilling

out fast now. 'I don't remember exactly. I just overheard a couple people talking about it. They said his parents found out about the video, and they're these crazy antigay activists – so I guess we know where he got that from – but they didn't even see the clip, so they didn't know it was from when he was a kid. They just heard he was caught cross-dressing, and – and—'

'Stop,' I said. I *definitely* did not want to hear the rest of the story. I could piece it together myself. 'Mouse, that's not our fault. It was just supposed to be funny – maybe a little embarrassing – but not actually hurtful. We didn't do that, okay? That's not on us.'

But no matter how many different ways I said it wasn't our fault, it still felt like a lie.

'We didn't mean to hurt anyone,' I tried again.

'I did,' Mouse said. His eyes met mine, and there was no apology there, only a kind of quiet wonder. 'Not all of them. But a few – the ones who hurt Jordan – I wanted to hurt them back. A lot. I still do. I . . . I kind of fantasised about something like this happening, but now . . .'

I sat back in my chair. 'Now you feel bad.'

He shook his head. 'Not bad, just not . . . better.'

I nodded, and we sat quietly in the dark for a while – the whir of computer fans the only sound. I wasn't sure what to feel good or bad about anymore either. If I could be wrong about Malcom, I could be wrong about anyone. We were doling out punishments, but who was to say they fit the crimes? The line between white hat and black hat had blurred, and everything was suddenly very gray.

'Hey, guys!' a voice called from the top of the stairs. It was Seth's dad. 'I don't mind you sneaking in the window, but you can't be down there until I've finished cleaning up the chemicals. It's not safe.'

'Sorry,' we called back in unison.

'Now, you can come up here and wait for Seth, or you can shimmy back out the way you came.'

We shimmied.

Out on the lawn, I brushed dirt off my hands and turned to Mouse, still crawling through the window behind me. 'It's getting late. We should just reschedule.'

Mouse agreed, and I texted Seth to cancel the session.

'You know,' I said, as Mouse finally cleared the window, 'if the videos – if all of this – isn't making you feel better, maybe we can stop now.'

He stood, pausing to inspect a grass stain on his right knee. 'What?'

The sun was setting, casting long shadows in the shape of sugar maples over the yard. Mouse was standing in one of those shadows, while I was in a patch of light that shone between them.

'The videos – the website . . .' I stumbled, not sure what I wanted to say but increasingly sure that we had come to a precipice and that one step more would be the step too far.

Mouse crossed his arms and squinted at me. 'What's up, Eli?'

'How long before we get it wrong? Before we destroy someone who doesn't deserve it? Right now, we're golden, but if we screw up, we won't be able to submit to the ACC. We won't—'

'It's not just about the competition.'

'I know, I know. It's about Jordan.' I heard the dismissive tone in my voice, and so did Mouse.

His crossed arms turned rigid. 'You don't understand, because he wasn't your friend.'

'No, but you are. And Seth is—'

'It's not the same.'

That stung.

It was one thing to sometimes feel like I was sitting in Jordan's chair; it was another to be told I didn't belong there.

'What if it was Zach?' Mouse asked.

'What?'

'All you care about is getting busted. But what if it was *your* friend who was dead?'

I flinched, unable to even imagine such a thing. 'That's not—'

'What if it was *your* friend burned until his skin was black and his eyeballs melted?'

'Stop it!'

'What if it was Zach's stain on the cafeteria floor?'

'Well, it wasn't!' I exploded.

Mouse relaxed his arms, a grim but satisfied look on his face. 'That's right,' he said. 'It wasn't.'

'I didn't mean ...'

'Everyone who hurt – who said – who—' Mouse pressed his lips together, trembling. 'I want them to pay. Every. Single. One.'

The darkness I'd only caught glimpses of before was now rolling off him.

'I want them to all go down in flames ... *just like Jordan.*'

He pulled his car keys from his pocket and turned away, and I stood speechless, watching him go – not a single bounce in his step.

32

'Hold still.'

Isabel gripped the top of my head to keep me from moving, while she finished dabbing my cheek with a sponge soaked in silver paint.

'So bossy,' I teased. I reached out to tickle her, but she dodged me, her concentration unbroken.

'If you mess me up, I will totally start over,' she warned.

'Please don't,' I said, holding comically still.

She laughed, but we both knew the truth: I would sit there for eternity letting Isabel practise make-up on me if it meant her hand in my hair and her lips within kissing distance. I couldn't have asked for a better distraction after my fight with Mouse.

Isabel traded her sponge for a large brush and dipped it in a sparkly powder.

'No glitter,' I said.

'It's not glitter. It's shimmer.'

'Oh, well, in that case, it's okay.'

She ran the brush over my forehead and chin. 'Close your eyes.'

I did as I was told and shivered when Isabel blew the excess powder from my face.

'There,' she said. 'Now *that* is a perfect Tin Man.'

I opened my eyes and leaned forward to look into one of her many mirrors. 'Straight off the Yellow Brick Road,' I agreed.

'I don't know why I can't get it to look like that for the show,' she said. 'Maybe because I'm too rushed.'

She put her face next to mine in the mirror, so we were cheek to cheek. 'But this—' She touched my chin. 'This is perfect.'

I returned the gesture. 'So is this.'

Our eyes met in the mirror.

There were no more words.

Isabel let out one small, shaky breath, and before she could inhale again, our lips and tongues were tangled.

My brain rocked back and forth between pure bliss and total panic. Was I doing it right? I hadn't kissed a girl since junior high, and she'd been so bad at it, I hadn't worried about my own skills. But Isabel – Isabel was great. I slipped back into the bliss, letting Isabel take the lead.

When we finally came up for air, her face was smeared with silver paint from nose to chin. I held up a mirror for her to see, and we laughed and made out some more. Then we used her make-up remover to clean each other up, which was almost as much fun as making the mess, and her mom never once interrupted us.

We eventually migrated to Isabel's living room, where we sprawled on the couch and pretended to practise Spanish, but really, we were doing more flirting than studying. I tried a few of the compliments Misty had taught me, and Isabel looked pleased. She even asked me to repeat one of them and then gave me a quick kiss while her mom was in the kitchen.

'I never thought I'd need Spanish,' I said, closing my workbook and winking at Isabel. 'But now I see the merits.'

She grinned. 'Not like algebra. Who needs that?'

'We all need that!' I sat up straight, prepared to deliver my math-makes-the-world-go-'round speech I gave whenever people said they'd never use it again after high school, but Isabel only laughed.

'Relax,' she said. 'I'm teasing. I know you computer geeks like your equations.'

Coding and calculating were really two different things, but I let it slide.

'So how do you plan to use your mad math skills?' she asked.

'What do you mean?'

'I mean, where are you going after graduation?'

'Graduation?'

'Yeah, you know – caps, gowns, tassels?'

Graduation: the grand finale at the end of this long comedy-tragedy play we called high school, the moment we were apparently supposed to have the rest of our lives all figured out.

'I have no idea,' I said honestly.

'No? I pegged you for an MIT guy.'

'I'm flattered.' I paused, then confessed, 'I don't know if I want to go to college.'

Isabel's lips parted in surprise. I explained to her about the app Zach and I wanted to develop and how the most successful tech companies were run by college dropouts. Then before I knew it, I was telling her about the ACC and the internship opportunities that could come out of it.

'Did you know Facebook interns make more in one summer than some adults make in a year?' I said. 'Imagine how much you could make turning that internship into a job. Why wait four years to get started?'

Isabel let out a low whistle. 'Wow, I see your point. But college – it's not just about the education, is it? It's about the experience.'

If the experience was anything like I'd seen in movies and on TV, I was happy to pass.

'I don't know if you've noticed, but I'm not exactly a keg-standing, tailgating, college kind of guy.'

She smiled. 'I noticed.'

'Hey,' I said. 'I shouldn't have told you about the competition. Don't tell Seth I mentioned it.'

'Why?'

'Because . . . I don't know.'

'Eli?'

I closed my eyes. I knew it was going to happen before the words even came out of my mouth. I wasn't sure if it was because Isabel was so easy to talk to or because I was just so exhausted from keeping things all bottled up, but one second I was a temple of secrets and the next, I was a Trojan horse, spilling my guts. I told Isabel everything – about the website, about Seth and Mouse seeking justice for Jordan and roping me in with the promise of a spot on their ACC team. I even told her how they'd blackmailed me with their knowledge of my Game Zap stunt, but I didn't mention my transgression with the police department. Some secrets weren't meant to be spilled. I didn't meet her eyes the entire time, and when I finally looked up, I wasn't surprised to see disappointment in her face.

'Eli, that site . . . it's so—'

'Shitty, I know.'

'I was going to say dangerous.' She watched me for a second, thoughtful. 'I wonder, though . . .'

'What?'

'I'm not saying it's okay for you guys to go all *renegado* vigilante, but – well, it does make me wonder how many people you've scared straight.'

And then I sensed it – pushing up from under Isabel's disappointment – that reluctant bit of awe. She was impressed.

I grabbed hold of that nugget of hope and quickly explained to her how we vetted every video and exactly why each and every person we featured deserved it. She pointed out that it wasn't up to us to decide who deserved what, but she was surprisingly less sympathetic toward Brett losing his college admissions.

'I work my ass off in school,' she said. 'And I still can't get an academic scholarship. But a guy like that mainlines some Incredible Hulk junk and gets a free pass to college? The *cojones*!'

'That was ... colourful,' I said.

And kind of hot.

'I'm just saying, if you're going to hack somebody – it's good that you hacked that guy. He deserved it.'

'Well, that one was Mouse, not me,' I said. 'But I don't really like the term "hacking" anyway.'

'Why not?'

It was hard to explain since I used the word myself, but

it was different when someone outside the cybercircle said it.

'It sounds like a crime,' I said. 'Like breaking and entering.'

'Isn't it?'

'Not when people leave their doors and windows open.'

And the internet was nothing but open doors and windows. Sure, every so often you had to pick a tiny little lock, but mostly, people invited you in without even knowing it.

'And what you're doing to get videos ... a door or a window?'

I groaned. 'A brick wall.'

She gave me a questioning look, and I told her about people getting scared and pulling their videos after the warning flyers went up at school.

'Personally, I'm done,' I said. 'We've done enough to show at the competition and any more could get us in more trouble than anything, but Seth and Mouse ...'

'They lost someone,' Isabel supplied.

I nodded.

'But you have to shut it down,' she said.

'I know. I'm trying.'

How could the same website that had made me feel so powerful now make me feel helpless?

'Eli?' Isabel's hand touched my arm. 'Are you okay?'

I closed my hand over hers and forced a smile. 'How do you say "hand" in Spanish?'

'*Mano.*'

I slid her hand up to my shoulder. 'And this?'

'*Hombro.*'

She leaned in close, her lips against my ear.

'*Oreja,*' she whispered.

My neck.

'*Cuello.*'

Then we were kissing again, and all thoughts of Friends of Bishop slid from my mind. After a few minutes, Isabel pulled away, lips wet and eyes bright, and gave me a sly grin.

'See?' she said. 'Everyone tells me their secrets eventually.'

33

Misty was right again, and I was surprised to find myself eager to get home and tell her so. I leaned my bike against the garage and burst through the front door.

'Misty!' I called into the kitchen, but she wasn't there.

'Eli?' her voice came from another part of the house.

'Isabel loved the compliments.' I poked my head in Dad's den – no one there. I called up the stairs. 'She said I even pronounced them right. Where are you?'

'Eli!' It sounded like she wasn't in the house at all. 'We're back here.'

I crossed through the empty living room to the back porch. 'I messed up the word for hair, I think. But she didn't care. She just liked that I at least tried, so thank you—'

I froze halfway through the back door, one foot on the cedar planks of the porch and my lips still forming the word 'you.'

Misty was there. And so was Dad. And so was a hideously large, embarrassingly tacky, blindingly bright, boulder of a diamond parked on Misty's left hand. She held it out in the sunlight like an offering to the gods, and for once, instead of feeling like the third wheel, I felt like the fourth.

I blinked at the ring, hoping it would disappear like a mirage, a hallucination of the heat, but it stayed stubbornly wrapped around Misty's finger.

'I was looking for you,' I said stupidly.

'Well, you found us,' Dad said, his arm tight around Misty's waist.

His mouth was smudged with colour from her lipstick. It reminded me of the way the silver face paint had smeared on Isabel, and I involuntarily pictured Dad and Misty doing the same thing Isabel and I had been doing, at the same time.

Gross.

'You caught us celebrating,' Dad said when I didn't respond. 'We have some good news.'

I'll be the judge of that.

'Uh-huh,' I said.

To Dad's credit, he kept the cheer in his voice to a minimum. 'You may have noticed Misty's new accessory . . .'

'I have eyeballs,' I monotoned.

Misty had lifted her hand to show off the ring but put it down again when she saw that I was deliberately not looking at it.

Dad cleared his throat. 'This shouldn't catch you by too much surprise, since Misty's already been part of our family for some time now, but . . . well—'

'We're getting married!' Misty squealed.

She actually squealed, which sounded strange in her smoky gravel voice – as though she were choking on her own excitement.

I wished she *would* choke on it.

'Congratulations.'

I said it with all the enthusiasm of an earthworm drying out in the sun.

Misty twisted the ring on her finger nervously. 'Thanks. So . . . did you say something about Isabel?'

She was trying to change the subject. As if we could possibly talk about anything else now.

'It was nothing.'

'Are you sure? Did she—'

'I said it was nothing.'

Misty's jaw snapped shut at that, and her eyes got watery in this way that made me feel guilty and pissed at the same time.

Out on the lawn, the sprinkler system kicked into gear with a hissing sound, and soon fans of water were casting rainbows over the grass, sparkling almost as much as Misty's ring.

Dad whispered something in Misty's ear and let go of her waist. 'Just give us a few minutes,' he said.

She nodded and crossed the porch toward the back door. I shifted to one side to let her by but didn't make eye contact, even when she paused next to me. I heard her take a breath, as if to say something, but I guess she thought better of it, because the next thing I knew, the door was closing behind her.

'Well?' Dad splayed his hands. 'What do you think?'

What did I think? Was he joking?

I think you should have discussed it with me first. I think marrying someone that much younger than you is a little bit creepy. I think, of all the ways you have put Misty before me, this is the absolute worst. I think it's why Misty has been so extra mom-ish to me lately, trying to butter me up to get my approval. And I think I'm an idiot for almost falling for it.

'It's your life,' I said out loud.

'It's *our* life,' Dad corrected. 'And your opinion means a lot to me.'

'Clearly.'

'Eli.'

'You're a big boy,' I said. 'You can make your own decisions.'

I expected Dad to switch into his default mode of cold and calculating – maybe hand out another grounding – but he only shook his head and leaned against the porch railing. 'I thought you two were getting along better.'

'Dad, seriously? I called her your midlife crisis not even a month ago. Now you think I want to call her Mommy?'

He ducked his head, a cowed look on his face that was totally foreign to me. There was something unnerving about seeing that kind of weakness in him. I should have felt vindicated, but all I felt was guilt for shitting on his celebration. I was so disconnected from Dad just then that the space between us was a physical thing, one more air gap to make me feel unplugged from the rest of the world – an outsider, this time in my own family.

We stood there mute, letting the sprinklers fill the silence with their *tut-tut* noise as they sputtered and turned. Dad coughed. The porch creaked. I wanted to scream.

It was too much. It was all just way too much.

I refused to go back into the house with Misty and that tumor on her hand, but I also couldn't stand there watching my dad shrink before me for one more second. I uncoiled like a spring, leaping off the porch. I skipped the stairs and went straight over the railing to land in the wet grass. My sneakers slipped beneath me as I ran around the side of the house to the garage, but I didn't slow down. I stayed in motion even as I up-righted my bike and hopped on the seat. I pedaled away at top speed, pumping my legs until they burned, but it still wasn't fast enough.

I didn't have a destination in mind at first, but soon I was steering my bike toward Seth's. I would apologise to Mouse, promise videos to Seth, and hack whoever I had to, to make sure they kept me on their ACC team. And next month, at the competition, I wouldn't hold back. I would make it impossible for recruiters to ignore me . . . for Dad to ignore me. I wouldn't leave the contest floor until someone offered me a job that took me out of that house, out of Haver, and out of Iowa entirely . . . so I could leave this bullshit happily-ever-after in the dust.

34

I managed to spend most of the weekend hiding out in Seth's basement, and the few hours I spent at home, I was either sleeping or doing my best to give Dad and Misty the silent treatment. By Monday morning, I couldn't wait to get to school.

I woke up late and shoved half of my desktop debris into my backpack, hoping most of what I needed for the day landed inside.

When I opened the door to my room, the intense smell of bacon smacked me in the face.

That's cheating.

Misty knew damn well that I had a weakness for bacon, even her undercooked version. A dirty play – but one that made my mouth water.

I dragged myself downstairs to the kitchen. The smile on Misty's face when she saw me was more of a smirk. She knew exactly what she was doing as she shoveled a fresh pile of bacon out of the fry pan and onto a plate, which she dropped in front of my usual chair.

I summoned every ounce of willpower I had, held my

breath against the savory aroma, and then made a show of bypassing the bacon and grabbing a banana from the fruit bowl on the counter instead.

Misty didn't miss a beat. She scooped the plate up and grabbed a bag of bread off the counter. 'Want me to put it in a sandwich for you? A little BLT to take to school for lunch? I can throw in some of that cake—'

I put my headphones on, deliberately letting them snap down on my ears, then pointed at them and gave her a quizzical look and a shrug.

Sorry, lady. Can't hear you over my music.

Misty pursed her lips to the side, her phony sunshine finally clouded over. She put one hand on her hip and used the other to point to the end of my headphones' cord, dangling at my waist.

'That move works better if you plug them in.'

I felt heat creep into my cheeks. 'They're soundproof,' I said.

Too late, I realised my answering her proved they were not, in fact, soundproof.

Misty shook her head at my stupidity, and now my face was really on fire. I slammed the banana back into the bowl and marched out of the kitchen. When I did finally plug the headphones in, I blasted my music so loud I could have legitimately blown an eardrum, and

I nearly burned the rubber off my bike tires speeding to school.

Just a few more weeks, I told myself.

A few more weeks until the ACC, a few more weeks of school, a few more weeks of Misty, of Dad, of Friends of Bishop. Then hopefully I would be unplugging from this drama and heading west to spend the summer in Silicon Valley. I could practically taste the freedom.

My hands were shaking as I locked my bike on the rack outside school.

'Just a few more weeks.'

'A few more weeks of what?' a voice asked.

I looked up to see Isabel leaning over the rack, her normally straight hair starting to curl in the humidity and a thin sheen of sweat on her face.

'A few more weeks until I get to spend the whole summer with you.'

Even as I said it, the truth of it split me in two. As much as I wanted to get out of Haver, an equal part of me wanted to stay right here with her. If I did land an internship from the competition, it would mean leaving Isabel behind, and who knew what would happen while I was gone?

'So, you already heard,' Isabel said.

I blinked. 'Heard what?'

'Oh. The look on your face ... I just assumed ...' She bit her lip. '*Ay*, Eli, *que desmadre*.'

I didn't know what that meant, but the tone of it tied a knot in my gut. 'Isabel, what's going on?'

'They're looking for you.' She lowered her voice to a whisper. 'For Friends of Bishop.'

'Who?'

'The police.'

'What?' I looked around, but fortunately no one was close enough to hear my alarm.

'The school is sending these notices home with us today.' She pulled a piece of paper from her back pocket and started unfolding it. 'I was in the front office before school, and there was this whole giant stack of them.'

I took the paper from her and read while she talked. 'It says the school district contacted police and wants to file charges – *criminal* charges.'

'But they don't know who to charge ... right?' I skimmed the page, but all the references were to the 'person or people behind the website.'

'Not yet, but they are really after you now.' She reached around the paper to point out a paragraph in the middle. 'It says they're consulting with the police department!'

'Shh.' I took Isabel's hand and held it steady. 'Don't worry about me, okay? I'll be fine.'

'You really think so?'

I had no idea, but I was panicked enough without Isabel freaking me out too, and since I couldn't seem to slow my own hammering heart, then at least I could calm hers.

'Eli, I thought you were going to shut the site down,' Isabel said.

'I tried. It's . . . complicated.'

She poked the paper in my hand. 'No, *this* is complicated. I heard Brett's parents went to the school board all pissed that they weren't doing more. Then they got some other parents riled up, and now this.'

I finished reading the paper and shook my head. 'They're basically asking parents to spy on their kids and then sell them out.'

'And from what you told me about your dad . . .' Isabel trailed off.

I refolded the paper and passed it back to her. 'Oh, I'm not showing him that. No way.'

'But he has to sign it—'

'They're not going to enforce that this close to the end of the school year,' I said. 'They just want us to know they suspect Haver students are behind the site. They're trying to scare us.'

And it's working.

My phone beeped.

I slid it from my pocket to check the screen.

Emergency meeting. Cafeteria. Now.

The cafeteria was half-full of kids sitting two or three to a table, and the sticky-sweet smell of imitation maple syrup assaulted my nose as I walked in. My stomach, still empty from skipping Misty's bacon manipulation, tugged in the direction of the aroma. The lunch line was up and running, but instead of the usual pizza and chicken-sandwich options, there were trays of eggs and sausage.

'Since when did the caf start serving breakfast?' I wondered out loud.

'Since this is where we do standardised-test coaching every spring.' It was Seth who answered. He appeared at my side and starting yanking me by the arm away from the food.

Asshole, my stomach grumbled.

'I'm a senior study buddy,' Seth said as he guided me toward a table at the edge of the room. Mouse was already there, his head down, hands in his lap. Seth pointed at a chair, indicating I should sit. 'We help underclassmen prep for the ACTs and SATs. So that's what this is, okay? It's me coaching two sophomores.'

'Got it,' I said.

Mouse said nothing.

Seth sat across from us and folded his hands like a teacher or parent about to deliver bad news to his kids. 'I don't want to alarm you, but you're going to get a letter from the school today—'

'I already saw it,' I said.

'Oh.' Seth looked at Mouse. 'Did you—'

Mouse held up a crumpled ball of paper in response.

Seth nodded. 'Okay, so you know, then.'

I opened my mouth to reply but was interrupted by a text.

Where are you?

The message was from Zach, and I cursed under my breath.

I'd promised to meet him at his locker before class. I hadn't seen him all weekend and wanted to show him some coding I had done. I was pretty sure I'd figured out how to get phones to interact with each other in an augmented reality game setting, and the flash drive with my work was burning a hole in my backpack, just waiting for Zach's approval.

Sorry, I forgot.
That's okay. I'll wait for you.

Shit.

Seth huffed. 'Can you stop sexting your girlfriend for one second?'

I waved him off and replied to Zach.

Can't make it. Show you the code
at lunch. Bring your laptop.

A reply bubble popped up. Zach was typing.
Then it disappeared. Zach was thinking.
Finally, he responded.

Whatever.

So that went well.

'Anyway,' Seth grumbled as I pocketed my phone. 'I've been thinking it might be time to shutter the site.'

I balked. '*You* think it's time? I suggested that last week and got my head bitten off.'

'I don't bite,' Mouse said, his voice monotone.

'Please don't say "I told you so,"' Seth begged. 'But you were right, okay? We should have shut it down sooner. We've done enough.'

'Enough?' I asked, hardly daring to believe my ears.

Seth met my eyes. 'We shut it down and get our story

straight for the ACC. With any luck, the snoops will forgive us when they find out we built the site for a competition.'

Something had been sitting on my shoulders, and I didn't even realise it until it lifted off and flew away. For the first time in weeks, I felt like I could breathe.

'Agreed,' I said.

We looked at Mouse, who shrugged. 'Fine.'

I wished he would bounce around or at least tap a toe. This new steady Mouse made me uneasy. Over the weekend, I'd assumed he was just peeved at me. Now I wasn't sure it had anything to do with me at all.

'You're sure?' Seth asked him. 'I know we didn't get to everyone we wanted, but—'

'I don't care.' Mouse looked up for the first time, and I saw the 'I don't care' in his eyes. He meant it.

Seth frowned. 'Now you suddenly don't care—'

'It didn't work,' Mouse said. 'The site was supposed to fix it, but it didn't work.'

'Fix what?' I asked.

'Everything. For Jordan. For us. For—'

'He means it's not justice,' Seth cut in. 'For Jordan.'

'It was supposed to fix it,' Mouse repeated. 'Supposed to . . .'

He trailed off, opened his mouth, closed it again.

Finally, he pulled his hoodie up over his head and slumped forward, elbows on the table. 'It was just supposed to fix it.'

'Well, it's over,' Seth said, coming a little unraveled. 'Friends of Bishop is over.'

His raised voice was enough to catch the attention of the next table over. They all turned their heads toward us, and for the first time, I noticed who was sitting there.

Ashley was apparently a senior study buddy too. She leaned back in her chair and called over to us. 'Are you talking about FOB?'

FOB? Since when did we become an acronym?

'I thought it was over too,' she said, 'because the last few videos were kind of boring.'

I kicked Seth under the table before he could respond.

Ashley turned so that she was partly facing us and partly facing the two junior girls at her table, hanging on her every word. She knew how to maximise her audience. 'But trust me – FOB is definitely not done.'

I retched inwardly at the cutesy nickname – coined by Ashley, of all people.

'How do you know?' Mouse asked with barely concealed venom in his voice.

I peered at him, looking for the hyper Mouse who spent life teetering on his tiptoes, talking too much and too fast but always with a smile. But all I saw was the shadow cast over his face by his hood. The darkness had swallowed him up.

'Well, I don't know for sure,' Ashley admitted. 'I just know what I heard.'

'Which is?' I asked.

She grinned, pleased by the prompt. 'Apparently some of them already got arrested.'

Oh really? That's news to us.

'And the school district thought it was over. But then a few new videos went up last week, and they realised someone was still out there.'

Still out there – stalking the cyberstreets, like the predators we are.

'So that's why they contacted police and wrote up all these letters everyone is getting today – because they're desperate to catch the last Friend of Bishop.'

Seth pretended to be impressed by her information, while I tried not to laugh. There was something hilariously ironic about the fact that Ashley Thorne thought she had the inside track on a website that was designed to take people like her down.

'Do you know who they are?' one of the girls Ashley was supposed to be tutoring asked, breathless.

Ashley turned away from us, leaning in to her more eager listeners.

'I have my suspicions, but I really shouldn't say.'

This should be good.

The girls pouted, and Ashley pretended to think it over before giving in.

'Okay, I'll just say I don't think they're kids from our school, honestly.'

Seth and I exchanged raised eyebrows and half smiles. If a bigmouth like Ashley wanted to spread a rumour that we didn't go to Haver, that wasn't such a bad thing.

'Why not?' one of the girls asked.

'Because I don't think Jordan Bishop even had friends – at Haver, anyway. I mean, he probably had friends *somewhere*, but who knows what kind of people he hung out with. Jordan was strange.'

Ashley paused for agreement, but the girls said nothing, stuck between respecting the queen bee and respecting the dead.

At my table, the half smiles melted away.

Ashley went on. 'I feel bad saying that, obviously, but Jordan was the kind of guy who – well, maybe it was better he committed suicide . . . because otherwise he would have come to school with a gun, you know what I mean?'

The air felt as if it had been sucked out of the room, and I was physically choking on the lack of oxygen.

Yes, you hateful bitch, we know exactly what you mean.

I sensed what was happening before it happened. Seth was on his feet, jumping up so fast, he drew attention from the tables around him, including Ashley's, but he didn't even look her way. He just slung his backpack on his shoulder and marched out of the cafeteria.

I knew where he was going. The second he'd stood up, I knew it.

Of course he didn't delete the video.

He probably had it on a flash drive – squirreled away somewhere next to his mom's lotion and his dirty magazines and whatever else he had to hide. But that video was coming out of hiding. No doubt, Seth was headed straight home to our secure computer, and in the click of a mouse, he would set Ashley Thorne's world on fire.

I looked at Mouse, stricken, but his face was dark – his lips set in an angry line. It was the most emotion I'd seen from him in days. Then he stood up and pounded after Seth – not his usual bounce but a determined run, and it was clear I was already outvoted.

I closed my eyes, trying to tell myself that Ashley was a monster – worse than anyone we'd put on the site so far – and maybe she deserved this. Her voice floated over from the next table, talking about multiple choice versus essay questions. She'd already moved past her evil assessment of Jordan.

In my mind, I replayed her other acts of cruelty, from the things she'd said about Isabel to the countless other ways she'd probably made people around her feel small – people in this very room. I sat there in the cafeteria, surrounded by her victims, and tried to feel like a hero.

But all I felt was queasy.

35

I knew the instant the video went live. I was in the hallway between first and second periods when phones began to ping, and the shuffle of feet went still. First there were gasps and giggles, then from a couple of guys – crude gestures and high fives.

It took a moment to realise I was the only one in the hall not looking at my phone. I pulled it out to avoid suspicion, but I didn't load the website. I already knew what they were all seeing: Ashley stripping down to her bra and striking poses that looked a lot more silly than sexy when viewed by an audience of classmates.

The video was inescapable. Everywhere I went, every corner I turned, it was in my face or in my ear. I caught a glimpse of it over a girl's shoulder in Advanced Lit; I heard a guy jerking off to it in the West Wing bathroom; and I witnessed teachers, red-faced, barking at students to put away their phones.

The only person I didn't see watching the video was Ashley, who had obviously – and wisely – gone home. I should have done the same. I spent half the day in a walking coma, with my eyes closed and my headphones over my ears. I skipped lunch, and Zach didn't even text me to complain. He'd probably given up on me.

Maybe I'd given up on me too.

I was secretly relieved after school when Isabel wasn't at her locker. I had expected a text from her when the video went live, and I wasn't sure how to interpret her silence. I would have to find out later, because right then, I had something important to do. I raced home, my bike leaving tire tracks in the soil where I sliced through the cornfield. If it hadn't been for Spanish, I would have cut out earlier, but then again, the damage had already been done.

I dropped my bike on the lawn and blasted through the front door, not bothering to stop in the kitchen, even though I was starving from not eating all day.

'Eli!' Misty called as I pounded up the steps. 'Hey, we need to talk—'

I slammed my bedroom door, cutting her off.

My fingers were already on the keyboard as my backpack hit the floor and my butt landed in my desk chair. I had never tried to manage our site from anywhere other than Seth's house, but that deal was done now. The most important thing was to shut it down – even if it meant exposing my own IP address.

I typed in the admin login and cursed.

They had changed the passwords.

I took a swig from a warm, stale can of Red Bull, left over from the weekend, set my music to heavy metal, and got to work.

It turns out, it's not so hard to hack your own website, since you know the code better than anyone – but Seth and Mouse were ready for me. On the other end of the connection, they were doing damage control – throwing up roadblocks every time I found a way in. It felt a lot like one of our ACC practise sessions, and I couldn't help but note that we'd all gotten pretty good at penetration and defence. It would have been fun if I hadn't been so damn desperate.

Seth and Mouse put up a good fight. Seth only texted me twice to call me a traitor and a pussy, and Mouse never looked away from the work to message me at all.

Sorry, was all I sent back.

Two hours later, Friends of Bishop was a ghost town. I didn't just take down Ashley's video; I deleted them all, one by one, until only the site's headline was left. Tumbleweeds might as well have been rolling across the screen. Then, because I was high on energy drinks and adrenaline, I actually created little tumbleweed graphics and sent them skipping around the home page.

I sent one more text to Seth and Mouse.

You're welcome.

Maybe they would thank me later and maybe they wouldn't, but I was pretty sure I was off the team either way.

I reconfigured access to the site's root directory, so they wouldn't be able to do any more damage, then I passed out from exhaustion before the sun had even set.

*

I woke up in my pitch-black bedroom on top of my covers and still wearing my clothes. I felt around the bed until my hand closed over my phone and squinted at the sudden brightness of the screen.

3:00 AM

And wide awake.

I turned on the lamp next to my bed, illuminating a small round plate with a peanut butter sandwich on the nightstand.

Misty.

My stomach growled. How long had it been since I'd eaten? Twenty-four hours? More?

I ate the sandwich gratefully, then stripped off my stale clothes and took a shower. I intended to fall back into bed, but by the time I stepped out of the shower, I knew I was done sleeping. My brain was too busy, wondering if Seth and Mouse had cooled off, if clearing the site had been enough to satisfy police, if Ashley would be back at school.

I took my time getting ready, deliberately avoiding my computer. I did that sometimes after a coding binge – took a second to see the world offscreen. But usually it was just that – a second – before I was back online. This morning felt different. I didn't even want to turn it on. I worked around it, instead clearing the cables and drives and dust off my desk. Then I emptied my overflowing hamper and scraped the dried toothpaste out of my bathroom sink.

It was still only 5:00 a.m. by the time I'd run out of things to do. I scanned my mostly clean room the way I would scan a line of code – looking for any tiny errors that changed the whole picture. I spotted one of those errors on the nightstand – the sandwich plate now sprinkled with crumbs.

I took the plate to the kitchen and rinsed the crumbs off in the sink, wondering what Misty had thought when she'd brought it up to my room only to find me passed out in yesterday's clothes and probably snoring up a storm. I bet she was worried.

I squirted some dish soap on the plate and gave it a good scrub. When it was clean, I set it in the centre of the kitchen island and stuck a Post-it where the sandwich had been with two scribbled words:

THANK YOU

Then I slipped out the front door just as the sun came up.

*

It was kind of nice cruising around Haver while it was still asleep. Our tiny downtown was washed in the warm first light of the morning, all the storefront windows turned to panes of solid gold from the rising sun. I rolled my bike up and down the main drag a few times, waving at shop owners as they arrived, yawning, to unlock their doors and start their days.

I watched them checking their phones, firing up computers inside their stores, and I was grateful, for the moment, to be unplugged.

When downtown got too lively for me, I aimed my bike toward school.

With any luck, the cybersnoops would give up the

search, and Friends of Bishop would soon be a memory. Maybe everyone at school would be talking about something different today. It was crazy how fast the world moved on to the next thing.

I reached the bike rack by the side door and locked up my wheels. Campus was strangely quiet. I checked my watch – half an hour until first period. Early, but not early enough to be the first person here, and the rack was full of wheels. Was there some morning assembly I hadn't heard about? Another phony Jordan memorial? The side door was locked, so I circled the building to the front.

And the scene there caused me to stumble over my own feet.

I was not the first person at school – not by a long shot.

36

A line of students stretched from the front entrance, where two uniformed police officers and a guy in a suit were collecting cell phones and other electronics.

'You'll get everything back at the end of the day.' Principal Givens was pacing up and down the line, his hair wild and his pants rumpled. He was waving his hands in an impatient way, trying to reassure students who were complaining loudly.

'But I need my phone for emergencies!' one girl cried.

'Can't we just turn them off?' another argued.

'This is illegal search and seizure!'

That comment came from a guy who looked more concerned about having his stash seized than his phone.

I joined the back of the line, trying to look casual and confused. Or casually confused.

I probably just looked constipated.

'What's going on?' I asked a guy in front of me.

'They're confiscating phones and tablets. I guess we can't have them in school anymore.'

'Oh,' I said, sweat beading up on my back. 'Was there a note about that?'

'No, they just decided all of a sudden. There are cops up there.' The boy pointed at the officers, and I nodded without looking. 'I think it has to do with that website. They don't want people taking videos with their cameras.'

A girl next to him turned to join the conversation. 'I bet that's not all. I bet they're going to go through our phones while we're in class – looking at all of our videos and pictures and stuff.'

'How would they do that? Everyone locks their phones,' the boy argued.

'They're the police. They have ways of getting around your password,' the girl said.

False – mostly.

Police usually couldn't crack even the most basic technology without the cooperation of the software companies that created it, and as a general rule, those companies were not cooperative. They erred on the side of customer privacy rather than law enforcement. And why not? They were in the business of profit, and we were the ones paying up – not police.

I suspected the phone collection was more of a show by the school to appear to be on top of a situation that had gotten completely out of hand. As for the police – well, I wasn't entirely sure why they were there, and the beads of sweat began sliding down my spine.

Up the line a little way, Principal Givens pulled at his hair, creating tufty white cones on either side of his head. Teachers had joined his crusade to calm students, and everyone appeared to be in a full-on frenzy. When we first launched the site, I thought it might be funny to see Haver High driven to chaos with a few keystrokes. But now, in person, watching people who were supposed to be in control totally lose it was a little scary.

The line moved painfully slow, and it was only growing longer as more kids showed up for school. I looked for Zach or Mouse or Isabel, but it was impossible to pick anyone out of the crowd. The line had really become more of a mob.

An angry mob.

Some students were shouting their protests, others were looking for hiding places in their clothes or bags, and a few even called their parents. Cars came and went, picking up students and ferrying them away. One mom pulled right up to the front door and got out, with the engine still running, to yell at the guy in the suit – who was apparently some district administrator. She called him several colourful names until the police officers gently suggested she get back in her car and go away.

By the time I reached the front of the line, first period had already come and gone, and my back was drenched under my pack. I shuffled up to hand over my phone, and a woman helping with the collection passed me a sheet of paper in exchange. In an instant, it was clear why police were there.

CHILD PORNOGRAPHY IS A FELONY OFFENCE.

I stopped moving. Or maybe the world stopped moving around me.

The headline, on Haver Police Department letterhead, was followed by a summary of Iowa laws – including some explicit information about videos of people who are underdressed and underage. My vision blurred as I scanned the page, glazing over a list of penalties that ranged from thousands of dollars in fines to years in prison.

Prison?

And here I'd been worried about whether my friends would forgive me – whether we could still be a team and figure out another entry for the off-site category. What a joke.

'Keep moving,' the woman barked.

Back off, lady. I'm having a meltdown here.

I looked over my shoulder. Where was Seth? Where was Mouse? Had they called their parents and bailed? Maybe I should have called Misty. The paper shook in my hands.

The woman huffed. 'There's a long line behind you.'

The cold fear inside me suddenly heated up to a boiling rage.

'Oh really?' I snapped. 'I hadn't noticed.'

'Excuse me, young man—'

'Maybe if you weren't violating our rights by taking our personal property, there wouldn't be such a long line.' My voice rose with every word, and I heard a few kids behind me call out shouts of support.

The woman looked scandalised, but I didn't care. I needed to release something just then or risk implosion, and she was the closest target.

'Just like you violated our rights with your stupid cybersnooping. Maybe if those laws didn't exist, neither would this line!'

The crowd close enough to hear erupted in a cheer, and I left the woman dumbstruck, holding my phone.

I pushed through the double doors but then stopped in the hallway, unsure which direction to go. If Seth and Mouse *were* here, I didn't know if I even wanted to see them. If they hadn't posted the video, none of this would be happening. It was their fault I had to tank the site, their fault police were at our door, their fault we might go to jail instead of to the American Cybersecurity Competition.

But it was your video, a little voice inside me said.

I squirmed.

I could look for Zach or Isabel, but one didn't know the truth of the trouble I was in, and the other hadn't called or messaged me once since the Ashley video went live. In truth, I was a little afraid to face either one of them.

The river of students broke around me, flowing in all directions as I stood motionless in the front hall – utterly stuck and, for the first time in weeks, utterly alone. The gap between me and everyone else had never felt so big.

I ended up skipping second period too. This seemed to be the day to get away with cutting class, and there were only about fifteen minutes left in the period anyway. I spent most of the time at my locker, half hoping one of my friends would come to me, since I was too much of a coward to go to any of them.

Across the hall, a group of guys clustered around a contraband phone.

'See? Told you. Tumbleweeds.'

'Bet they got busted.'

'Then why all the cops today?'

'Put it away. A teacher's coming.'

I waited another ten minutes. No sign of my friends. I wasn't sure I still had any.

On my way to third period, I finally got brave enough

to check out the East Wing, to see if Seth and Mouse were in their usual spot, but the only people in the hall were a pair of girls staring at a locker with their hands cupped over their mouths. Their whispers carried in the mostly empty corridor – not that they were really trying to keep their voices down anyway.

'Who do you think did it?'

'I don't know, but if anyone deserves it . . .'

'Don't say that.'

'It's true, though. You know that striptease wasn't even for her boyfriend? It was some other guy.'

'I know. It was that junior, Adam something. I heard police questioned him and confiscated his computer.'

I slowed down as I walked by, and over the girls' shoulders, I clearly saw the thick lines of a black Sharpie marker scrawled across a locker door.

SLUT

Even if I hadn't seen Ashley at that very locker in the past, I would know it was hers.

'So one guy dumps her and the other gets arrested for pimping her out online. She sure knows how to pick 'em.'

The girls giggled, and I was ashamed to have played a part in providing their entertainment. They were probably girls Ashley had mistreated in the past, but did that give them permission to laugh at her misery?

I was no better, though. I had laughed at Brett. I had thought he deserved his shame. So did Seth and Mouse. So did Isabel even. Everyone was sitting in judgment over everyone else, enjoying each other's misery, and I could no longer see the line between us and them.

I stopped at a random locker and pretended to work the lock.

'She skipped school again today,' one of the girls said.

'Well, obviously. She couldn't show her face after that.'

'Why not? She showed everything else.'

Their giggles turned to hysterics, and they finally wandered away from the locker. I closed my eyes and threw my head back, letting out a long breath. When I opened my eyes, I was looking at the wall above the lockers, where one of Haver's No Bully Zone signs was partly peeling off the wall. It was once bright red, but like its message, the sign had faded over time.

I reached up, closed my fingers around the loose corner and tugged. The plastic sign hit the floor with a hollow *thunk* that echoed down the empty hallway.

37

'Eli!'

My head whipped around at Isabel's familiar voice. I started to smile, but faltered when I saw the way she was barreling down the hallway, her expression fierce.

She was talking fast and loud – practically shouting – and I could only catch snippets.

'Pinche pendejo ... poco fiable ... ¡no vale madre!'

I swallowed hard. It wasn't nearly as much fun to hear her swear in Spanish when the cursing was directed at me.

She came at me so hard, I backed up against a locker, banging my head on the smooth metal. She put a finger in my face, the other hand on her hip.

'What the hell were you thinking, Eli Bennett?'

'I wasn't – I didn't—'

'Was this for me? Tell me this wasn't for me!'

'What?'

I was genuinely confused, and not just by her sudden interrogation. I was also struggling to understand how part of me wanted to run away from her and part of me wanted to smash my lips onto hers. I compromised by pressing myself flatter against the lockers.

'I didn't ask for this, Eli.' She was breathing heavily from her sprint down the hall. Her gum was cinnamon today. 'I don't need anyone to fight my battles, and I don't really care what Ashley said to me or about me. I'm not vengeful person. I'm a – a – a *high-road* person.'

She stood up straight as she said it, lifting her chin a little and finally dropping her finger from my face.

'Okay,' I said. 'I get it—'

'So did you?'

'Did I what?'

'Did you do it for me?'

I tried to tell her I didn't do it at all, but when I opened my mouth, no words came out. Maybe I didn't post it, but I recorded it, and I didn't know which was worse. I ran a hand over my face.

Shit, I can't even tell right from wrong anymore.

Or, in this case, wrong from wronger.

'Say something,' Isabel commanded.

But I couldn't. The lies and excuses and confessions and apologies were all stuck inside my throat – fighting to be the first to make it to my lips.

Isabel shook her head at my silence. 'I was wrong, Eli. You didn't tell me all of your secrets after all.'

She gave me one more beat to say something – *anything* – and when I didn't, she stormed back the way she'd come.

As soon as she disappeared around the corner, leaving me alone, I managed a feeble whisper.

'I didn't do it.'

No, that's not true.

I wanted so badly to deny responsibility for Ashley, for Brett, for all of it. But I couldn't ignore the claw of guilt clutching my chest, making it difficult to breathe.

'I didn't mean to.'

Getting warmer.

The claw loosened its grip ever so slightly.

'I'm sorry.'

And even though no one was around to hear it, it felt good to say it out loud, and all the oxygen came rushing back into the hall.

A bell rang. Third period had started. Or maybe it was over. I'd totally lost track of time.

Doors opened and down the hall, students spilled out, filling the world with a cacophony of voices and footfalls.

Over, then.

I'd managed to miss the entire first half of my day. I should have just gone home.

But I didn't want to be home any more than I wanted to be at Haver. What I really wanted – what I *needed* – was a friend to give me advice. The kind of friend who always knew the right thing to do, the kind who would be there for you even when you didn't deserve it – even when you'd been a total shit to him.

I don't remember racing out of the East Wing or flying down the stairs to the first floor. I don't recall crossing campus or who I passed on the way. I only know I got to the cafeteria in two minutes flat. I spotted Zach at our table from across the room and let out a sigh of relief. He was there, waiting for me, despite the fact that I'd blown him off yesterday – or maybe because of it. Possibly he was there to tell me off. I deserved it. And he deserved the truth.

'Hey,' I said when I reached our table.

'Hey.'

'So.' I fidgeted, unsure if I should sit. I knew what I wanted to say, but now that I was here, I didn't know how to begin.

'So, yesterday . . .' he prompted.

'Yeah, sorry. Seth called an emergency . . . practise.'

Still lying. What is my problem?

It wasn't that I wanted to lie to Zach. It was that I was suddenly aware of the other people who sat at our table, who were now watching Zach and me with interest.

'For the ACC,' Zach said. His voice was a little hollow,

and I could sense that he knew it was more than that.

'Right. Except, no – not really. Can we go somewhere else to talk ...'

But Zach was no longer looking at me. His eyes were narrowed to slits and aimed at something over my shoulder.

I turned slowly, already sure of who I would see.

Seth was marching toward us, banging into people as he beelined for our table.

'I have to talk to you,' he said.

I brushed him off. 'Later.'

Zach stood up, hands curled into fists. 'I think you've got the wrong lunch hour, dude. Seniors eat at noon.'

'Why don't you sit down and mind your own business?' Seth barked.

'Guys, stop!' I cried.

I noticed a slight hush fall around us and saw several bemused faces at the closest tables. I couldn't blame them. We must have been a sight to see, three nerds facing off like wannabe tough guys. Everyone probably thought we were about to rumble over who stole whose calculator.

Zach started to snap a retort at Seth but then pressed his lips together and turned to me instead.

'Eli, what the hell is going on?'

'I want to tell you,' I said.

'Then tell me.'

303

The quiet spread, as more tables caught on to the geek-brawl about to go down. I felt every set of eyes watching, every pair of ears listening.

'I can't,' I said. 'Not now.'

Zach huffed. 'You know what? I don't even care anymore. I'm out.'

He grabbed his backpack off the floor and pushed past me.

'Wait!'

I started to follow him, but Seth skipped ahead of me, blocking my path. 'Eli, I'm serious. We have to—'

'I said *later*!' I shoved Seth out of my way, and he stumbled into an empty chair, knocking it over with a clatter.

A few people gasped. A few more giggled at Seth's expense. But as I hurried after Zach, most of them went back to eating their lunch, disappointed that there hadn't been more of a show.

Zach had a couple of yards on me, but I was close enough to see that he turned left out the cafeteria doors, toward the side exit, instead of right toward his next class. I pounded down the hall after him, shouting his name. He heard me – everyone in Haver probably heard me – but he didn't turn.

And behind me, an ever louder voice than mine hollered

my name. Seth was chasing me chasing Zach. Heads poked out of doorways to watch. We were just providing all sorts of entertainment today.

Zach was faster than me, and by the time I slammed out the side door behind him, he had already unlocked his bike from the rack and was hopping on.

'Zach, wait!' I was panting, and it felt like my heart was going to burst out of my chest, but I didn't slow down, even when Seth exploded through the door after me, still screaming my name.

I got my own bike under me and nearly ran over Seth as he caught up.

'It's important!' he cried.

There was desperation in his voice, and outright fear too, but I couldn't stop to find out why. If I blew off Zach one more time, it could be the last time. Seth and Mouse had showed me I could expand my circle of friends beyond Zach, but I'd done it to the *exclusion* of Zach. I needed to fix that now.

As I pedaled into the street, I heard Seth's breathless cry one last time.

'Only seniors can leave campus for lunch!'

After all the rules – all the *laws* – we had broken, this was the one he considered sacred?

If I weren't facing potential pornography charges, if I

hadn't lost my girl and maybe my best friend, if I hadn't become the bad guy somewhere along the way . . . I might have laughed.

But at that moment, pumping my legs until they burned and watching Zach become a speck in the distance as he widened the gap between us . . . I just wanted to cry.

38

I lost Zach for good at a stoplight downtown. I tried to run the red and nearly got killed by a guy looking at his phone and laying on the gas. He glanced up just in time to slam on the brakes and gave me the finger. I returned the gesture and backed up onto the sidewalk to wait for the green light. By the time it turned, Zach was long gone.

I knew he wouldn't go home. Cutting school in the middle of the day was not okay in Zach's family. But after an hour of circling town, I couldn't figure out where he'd disappeared to. The old guys playing chess in the park hadn't seen him; the arcade was deserted; and I didn't see his bike in the rack outside the library.

I finally gave up and went home, feigning a stomachache when Misty questioned my early arrival. Up in my room, I decided to call Zach, even though I knew he wouldn't answer . . . and only then did I realise my phone was still at school. I cursed and yanked my headphones from my neck to hurl them across the room.

I flopped back on my bed. Maybe it was for the best. Every time I opened a phone or a computer or anything else with an internet connection, I seemed to do damage.

Downstairs, I could hear Misty clanging around the kitchen, and for once, the music she was playing wasn't awful. I took one last look at my computer, then tossed a dirty T-shirt over the monitor and went down to see if I could help her not-ruin dinner.

She was standing in front of the open refrigerator, a gallon of milk in her hands. I watched as she checked the expiration date, gave it a sniff test, then shrugged and put it back on the shelf.

She turned around, holding a carton of eggs, and startled when she saw me.

'Hey, feeling better?' she asked.

'Oh yeah . . . I took some aspirin. No more headache.'

'I thought it was your stomach.'

Shit.

I choked, not sure how to respond, but Misty only shook her head. 'Don't make a habit of it, okay?'

'Okay.'

'And give me a hand here.'

'Yeah, that's why I came down.'

Misty almost dropped the eggs, but she caught the carton at the last second and set it gently on the island. Her eyes met mine, guarded, like she was bracing to be the butt of a joke.

'You came down to . . . ?'

'I don't know, see if you need help with anything.' I shrugged. 'Is that so strange?'

'Yes.'

Okay, she had me there.

'Let's just say I need a distraction,' I said honestly.

Misty's eyes narrowed, but she seemed satisfied with that answer and slid the eggs across the island to me, along with a large silver bowl.

'Crack those in here. I found a gluten-free cake recipe I want to try out.'

'Sounds delicious,' I said with every ounce of sarcasm I could muster.

She raised a wooden spoon like she was prepared to hit me with it, but she was laughing as she let it fall into the bowl with a clatter.

'Gluten is poison,' she said, launching into a detailed description of an article she'd just read in *Cosmo* or *Vogue* or some equally scientific magazine. I let her drone on in her gravel voice without questioning her facts or even rolling my eyes. I was feeling especially generous, I guess. Or maybe I just wanted to pretend that I was someone else for a minute – someone other than a computer-cracking, possibly perverted, lying, stinking, future felon.

We worked on dinner mostly in silence: she chopped, I mixed; she baked, I sautéed; and when a decent song came on, she sang and I danced ... just a little.

Dad's face when he came home to find us in a kitchen kumbaya was priceless. For a second, I thought he was going to go outside and come back in, just to make sure he had the right house.

After dinner, we ate Misty's gluten-free cake in front of the TV, and it wasn't at all terrible. I was shoveling the last bite of frosting into my mouth when Dad flipped to a news channel. And because I couldn't possibly get one night off from the drama, video of Haver High filled the screen.

The cake stuck in my throat.

'... police report has now been filed. It's not clear what charges the person or persons behind the site – the so-called Friends of Bishop – will face. For now, investigators say they just want to talk to them.'

The video switched to older footage of school – from the days after Jordan's death, when there was crime tape all over inside and TV cameras all over outside.

'The website's name could be a reference to Jordan Bishop, the fifteen-year-old freshman whose suicide last year triggered a national uproar ...'

Misty turned up the volume the way she always did when the news talked about something awful – like she couldn't get enough. It still wasn't loud enough to drown out the sudden pounding in my ears. Could Dad and Misty hear that?

I sank back in the couch, but it didn't swallow me up like I'd hoped. *I should change the channel*, I thought. *I could grab the remote right now and flip to sports. Dad likes sports.* But I didn't move, and I couldn't look away.

The video changed once more, and the cake that had been stuck in my throat now threatened to come charging back up. Game Zap logos flashed across the screen, above a banner that read: 'Is Haver a haven for hackers?'

The reporter's voice continued.

'. . . may recall several years ago . . . investigators looking into a cyberattack on a gaming network that exposed the credit card information of tens of thousands of customers . . . traced an IP address to Haver, though they were never able to identify a suspect. About a year after the Game Zap hack, another cyberattack nearly cost the life of a Haver police officer . . .'

I gasped a little – loud enough for Dad and Misty to hear – and I covered it up with a fake cough.

The image on the screen now was of a house with windows shattered by bullets – a house where an undercover officer and his family lived, up until the day his home address was released to the public for anyone to see.

My heart was hammering so hard now, I couldn't concentrate. I barely even heard the reporter, but I knew she was recounting how gang members had gone after the officer – how if they'd come just one day later, they might have killed his wife and children.

Was Haver a haven for hackers?

Just one.

Sure, Seth and Mouse were the real Friends of Bishop, but they were first-time offenders, and their crimes paled in comparison to mine. They only knew half of what I'd done, and that was half more than anyone else knew. Isabel was right. I still had secrets. They surrounded me, devoured me.

My secrets built the buffer between me and the rest of the world. I could never tell a soul about the Haver PD hack, because just like a single connection to a computer will destroy its air gap, a single secret shared could tear down my own personal safe zones.

I pulled my knees up to my chest and sank into my end of the couch. Dad and Misty suddenly felt very far away.

39

'My email got hacked once,' Misty mused when the report was over.

'Well, that's what happens when your password is ABC123,' Dad teased.

Misty tucked herself under Dad's shoulder and poked him in the ribs. 'I would never have such a dumb password. Take it back.'

Dad tickled her instead.

I would have told them to stop their gross flirting right on top of me, but I was still in silent freak-out mode.

'Did you know about that website?' Dad asked me.

'Obviously. I *go* to Haver.'

Always nice to have disgust to fall back on when you don't want other emotions to leak out. It helps when parents ask ridiculous questions. Makes the disgust easy to tap into.

Dad grumbled, 'So much for all those cybermonitors our tax dollars are paying for, if a couple of hackers can outsmart the whole of them. I'd rather give my money to the jokers behind that site.'

A little ray of pride burst through the dark cloud of panic, and I almost smiled.

Dad shook his head. 'Punks.'

Almost.

When the news moved on to weather and sports, Dad said something about having a lot of work to do and retreated to his office. I hoped Misty would follow him, but she stayed and eyeballed me with one of her annoying X-ray stares.

'So is that site the big thing at school right now?'

The problem with Misty was that she paid too much attention.

I steadied my breathing.

Bored expression. Eye contact. Shrug.

'Yeah, I guess.' I knew that wouldn't be enough, so I added, 'They took our phones today.'

'Whoa. Seriously?'

I relaxed a little. She didn't seem suspicious.

'Yeah, I left mine at school.'

'You forgot your phone?' Misty said with an exaggerated jaw drop. Then she leaped off the couch to the front window, swept the curtains aside, and peered up to the sky. 'Nope, no pigs flying.'

I chucked a pillow at her.

She caught it, laughing, and flopped back down on the couch. 'So do you know the girl in the naked video?'

'She wasn't naked—'

'You watched it?' Misty cried. Then she held up a hand and closed her eyes. 'No, don't tell me. I don't want to know.'

'Her name's Ashley,' I said. 'She hasn't been back to school since it came out.'

Misty apparently heard the remorse in my voice and mistook it for something else.

'Ashley, huh?' She grinned. 'Pretty concerned about this Ashley, are you?'

'No, that's not—'

'What about Isabel?'

I huffed. 'You're missing the—'

'Two girls. That's quite the balancing act there, Eli. I'm impr—'

'Forget it.' I jumped up and started to walk away, but Misty caught me by the wrist.

'No, wait. I'm sorry. I'm listening, I swear.'

Reluctantly, I sat back down.

'I don't know her that well – or at all – but she's a pretty awful person, so some people think she kind of deserved it.'

'Uh-huh,' Misty said. 'And what do you think?'

'I'm not sure anyone deserves to be humiliated like that.'

Misty stayed silent, waiting for me to fill the space.

'Someone wrote "slut" on her locker,' I said, letting it all pour out now. 'And these girls – I don't know if they wrote it or just saw it, but they were laughing at it . . . at her.'

'Girls she was mean to?' Misty asked.

'Yeah, I think so. How did you know?'

'I was a girl once too.' She winked, then got serious again. 'I've also been called a slut a few times . . . as you can imagine.'

She said the last part very quietly and cast her gaze to her lap, where her hands had gathered up a blanket and were now wringing it like a dishrag. I didn't press her for more information.

'So, Isabel . . .' Misty said slowly, changing the subject for both of us. 'She's still the one?'

I sighed and let my head fall back on the couch. 'Oh man. I don't know anymore. She really freaked out on me today.'

'Why?'

Why? Because I'm responsible for that whole crime wave we just saw on the news, and she thinks I did it for her. And now that I think about it, I kind of did.

It was true, I realised. I probably would have left Ashley alone if it weren't for the things she'd said about Isabel, and I definitely wouldn't have given Seth the video if she hadn't treated Isabel like gum on the bottom of her shoe at the concert.

I lifted my head, choosing my words carefully. 'She thinks I got in the middle of this girl fight she's in. She and . . .'

Don't say 'Ashley.'

'She and this other girl have a kind of competition going, and she thinks I tried to help fight her battles for her, which I totally didn't do – not on purpose, anyway. But even if I had, what would be so bad about that? I thought girls wanted knights on horses and all that.'

'Oh, young Eli.' Misty did her best Yoda impression. 'Much to learn, you have. Complicated, girls are.'

She managed to make Yoda sound like he'd been smoking a pack a day for a century.

Girl problems were the least of my worries, but talking about Isabel – or anything other than Friends of Bishop – was a welcome distraction.

I lifted one corner of my mouth in a half smile, despite my mood. 'You are kind of a nerd, you know that?'

She returned the smile. 'I do know that. I also know some girls – the best girls – don't want to be rescued.'

'But you let Dad . . .' The words died on my lips, but she could fill in the blanks.

'Eli, your dad did not rescue me. Yes, he swept me off

my feet, but do you think I wanted to be swept right out of my home state and away from all my friends and family?'

It was my turn to look down at my hands.

'I love your dad,' she went on. 'But I do not love snow. I do not love the smell of manure or the tiny airplanes we have to take to get to this tiny town's tiny airport. I do not love the fact that I have to finish my degree online, because there is no college within a hundred miles of Haver.'

I bristled. It was one thing for *me* to think Haver was a dead-end loser town, but it wasn't cool for outsiders like Misty to point it out.

'Sorry it's such a snoozefest,' I said.

'I didn't say that.' She sat forward on the couch, elbows resting on her knees. 'But I had to give up a lot of things to come here. I miss sunshine. I miss the beach. I miss my family . . . my *other* family.'

'Sorry,' I mumbled. And this time I meant it.

She put a hand on my shoulder. 'No, I'm not telling you this to make you sorry. I gained so much more than I lost. I went from TV dinners for one to homemade meals for an entire family . . . however terrible they may be.'

I let out a soft laugh.

'The point is,' she said, 'it was my choice. Your dad is not my hero. He's my partner. And that's what you should be for Isabel. Don't try to rescue her from some "mean girl."

If you get in the middle, you end up standing in front of her, blocking her way. Just stand next to her, so she knows you're there.'

Well, damn. That actually made a lot of sense. Now if only I could tell her my real problems and have her solve those too.

I lifted my head and met Misty's eyes. 'Thanks.'

'Any time.'

Why did she have to be so nice? It made me feel like a shit.

'I probably don't deserve . . . the way I've been acting . . .'

She waved me off.

'Eli, I may not be your mom, but I've always got your back.' She twisted her engagement ring. 'It's kind of my job now. But even if it wasn't, I'd still be on your side. Got it?'

I nodded. 'Got it.'

A knock at the door interrupted our bonding moment before it got too mushy, and I would have been grateful if I hadn't been so damn jumpy. In my paranoid state, I pictured a crowd of police on the front porch, ready to bust down the door. Misty stood up to answer the knock, and I couldn't stop the panicked cry that flew out of my mouth.

'No, don't!'

She froze, looking down at me with a combination of confusion and concern.

319

I opened my mouth to speak, but I couldn't come up with any words to explain the outburst, so I just ended up gaping like a fish caught on the end of a line.

A voice from the other side of the front door spoke.

'Eli, I know you're in there. I saw your bike.'

Zach.

I was flooded with relief and rolled over the back of the couch to beat Misty to the door. I flung it open, and there was Zach, all in shadow, with the sun setting behind him and a grim look on his face.

'We need to talk.'

40

I stepped aside to let Zach in, but he shook his head.

'In private,' he said.

Behind me, Misty was lingering in the living room, taking her time picking up our dinner mess and trying to look like she wasn't eavesdropping.

I could see Zach's point.

I followed him out to the bench under the giant maple.

As soon as we sat down, he whipped out a phone – *my* phone – and handed it to me.

'Oh man, thanks! How did you—'

'I went back to school,' he said, looking sheepish. 'I didn't want to miss Chem lab.'

I laughed. 'I should have figured. Of all the places I went looking for you ...'

'Señora Vega told me to give you this.' He yanked a paper from his backpack.

I took it tentatively. 'Let me guess – she's automatically flunking me for cutting class today?'

'Not exactly,' he said.

I turned the paper over, surprised to see our vocab quiz from the week before.

I blinked twice at the A+ on the top of the page and the words next to it – '*Excelente. Mucho mejor.*'

Well, there was one thing I hadn't failed at today.

'So you were looking for me?' Zach asked.

'Yeah. That thing in the cafeteria – with Seth – I wanted to tell you . . .'

'Tell me what?' Zach pressed.

The razor focus in his eyes just then, the way he leaned in . . .

'You already know.'

The relief was palpable, but I wasn't completely off the hook. I owed it to Zach to tell him the truth out loud. So, I took a deep breath and did just that.

I told him all about the real-world-application section of the ACC and how Seth and Mouse had turned it into their personal revenge mission. I told him about the way Ashley treated Isabel and what I'd done to get back at her and how much I regretted it. I confessed to every computer we'd cracked and every secret we'd spilled.

And the last truth I told him was that I hadn't put up much of a fight. I'd wanted to be on their team so badly and hated the cyberlaws so much, I was willing to let the collateral damage pile up around me.

I just didn't know it would bury me.

By the time I finished, darkness was falling on our street, and Zach's head was in his hands.

'This is a mess,' he said.

'I know.'

'You guys broke the law.'

'I know.'

'You're such an idiot.'

'I know – wait, what?'

Zach lifted his face, and even in the twilight, I could see the disappointment there. For a second, Zach looked just like my dad.

'Come on, Eli. You're smart enough to know what you were getting in to.'

I jumped off the bench. 'Me? What about—'

I was interrupted by my phone ringing. I pressed Silent without checking the screen.

'Seth March is too disconnected from reality to understand the consequences of his actions,' Zach answered my unfinished question. 'And that kid, Mouse . . .'

'What about him?' I challenged.

Maybe Seth and Zach would never be best buddies, but Mouse had been nothing but cool to Zach at the concert. And until recently, he'd been nothing but cool to me, too.

Zach frowned. 'I don't think he's who you think he—'

My phone rang again.

'It's been doing that nonstop,' Zach said. 'You might want to answer it.'

I checked the screen and silenced it a second time when I saw Seth's name.

'It wasn't supposed to get this big,' I said, pacing back and forth. 'I thought we'd just embarrass a couple people who—'

Another ring.

Zach threw his hands up. 'Just answer it already. Your new friends obviously need you.'

'That's what this is really about, isn't it?' I stopped pacing to stand directly in front of Zach. 'You're jealous.'

'Of what?'

'Of me – hanging out with other people, doing the ACC—'

'Breaking the law, ruining people's lives!' Zach countered.

I shushed him, even though I doubted my neighbors were lurking on their lawns in the dark, listening to us.

'Maybe you're jealous that I met a girl, or that my website got so much attention.' Heat crawled up my neck into my face. I knew what I was saying was stupid, but now that the words were spilling out, I couldn't stop them. 'You just can't handle the fact that I have my own life now – that I have a life at all. So yeah, I think you're jealous.'

Zach reared back as if he'd been slapped. 'Wow, that is so off base.'

'Is it?'

He stood. 'Yeah, it is! I totally supported you with Isabel and the competition, even after you lied about it. I went to your stupid concert and forced myself to be nice to all your stupid new friends—'

'Gee, sorry to have torn you away from your fun weekend of sitting around, jerking off! Sorry I tried to include you!'

Zach got right in my face and spit as he talked. 'Man, you've got your head shoved so far up your ass, you can smell your own belly button!'

There was a pause as we stood toe to toe, fists clenched and panting, letting Zach's comeback sizzle in the air.

Then a ray of light cut through the storm gathering between us.

'Smell my own belly button?' I smirked.

Zach cracked a smile in spite of his fury. 'It's all I could think of.'

'Smells like lint.'

'Probably smells more like cheese, you dirt ball.'

I let out a laugh, and all my tension escaped with it. I

sagged back down to the bench. 'I'm sorry, Zach. Really.'

Zach sat too, and the slight smile on his face clashed with the serious look in his eyes. 'So now that your head is clear of your ass ... there's one other thing.'

'I swear, I've told you everything,' I said.

Almost.

'No, it's something I need to tell you.' Zach scratched his ear and seemed to decide something. 'Actually, I think it would be better if someone else told you. Are you up for a ride?'

I hesitated. I'd about had it with mysteries. But I trusted Zach ... and I owed him one.

My phone rang again as we collected our bikes, and when I cleared the screen this time, I saw seventeen missed calls. I clicked the number to view them and swallowed hard. Every single one was from Seth.

My thumb hovered over his name, tempted to call him back to see what was so damn urgent, but I already knew. I knew it when he chased me out of school with that desperate look in his eyes. Seth had finally figured out how deep the shit he was in really was, and now he expected me to throw him a rope to pull him out. But I was there drowning right next to him, and I was afraid his flailing would just drag me further down. So I pocketed my phone and pedaled off in the dark after Zach.

*

Zach wove a path through downtown and finally rolled to a stop in front of the arcade. I followed him inside, listening to the familiar *Pac-Man* tune that played in place of a door chime as we entered. I was used to seeing the place packed with kids waiting three-deep in lines behind the best games, so it was strange to see it deserted and quiet, save for the constant hum of electricity and the occasional explosion of sound from the pinball machines. I wondered why the owners bothered opening on a Tuesday.

I trailed Zach as he circled the arcade, finally finding what – or apparently *who* – he was looking for in a back corner, behind the wheel of a racing game.

'Eli,' Zach said. 'This is Brett Carver.'

I stopped in my tracks, several feet away. Was this a trap? A betrayal? Maybe Zach hadn't forgiven me after all and had lured me here for a showdown. I wanted to ask him all of this, but instead, I fixated on the back of Brett's head.

'Hey,' I said.

Brett's virtual car crashed, and he turned to wave.

'Brett has the highest score on *Maximum Velocity*,' Zach said, his arm sweeping toward the row of pseudo car seats on either side of Brett. 'He's been coming here a lot, since ...'

'Since I pretty much got kicked off all my teams,' Brett supplied.

He sounded matter-of-fact about it, and I figured if he wasn't pissed at me, then Zach hadn't told him who I was or what I'd done.

Or maybe Zach had just been waiting for me to confirm his suspicions.

'Brett's banned from sports because of that website,' Zach said. 'The one with all the videos.'

'Oh right,' I said, picking up on Zach's pointed tone.

He hadn't outed me. So what was he up to?

Brett tilted his chin at Zach. 'This is the guy?'

Zach nodded.

Brett slapped the seat next to him – an invitation – and I perched on it reluctantly, while Zach slipped between two pinball machines and disappeared into the maze of games.

'So you're a friend of Zach's?' Brett asked.

For just a second, I heard 'Friend of Bishop' instead of 'friend of Zach,' and I made a strangled noise. Brett must have thought I was choking, because he leaned over to pat my back.

'You all right, bud?'

I'm not your bud.

'I'm fine.' I brushed his hand away. 'What's this about?'

Brett arched one eyebrow. 'You tell me, man. This is

328

your party. All I know is my pal Zach asked me to meet him here. Said he was bringing you. Said you might be buying too much into that bogus website. Guess he wants me to set you straight. Can't believe everything you see on the internet, y'know?'

There was a lot to unpack in what Brett had just said, but I didn't hear much of it past the word 'pal.' Is that what Zach and Brett were? *Pals?* I rolled the word around in my mouth, disliked the taste of it. Is this where Zach had been while I'd been cramming for the ACC with Seth and Mouse?

I said nothing, afraid of stepping on a land mine, and Brett filled the silence.

'That site is mean as shit, but I guess I kind of deserve to be on it.' He leaned back in his seat, one hand absently spinning the game's plastic car wheel.

'For the stuff you did to Jordan?' I said.

He blinked, his forehead creasing a little. 'No, for taking junk to up my game.'

'Oh.'

'Why does everyone think I did something to Jordan Bishop? Just because that's the name of the website?' He twisted around to face me straight on. 'See, that's what I mean. Can't believe everything online.'

I frowned. 'You really have *no idea* why they went after you?'

'I don't even know who *they* are,' Brett said. 'No one does. So how do I know why they did it? I'm honestly surprised they didn't try to blackmail me or something. If they had showed me that video and threatened to release it, I would have done anything they wanted. They could have totally made me their bitch. Instead, they just put it out there. Makes no sense.'

Was this guy really that dense?

'I think they made it pretty clear on the site,' I said. 'They're taking down people who took down Jordan.'

Brett shook his head. 'But that wasn't me. I mean, sure, I probably LOL'd if one of my friends dragged him on social ... but I didn't have any beef with him.'

'Maybe you just don't remember. If you were in a 'roid rage—'

'*'Roid rage?*' Brett snapped back. 'What is this, an intervention? Who even are you?'

I'm a Friend of Bishop.

'I'm no one. But I saw that kid set himself on fire. And I've heard what people called him. "Faggot—"'

'That wasn't me.'

'"Queen."' I was practically spitting.

Brett scratched his cheek. 'Ugh. Yeah, that one was me. I forgot about that.'

'And "trailer trash."'

330

'*Everyone* called him trail—'

'You said he'd be better off dead and—'

'Whoa!' Brett leaned back, his hands in the air. 'No way. I would never say anything like that.'

I spluttered. 'Your friends said it then. And you LOL'd, right? You laughed. You said so.'

'No!'

'Bullshit!'

Brett stood up now, looking like he wanted to get away from me – a guilty move in my opinion. 'What do you care, man? You don't even know me!'

'I know people *like* you.' I was shaking all over.

'Zach, who is this guy?' He called out through the clamor of machines, but Zach didn't come. 'Is this some kind of setup?'

Funny, that's exactly what I'd been thinking. And like me, if he was afraid of a sting op, he probably had something to hide.

Brett looked back at me and seemed to be debating whether to defend himself or knock me out. He settled on the former.

'Look, I ought to beat your ass for getting up in my business, but since you're a friend of Zach's, I'll tell you what I told him: I may be an asshole for going along and not sticking up for Jordan, but everyone was ragging on him – *everyone*. And my crew didn't tell him to off himself.'

My hands were rolled into fists.

'Well, *someone* said it. He didn't kill himself for nothing.'

'Yeah, someone said it!' Brett shouted. 'I saw it! I was in that chat!'

I knew it. He *was* guilty. We were right to put him on the site. We weren't the bad guys. I was looking at the bad guy.

'So you admit it!' I stood too, facing off against Brett in the narrow aisle between racing games and pinball machines. 'You were there.'

'But I didn't – I just saw—'

'Saw your friends being d-bags.'

'It wasn't my friends!' Brett exploded, throwing his arms wide.

'Then who was it?!'

'Some guy called *Mouse*!'

41

The sounds of the arcade faded around me, and in their place, a dull buzzing noise filled my ears. But I still heard Brett's words banging around in my brain.

He's wrong.

It couldn't have been Mouse. It made no sense.

Zach appeared just then, looking ready to step in between us, so I figured he'd heard everything. I wished he'd just told me, but maybe he knew I wouldn't believe it, coming thirdhand.

And here I'd thought Zach and Mouse could be friends.

As if from a great distance, I heard Brett say to Zach, 'Your friend's a dick.'

'Show him,' Zach said.

'Why should I? I don't have to prove anything to—'

'Please.'

They spoke like friends, and it was a punch to the gut – not because Zach had expanded his social circle, but because I'd been too busy to even notice.

Slowly, slowly, the buzzing in my ears faded, and the

*ping*s and *whir*s of the machines around us came back online. I was vaguely aware of the scowl on Brett's face as he pulled his phone from his pocket.

'This is none of your business, but if it gets you off my back . . .'

He swiped the screen a few times and then passed the phone to me.

For a second I was confused. I was looking at the Chat Mob app that had been shut down after Jordan's death. It wasn't possible.

Then I realised it wasn't the defunct app at all but *screenshots* of it – of a conversation that should have disappeared with the app.

B.Carver: *How did Bishop even get in here? This is a private chat.*

Jordan: *I am everywhere. I own the internet.*

Boss: *You own nothing. You don't even own that piece of shit car your mom drives.*

PeterPan: *Hey J, you think if I blow Fogerty too, he'll bring my B up to an A?*

B.Carver: *You don't have to do that, Pete. I hear Fogerty takes cash for grades. Too bad Queen Jordan can't afford the rates.*

I scowled up at Brett, who stared back defiantly.

'What was your problem with Fogerty, anyway?' I asked.

'Athletes need to maintain certain grades,' Brett said. 'Some teachers are more understanding than others.'

'Fogerty's not a sports fan,' Zach supplied.

And neither was Zach, so why was he so buddy-buddy with this jock? They didn't have anything in common. Except a lot of free time now that Brett had no sports and Zach had no me. I felt responsible for both of those things and looked back down at the phone to cover my guilt. The chat continued in the next screenshot.

PeterPan: *Maybe you should sell your trailer J. Would that buy you an A?*

Jordan: *Maybe you should suck my D, assholes. Then cross your nuts I don't hack your transcripts and turn all your grades to Fs. How do you like those letters?*

B.Carver: *Bluff.*

Jordan: *Try me.*

Boss: *Careful, Carver. I think he's flirting with you.*

I swiped to the next screen. It seemed to capture a later portion of the conversation, and I wondered what Brett had conveniently left out. In this shot, more people were in the room.

PeterPan: *Who invited these shits into the chat?*
Jordan: *I did.*
Boss: *Looks like Jordan isn't Fogerty's only fag. He's got friends.*
March: *We're not his friends.*
Mouse: *And we're not fags.*

I gagged on the bile that rose up in my throat. March and Mouse. It didn't take a genius to solve that puzzle.

Jordan: *They're my bitches. ;)*
B.Carver: *Ha! J confirms it. He has a harem.*
Boss: *Knew it. Queers.*

'Why did you save these?' I asked Brett, without looking up.

'I used to screenshot all my Chat Mob conversations. I kept that one after ... well, in case someone ... they were looking for people to blame.' He cleared his throat, lowered his voice. 'I wanted to be able to prove I wasn't the worst.'

I swiped through the last two images and read the worst for myself.

March: *I'm not your bitch, Jordan. I'm not your anything.*

Mouse: *Me neither.*

Jordan: . . .

Mouse: *The only bitch here is you . . . Fogerty's bitch.*

Jordan: *Screw you guys.*

PeterPan: *Damn, boys! I think J just said he wants to screw you.*

Jordan: *I invited you to back me up.*

March: *Then you made a mistake.*

B.Carver: *LOL.*

Boss: *Burn! The new guys aren't so bad.*

March: *You'd be better off inviting Fogerty.*

Mouse: *You'd be better off dead.*

I swiped the screen again, but the chat shots were done. And my world was upside down.

'See?' Brett said. 'Friends of Bishop ought to go after those chumps. I think Jordan legit thought they *were* his friends.'

'Congratulations,' I said, tossing the phone back to Brett. 'You weren't the worst.'

He caught the phone with one hand and slipped it into his pocket. 'Told you.'

Not the worst. But not innocent either.

I didn't have to say it out loud. He saw it in my face, and maybe, deep down, he saw the truth in himself. He could only hold my gaze for a few seconds before his eyes dropped to the floor.

'I'm just saying, no one got busted for what happened to Jordan, because half of Haver would have had to go down for it. I don't know who's calling themselves Friends of Bishop, but he sure as shit had a lot of enemies.'

I had no answer for that, and after a moment of silence, Brett nodded a goodbye to Zach and pushed past me, out of the arcade.

When he was gone, Zach stepped forward tentatively, an apologetic look on his face. 'I met Brett here a couple of weeks ago, and we got talking. He's a good gamer. He's thinking of joining the chess team now that he . . .'

Now that he's off all teams, and his future is shot.

On any other day, I would have registered some surprise at the fact that a guy like Brett Carver could play chess, but my yardstick for surprise had just changed dramatically. Changed and warped and twisted back in on itself.

'It wasn't just that one chat,' Zach said when I didn't respond. 'If you know where to look, there were a lot of—'

'Stop.' I put my hands to my head, to keep it from

338

popping off. 'Zach, it can't be right. He photoshopped the chat pics or—'

'Why would he do that? No one even knows he has them.'

'I know, but . . .'

'And why would he make up *those* names, March and Mouse?'

Shit. I don't understand.

I needed to talk to Mouse, to Seth . . . *Seth.* I pulled my hands from my head and dug in my pocket for my phone. No new calls. Seth had given up at number 17. He had also sent four text messages:

> Call me.
>
> Call me.
>
> Seriously call me.
>
> Please.

And three voice mails.

I listened to the first one. He must have been in a car or riding pretty fast on his bike when he left it, because I mostly just heard a roaring wind. I caught enough to get that he couldn't reach Mouse and thought something was wrong.

I clicked to the next voice mail.

'What are you doing?' Zach asked.

I waved for him to be quiet, and put a finger in my non-phone ear to hear better.

Eli, what the shit? Answer your phone! I think I know where Mouse is. I got him on the phone for a second, and he said something about an audience and the Yellow Brick Road. I think he means The Wizard of Oz – invited dress rehearsal tonight. Everyone's going to be at school . . .

Still listening, I started moving toward the exit, waving for Zach to follow me.

. . . heading there now. I think he's going to do something crazy. If you get this, meet me there.

'We have to get to school,' I told Zach as we grabbed our bikes.

He nodded at the urgency in my voice and didn't ask any questions.

I tucked my phone under my chin to listen to the last message as we rode away at top speed, dodging people on the sidewalk. Seth's voice, panicked in his first two voice mails, was now hysterical.

> They won't let me backstage! Fucking theater nerds!
> Think they're the police of the auditorium! I know he's
> in there somewhere – backstage or, shit, in the rafters.
> Who knows? Where are—

The message cut out. Or, at least, I thought it did. A second later, I heard Seth breathing and realised it was still playing. His voice was almost a whisper when he spoke again.

> Eli, there's something we didn't tell you

I hung up.

'No shit.'

Phone still in my hand, I immediately dialed Isabel.

Please pick up. Please pick up.

It went to her voice mail after one ring. She ignored the call, either because it was me or because the show was about to start.

'Do you know anyone in the play?' I asked Zach as we turned out of downtown and onto the stretch of road that would beeline us straight to school.

He shook his head, panting with exertion. 'No. What's going on?'

'I'm not sure yet.'

I looked down at my phone once more, my bike weaving dangerously, and opened a text message to Isabel.

Call me. 911!

I didn't know exactly what the emergency was, or what Mouse was up to, but I knew in my gut that we needed to get backstage. I leaned forward on my bike handles, pushing in a fast line down the centre of the street. Ahead, the Haver High rooftop appeared over the trees. I pedaled harder.

My phone rang. Isabel.

I answered without a hello.

'Look, I know you're mad at me, and I understand if you hate me forever, but right now, I need your help. It's important, and it's not for me.'

'Okay,' she answered, without hesitation, without any questions at all.

And in the midst of everything, with my lungs about to burst and my life about to implode and my friend about to do God-knows-what, I realised that I might be in love with her.

'Thank you, thank you!' I said. 'I need you to keep an eye out for Mouse.'

'Mouse?'

'Yes. Just trust me. And one more thing. Can you open the stage door for us?'

'The show is starting,' she said. 'And I'm downstairs in the green room.'

'Isabel, please.'

'Okay, okay. I'll open it. You have one minute!'

'We'll be there.'

I tucked the phone back in my pocket just as we reached the edge of the school grounds. The auditorium's lobby doors were open wide, spilling a golden light onto the lawn. We skirted the light and rolled over the gravel strip that led to the back of the building. And then the darkness reached out and grabbed me.

42

The darkness that took hold of me was actually Seth taking hold of my bike handles.

He bolted out from the deep shadows draping the auditorium's exterior walls and planted himself in front of me. I skidded to a stop just in time, spraying rocks that pinged off the wall and ricocheted back, stinging my legs and arms.

'Shit, Seth!'

'Where have you been? What's he doing here?' He shot Zach a dirty look.

'He gave me my phone, or I wouldn't have even gotten your four hundred messages.'

Now that I was here, my shock had given way to anger and confusion.

How stupid was I to believe Seth and Mouse were my friends?

And if the website wasn't justice, what was it?

I had so many questions, but the one that reached my lips first was simply, 'What is going on?'

But Seth was already walking away. We dropped our bikes to hurry after him.

'Ask him about Jordan,' Zach urged in a whisper that carried down the length of the alley.

'What do you know about Jordan?' Seth spun to a stop, gravel crunching under his heel.

'I know you said some pretty messed-up things to him for a guy who claims to be a Friend of Bishop,' Zach said.

Seth gaped, first at Zach, then at me. 'You told him?'

'Yeah, I did,' I said. 'Because I can trust him – unlike you.'

A door opened just ahead of us, fluorescent light slicing across the gravel drive like a white knife. Isabel's head poked out of the doorway, and she squinted into the dark.

'Eli?'

'We're here,' I said, hustling toward the stage door with Zach and Seth in my wake. 'Have you seen Mouse?'

'No,' she said. 'Why would he even be here?'

I looked at Seth to explain, but he only crossed his arms and tapped a foot, impatient to get inside.

'Is it okay if we just look around for a few minutes?' I asked Isabel.

'Okay.' She kicked a large rock under the door to wedge it open, then she backed up into the landing of a brightly lit, narrow stairwell. 'I have to get back to the green room. That's in the tunnels, so I'll look there. I'll call you if I see him.'

If she was still mad at me, I couldn't hear it in her voice. Whatever fight we were in was on pause until my emergency was over. Yeah, I was pretty sure I loved this girl.

'Thank you,' I said.

She pointed to a second door, behind her. 'That leads backstage. The show already started, so you have to be quiet. Upstairs will take you to the catwalks. You can't really walk on them, but it will give you a good view of the audience, in case he's there.'

I thanked her again, and she disappeared down the staircase that led to the basement.

Seth started to follow her inside, but I stopped him with a hand to the chest.

'First you have to tell me what we're doing here. What is Mouse up to?'

'I don't know.'

'I don't believe you.'

Seth opened his mouth to respond, but then all at once, his face crumpled and dropped into his hands.

'You're right,' he said.

'I am?'

I had braced for a fight, not a confession.

'We didn't lie. But we ... we left some things out.' Seth lowered his hands but still didn't meet my eyes. 'What happened to Jordan ...'

'Was he even your friend?' I asked.

My muscles were coiled tight, and I felt like I might throw up. Had I really been on the wrong side all along?

'He was,' Seth said. 'I mean, not at first. First we were just teammates. I met Mouse and Jordan last year when you all came in as freshmen. I tried to start a coding club, and they were the only ones who signed up.'

I exchanged a look with Zach and saw my shock mirrored in his eyes. I remembered being a newbie last year, seeing flyers for the club our first week of school. We were both interested, but I was too scared to join anything right away, especially something that sounded like a nerd club, so I had talked Zach out of joining.

Maybe things would have been different if I hadn't been such a chickenshit. Maybe we would have all been friends, and Zach and I would have been there to stick up for Jordan.

Or maybe we would have ended up standing exactly where Seth was right now.

I shivered.

'Three people wasn't much of a club,' Seth went on. 'So we decided to enter the ACC instead. After that, we really were friends. But then . . . then Jordan started . . . *annoying* people online.'

'He was a troll,' I said.

347

I reached deep inside for some sense of surprise but came up empty. Maybe a part of me had known all along, but you feel guilty thinking about a dead guy like that. Crazy how death can change a person, even after they're gone. An internet creeper, postmortem, can suddenly become the perfect victim.

We'd eviscerated Jordan's enemies. But how many were unjustly punished? How many had he hit first?

The alley tilted a little, and I thought I might be sick.

'He was never a troll to us,' Seth said. 'He wasn't a bad guy. He just liked to have fun with people online. It was kind of funny, and we stuck up for him ... maybe even egged him on a little ... at first.'

'And then?' I pressed.

'And then they came after us – me and Mouse. Anyone who defends a troll must be a troll too, right? It was making things ... difficult for us. Online. At school. He was dragging us down. The things people said to us ...'

'Worse than what you said to Jordan?' I said.

Seth sucked in a breath.

'Yeah, I know about that.'

'We got put on Ashley's "Pretty Pervy" list because of him,' Seth said, defensive now. 'Whatever he had going on with Mr. Fogerty – and maybe it was nothing, I don't know – but we got sucked into it too. Brett Carver and his crew started calling us Fogerty's Fags. Jordan wanted to go after those guys online, but we thought it would just make it worse. We asked him to leave it alone – or at least leave us out of it. We begged him . . .'

Seth's voice cracked.

Next to me, Zach folded his arms and shuffled his feet, rolling gravel under his sneakers. He'd been pretty anxious for me to know the truth earlier. Now he looked unsure.

'Um, why don't I start upstairs?' he said. 'It will take a while to look at everyone in the audience from the catwalks . . .'

'Go,' I said.

He scurried through the open door and up the stairs before I could change my mind.

Seth took an unsteady breath and continued. 'Jordan wanted to go to war, but we were too chicken. You can't win against guys like that, y'know? Or at least we didn't think so then. After Jordan . . . afterward, Mouse said we were cowards. He thought we should have had Jordan's back.'

'And what did you think?' I asked.

'I thought we had to protect ourselves,' Seth said.

'You turned on him.'

'No . . . or, not right away, anyway. We tried to just

349

kind of … *ignore* him at first, but he didn't really get the hint.'

'I think he got it in the end.'

What I'd read on Brett's phone hadn't been a hint so much as a Mack truck slamming into Jordan.

'He thought you had his back. He thought you were his friends.'

'We were.' Seth blanched. 'We shouldn't have … We didn't mean to …'

He couldn't finish the thought, and I didn't need him to.

The whole picture finally became clear, and I could see it from all angles at once, which was a maddening thing. When Jordan started spiraling out of control, he thought Seth and Mouse were along for the ride, but they were just caught in the undertow, trying to come up for air. He brought them attention they hadn't asked for. I could imagine the desperation they must have felt when they deflected their own abuse and redirected it back toward Jordan.

And I could imagine Jordan being crushed by that betrayal.

I had to put a hand on the open door to keep from falling over. The whole world had gotten it wrong. Jordan Bishop didn't care what a bunch of 'bullies' said at all.

'He didn't do it because of them,' I said, aching with pity for the boy I never really knew. 'He did it because of you.'

Seth was desperate to make me understand. 'We didn't know he would—'

'All the things you told me people called him . . .'

'You weren't there.'

'Trailer trash,' I quoted. 'Scum.'

Seth shook his head and put his hands in his hair. 'Stop.'

'How many of those did you ignore?'

'Please.'

'How many did you say yourself?'

'Don't,' he said. 'There's nothing you can say – nothing you can even *think* that will make me hate myself any more than I already do. I *hate* myself, Eli. I HATE MYSELF!'

Seth was crying now, his hands still twisting in his hair, his upper body rocking forward and back.

I didn't want to see this. I didn't even want to *know* any of this.

'I thought you guys just felt guilty that you didn't stick up for him,' I choked out. 'This is too much.'

'Too much for *you*? I live with it every day.' Seth sniffed back his tears. 'That's my punishment – that I have to live with it. But Mouse . . . he was so messed up for so long. When I got the idea for the website . . .'

'So you did plan for it to be a revenge site all along.'

More secrets. More lies.

Seth's face was filled with regret. 'When Jordan ... it was like Mouse died too – like I had lost them both. And then suddenly, with the site, I got my friend back. He was human again.'

'Still think of yourselves as human, huh?'

I didn't mean to kick a wounded dog, but I had to say something to fight off the urge to comfort him. I felt frayed at the edges, and all my loose threads were reaching out to Seth in sympathy. Sympathy he didn't deserve.

'But it didn't last,' Seth went on as if he hadn't heard me. 'I guess he expected the website to fix it all somehow – to undo what we did, or make up for it. All Jordan ever wanted was for us to take his side and stand up to his enemies, so Mouse thought – *we* thought – the least we could do now is the one thing we wouldn't do for him then. But it didn't change anything. And now Mouse ... well, you've seen him.'

I pictured the bouncing Mouse I'd first met weeks ago – the one who talked fast and was constantly in motion, the boy with the orange-and-blue shoes and the disarming grin. But under it all had been that darkness, and it turned our bouncy friend into the still, emo kid in the cafeteria yesterday – haunting us more than helping us, a shadow of himself.

'I have seen him,' I agreed. 'It would have been nice to know what I was looking at.'

Seth slumped against the building. A second ago, he'd been anxious to get backstage. Now he just seemed lost . . . and so small, it was hard to believe he was two years older and allegedly the smartest kid at Haver. It was even harder to believe that after all his lies, I still gave a shit about him – and about Mouse – and I couldn't walk away.

I took a deep breath. 'So are we going to go get him or what?'

'What do you think he's doing in there?' Seth whispered, fear in his voice.

I threw up my hands. 'Maybe he's just trying to get video of people falling down during their dance numbers.'

Seth, sagging in the shadows of the alley, didn't laugh.

Yeah, probably not the best moment for comic relief.

But it was better than saying what we were both thinking. Mouse wanted vengeance and the website hadn't been enough. How many of Jordan's enemies were inside that theater? How many would Mouse have to take out before he atoned for his own mistakes?

I knew now that the darkness I'd seen in Mouse was his own guilt, eating him from the inside out. I didn't want to imagine what that darkness would look like when it fully escaped.

I kicked the rock out from under the door. 'Are you coming or not?'

43

The backstage area was dark and crowded and smelled of old, wet wood, just like the auditorium always did. It struck me, as the stage door closed behind us, that the last time I noticed that smell – the last time I was in this space – it was April Fools' Day, and I'd been watching a parade of Jordan Bishop's pictures, thinking the memorial was pointless since the kid obviously didn't have any friends. One month and an entire lifetime later, here I was looking for one of those friends ... one of *my* friends.

I blinked as my eyes adjusted to the darkness – deeper backstage than it had even been outside. Here and there, pinpoint lights illuminated the ground so people wouldn't trip over themselves. Seth and I stood shoulder to shoulder, encircled by students in colourful outfits and funny hats – Munchkins ready to sing Dorothy down the Yellow Brick Road.

A sudden roar filled the auditorium – the tornado destined to carry Dorothy and her dog out of Kansas and into Oz. The sound effect drowned out backstage whispers and rustles, and made it impossible for Seth and me to hear each other. I motioned to him that I was going to circle around to the other side of the stage. He replied with his own gesture, indicating he would check the immediate area.

I glanced up to the rafters, looking for Zach, but I was too blinded by bright, high-hanging lights to see anything. When I looked back down, I could have sworn I caught a glimpse of Mouse among the Munchkins, but it may have been the echo of the lights in my eyes, because when my vision cleared, he was gone.

Onstage, Dorothy's house landed with a crash, and behind the curtain, I plunged into the crowd of dancers. A few of them stood at least a head taller than me.

Some Munchkins.

When I reached the centre of the group, I could see the other half of the backstage area was pitch-black. Set pieces loomed tall and flat, like giant books lined up on a shelf, the narrow spaces between them full of deep shadows. It was a perfect area for Mouse to hide. I wondered how he planned to stay hidden – what he might be plotting there in the dark.

I was nearly free of the Munchkins, when all of a sudden they moved as one, rushing toward a part in the curtain and sweeping me along with them. I spun around in the confusion, fell over my own feet, and grabbed at someone's suspenders on my way down. The suspendered Munchkin managed to stay upright, but I'm pretty sure he kicked me on his way to the stage.

'No crew allowed in this area,' someone hissed as they hopped over my prone form.

A second later, the curtain had closed, and I was alone on the ground. I got to my knees and gave the finger to the Munchkins, even though they couldn't see me. Then I tiptoed over to the darker side of the stage, slipping into a slim pathway between two of the huge set pieces.

Beyond the curtain, the chorus of 'Follow the Yellow Brick Road' came to a crescendo.

I wove in between the set walls, making my way toward the front of the stage. I had nearly cleared the last set piece when something assaulted my nose, and it wasn't the wet-wood smell that defined the auditorium. It was much worse.

I gagged.

What the . . .

I barely had time to form a thought when the music that had built to a thunderous climax suddenly cut off, along with the lights.

This is it, I thought. *Whatever Mouse is doing, he's doing it now.*

But the next thing I knew, Munchkins were skipping offstage and rushing to the other side of the theater, away from me and the sickening smell. The song hadn't been cut off. It had just come to a dramatic close.

I let my nose guide me around the last set piece, and though it was still pitch-black, I could sense now that there was nothing between me and the auditorium but the heavy drop of burgundy velvet curtain that kept the backstage area hidden. I wonder if it also hid the smell from the audience. The aroma was so strong now, I had to pull my shirt over my face.

Oh no. Oh no.

Terrified, and understanding all at once, I stumbled in the dark toward it ... the sickly sweet smell of gasoline.

One hand holding my shirt to my nose, the other groping blindly ahead of me, I moved forward on pure instinct, stepping carefully to avoid falling again, but I still slipped a little where the gasoline had spilled on the floor.

I knew that's what I was sliding on even before the auditorium lights came back up and confirmed it. In the glow that floated down from the catwalks overhead, I could see the shimmering rainbow of fuel snaking across the floor.

I followed the trail with my eyes and there, standing at a part in the curtain, like a player about to take the stage, was Mouse, his clothes soaked in gas and a box of matches in his hand.

44

The curtain fluttered slightly, and I saw Mouse more clearly. He was drenched from head to toe, in a puddle between two empty gas cans. He bounced a little in place, making a small *splish-splash* where his heels hit the gasoline. But while his feet had found their bounce again, the hand holding the matchbox was steady.

'Hi, Eli,' he said.

As if he was expecting me. As if we were back in Seth's basement and I'd just arrived for a practise session.

'Mouse, what are you doing?' I asked, even though the answer was obvious.

'We didn't speak,' Mouse said.

'What?' I inched closer, forcing myself to lower my hand from my face, even though I was choking on the smell.

'At the assembly,' Mouse said, gesturing behind him to the auditorium. 'We didn't speak for Jordan.'

How is he not gagging? He's swimming in it.

Two steps closer.

I retched.

One step back.

Space, backspace. Space, backspace.

'And we didn't speak when people started tearing him down.' Mouse fiddled with the matchbox, opening and closing it. 'We didn't stick up for him. Instead we ...'

The matchbox crumpled in Mouse's fist.

'I know,' I said.

It's all I could get out, because I was holding my breath against the gasoline.

Mouse looked at me, surprised for a second, then his face folded into shame and tears. 'I didn't mean it.'

'I know that too.'

Another step forward.

Space, backspace.

'I want to speak now,' Mouse said, dragging a sleeve across his face.

'I'm listening.'

'Not to you. To them.' He made a vague gesture behind him, and I wished with everything in me that someone onstage would spot us through the crack in the curtain and come put a stop to this sideshow nightmare.

'I want to tell them the truth,' Mouse said. 'I want to tell them. And then I want it to be over. Like it was for Jordan.'

A part of me had been right. Mouse *had* come here

tonight for revenge – just not on the people I thought. He planned to punish himself.

I took one more step toward Mouse, and this time, he backed away, pulling a match from the crushed box and holding it out like a warning.

'Okay, okay,' I said, my hands in the air. 'I just want to—'

'Mouse, what the ...?!' Seth came skidding up so fast and loud, he almost knocked me down.

The voices onstage faltered at the commotion behind the curtain.

Come! I willed them. *Come end this.*

But the show must go on, and the actors slid back into the scene, a new musical number rising up to muffle our voices.

Seth slipped, like I had, on the wet floor, and gripped my arm for support. But even after he got his feet back under him, he didn't let go. Viselike fingers crushed my bicep as he took in the scene before him, mouth open but no words coming out.

Mouse smiled – *he actually smiled* – at Seth. He was still holding up his match, mere inches from the strike pad that would create a spark and light him up. The space between match and pad was just like the invisible gap around a secure computer – only empty air, but somehow full of energy, powerful in its potential.

'Down in flames, right?' he said to his gaping friend. 'Just like Jordan.'

But I knew Seth wouldn't allow it. I was so grateful for his arrival, because bossy, bigmouth, know-it-all Seth March was going to shut this shit down right now. He would bend Mouse to his will, as always – convince him this idea was a disaster – and drag his ass back home for a second round of 'what the hell were you thinking?' lectures.

I waited for the dam to burst.

Any minute now.

Seth stayed silent.

Come on.

Nothing.

I glanced sideways at him, afraid to take my eyes completely off Mouse, and what I saw was terrifying. Seth was nodding – almost imperceptibly – but nodding all the same. Then, tears were sliding down his face, and terrible, stupid words were falling out of his mouth.

'You're right,' he said. 'You're right.'

Seth's knees buckled, and he hit the floor, his body racked by silent sobs.

Mouse watched him go down, a look of pity on his face.

'You don't have to come,' he said. 'It's okay if you stay.

But you have to tell everyone the truth, Seth. Tell them what we did.'

Seth rocked back and forth in response, and Mouse pinched the match, poised to strike.

To my left, a puddle of despair. In front of me, a powder keg about to blow.

And it was enough.

Enough.

'Enough!'

It came out in a strangled cry, and I realised I was breathing heavy, fumes and all. Either I was getting used to the gasoline, or I was using it to fuel my rage.

'This is done.'

I was done.

Done with lies. Done with vigilante justice. Done watching my friends fall apart.

Friends.

I knew the truth of the word in that moment. We might have called ourselves Friends of Bishop, but these were friends of *mine*. And they were crumbling.

'He doesn't deserve your tears,' I said to Seth, then to Mouse, 'or your suicidal apology.'

Mouse's hands froze in place, and Seth's sobbing slowed to a sniffle. It was as if my words had shocked them into slow motion.

I could not fathom their pain, and I felt a deep pulsing sorrow of my own for the boy who had been betrayed, but from everything I'd heard, he was not innocent. And the worst crime he'd committed had been the lifetime of guilt he'd laid on his friends.

Seth and Mouse found their voices.

'But he—'

'You don't know—'

I cut them both off with a sharp wave of my hand.

'No. I've had it with the martyrdom of Jordan Bishop.'

In fact, I was pretty *pissed* at Jordan Bishop.

What he'd done that day in the cafeteria was selfish, even if he didn't mean for it to be. I couldn't imagine hurting so bad that setting fire to your own skin was preferable to the pain inside. But I knew this much: that kind of pain didn't come from just one place. It couldn't all be laid at Seth and Mouse's feet. Yes, they had hurt him, but just like our web videos hadn't been enough to make up for the cruelty Jordan experienced . . . his suicide, too, was a punishment that didn't fit the crime.

'I know you feel like you betrayed him, but you were scared. You made a mistake. This is too harsh a price to pay. It's not fair.'

Slowly, Seth got to his feet, listening. But Mouse wouldn't hear it.

'Fair? Is it *fair* that no one was ever punished? That *we* were never punished?'

'Mouse, it's not your fault that he—'

'It *is* our fault!' Mouse shouted.

The actors onstage fell quiet again, and this time, the silence stuck.

'He didn't care what anyone else said to him.' Mouse was in a rage, his bouncing turned to a violent shaking. 'But our words – our words *killed* him!'

'That's bullshit!' I hollered back, barely aware that the entire audience was probably listening now. 'Jordan was a—'

'Don't you talk about him like you knew him!'

Our voices exploded through the silent cavern of an auditorium.

'Well, that's all we talk about, so I practically *do* know—'

'You don't know shit! The things we said . . .' He glanced at Seth, who was now shaking at my side, then back to me. 'I told him he'd be *better off dead.*'

I tensed, not wanting to hear that truth again.

'Don't do this to yourself,' I pleaded.

'We pushed him.'

'Stop it!'

'We *broke* him.'

'No!'

'*We* did that. *We* did—'

'HE LIT HIS OWN MATCH!'

There was a gasp somewhere onstage, a slight rustle in the audience, and then a terrible hush. It was the kind of thing you weren't supposed to say – the kind of thing that couldn't be unsaid, just like Jordan's fiery goodbye couldn't be unseen.

Mouse and Seth both looked smacked in the face.

'I'm not excusing what you did,' I said. 'You played your part, but his death isn't all on you. It's on Brett and his crew; it's on people like me for not paying attention.'

The curtain behind Mouse was shoved to the side by someone onstage, and I was blinded by the sudden wash of lights that all seemed to be pointed right at us. I nodded to the crowd – a hazy blur beyond the sudden and intense glow. 'It's on them, for thinking they can fix it by silencing it. And it's on Jordan too. He set a lot of things on fire that day.'

'You don't understand,' Mouse said, his voice aching with regret.

Out of the corner of my eye, I saw people making their way across the stage to us, the curtain rippling in their wake. The crowd beyond the stage lights was now a shifting mass of colour and a swell of voices.

'That smell.'

'Gasoline.'

'Who are they?'

'Matches!'

'Call 911!'

Yes, I thought. Call for help. Maybe I could distract Mouse long enough to keep him from setting himself and possibly this whole place on fire.

'Everyone thinks that no one was punished for Jordan's death,' I said. 'But that's not true. You've been punishing yourself every day.'

On the periphery, a small group was gathering: Munchkins, Flying Monkeys, Isabel, Zach, and someone who looked vaguely the size and shape of a grown-up. I couldn't break eye contact with Mouse to say for sure. They were silent, watching me try and fail to talk my friend off a ledge.

'We're all responsible.' As I said the words, I felt them soar past Mouse and into the auditorium, settling on the hundreds of people in the audience. 'We all killed Jordan Bishop.'

Mouse nodded, tears slipping down his cheeks, and I realised my words had only pushed him closer to the edge. He moved the match as if to strike, and I took one last shot.

'Don't do to us what Jordan did to you.'

I'd been struggling with what to say, but that felt right. I'd finally hit on the right thing.

Mouse's face crumpled.

It was the wrong thing.

With a look that was at once devastated and determined, he pressed the match head to the strike pad. The time for talking was over.

I lunged toward him, feet sliding, arms stretched – but he was too far away.

I couldn't reach him.

I couldn't stop it.

And then Seth was there.

Seth on top of Mouse, matchsticks flying.

Seth and Mouse on the floor, splashing in the gasoline.

My knees hit the wooden stage planks as I collapsed with relief.

The curtain fell back into place, plunging us once more into near darkness.

The adult-shaped person swooped in, cradling Mouse, who was now wailing in the fetal position.

A hand touched my shoulder – Isabel.

No, Zach.

Both together.

They were pulling me up off the floor.

I heard a voice – someone onstage making an announcement to the crowd – then the rustle of bodies shuffling to the exits.

On both sides of the curtain, the show was over.

45

There were sirens. That much, I remember. Sirens and stretchers and a lot of freaked-out adults.

But everything after that was a blur. I didn't know how I got home or what happened to my bike. I didn't recall talking to police or whether I'd said goodbye to Zach or Isabel. I just remembered Mouse and Seth in a pool on the floor, and the next thing I knew, I was slumped against the kitchen island under too-bright lights.

My clothes still reeked of gasoline.

Misty's fingernails clicked against the counter as Dad thanked an officer and closed the front door. He came back to the kitchen, arms crossed, his face a mask of ice, but underneath that cold surface, I could see emotions shifting and churning, and I understood something about my dad in that moment. It wasn't always anger he was controlling with his constant calm. Sometimes it was fear.

'I'm sorry,' I choked out.

'For what?' Dad asked. 'For lying to us? For breaking the law?'

'Paul, stop,' Misty pleaded in a hushed voice.

'I didn't even know you were capable of – of—'

'Of being so stupid?' I supplied with a sniff.

'Of this level of skill. Your coding . . . I – I had no idea.'

I blinked and met his gaze. I couldn't be hearing right. I was vaguely aware that I'd spent the past half hour spilling my guts to the police about how we'd managed to keep our site hidden from snoops, while Dad paced back and forth behind the officer in stony silence. I knew he'd been listening, but now I realised it was more than that. For once, he'd really *heard* me.

I hesitated. 'Are you – you're proud of me?'

'On the contrary,' Dad said, his face pale but mask still in place. 'I am profoundly disappointed.'

Of all the words he could have picked – that was the one with the sharpest edge, and it sliced right through me.

I came undone.

Misty rushed up to hug me as the first tears fell. I sagged into her tiny arms, collapsing under the weight of all that had happened in the last twenty-four hours – in the last four weeks.

Over the top of her head, I saw Dad's mask morph – from calm to confusion to concern to something else I didn't quite see, because suddenly his arms were snaking around Misty and I at the same time, wrapping us both in a hug.

371

I sank into those arms, wondering how I never knew they were so big.

From inside the bear hug came Misty's muffled voice. 'Ugh, Eli. You smell *awful*.'

I smiled through my tears, and Dad laughed.

'So,' I sniffled, feeling like a little kid. 'Am I – I'm not in trouble?'

Dad's voice was close to my ear when he answered. 'Oh, you're in trouble. You're in *so much* trouble.'

And his arms squeezed tighter.

*

The sun was scorching as I waited on the sidewalk, watching the line of cars creep by. So far, none of them was my ride. I wished I could just walk home, but Dad was getting better at this grounding thing. He'd created his own definition, and it included constant supervision from the time I stepped off school grounds until I came back the next day.

I squinted into the sunlight reflecting off car windshields. Still no sign of Misty.

I stood sweating in the June humidity.

It was the last week of class, and I was literally counting the days until summer break. That's when the whispering at school would end.

Police couldn't release our names since we were juveniles, but after Mouse's *Wizard of Oz* meltdown, it was pretty much the worst-kept secret in Haver that we were Friends of Bishop. Half the kids at school looked at us with awe or fear, and the other half looked like they wanted to catch us in a dark corner to show us what they thought of our website.

I wanted to escape them all in equal measure.

Everyone saw us as either hero or villain, but if I'd learned anything from all of this, it was that it was possible to be both, and I wanted to be neither.

'Hey, Bennett!'

Speaking of villains.

'What do you want, Malcolm?'

He lumbered up next to me, his red hair looking more blond in the sun. 'Now is that a nice way to greet one of the few people at Haver still talking to you?'

I turned away from him, willing Misty's car to appear.

'I have a proposition for you,' Malcolm said to the back of my head, ignoring the fact that I was ignoring him. 'I thought you might be strapped for cash, what with your legal fees and everything . . .'

'Get to the point.'

'The point is, I have to take summer school. Apparently I didn't exactly pass World History.'

I felt a stab of empathy. I had managed to pass Spanish by the skin of my teeth, and even then, Señora Vega had suggested I get a tutor over the summer.

'And?' I prompted.

'And, seeing as you're supposed to be a genius or whatever, I thought you or one of the other *Friends* might be able to tutor me.'

'By "tutor" you mean write your papers, right?'

'Well ...'

'No.'

'It's just ... I have to get a job this summer. I'm saving up for something important.' He lowered his voice. 'Some*one* important.'

I swallowed, remembering his searches on my key-sniffing software.

Prenatal care ... paternal rights.

I felt bad for him, despite our history, but I had my own problems, and I told him so.

He gave up surprisingly easily. 'Yeah, I figured. It was worth a shot.'

Misty finally appeared, six cars back in the row, and she hopped out of the driver's seat to wave from a distance.

I waved back to let her know I saw her.

'Wow.' Malcolm let out an appreciative whistle. 'Your babysitter is bangable.'

Once upon a time, the comment would have made me cringe, but every day I gave a little less of a shit what anyone else thought, and the shame I would have felt two months ago was now just a twinge of annoyance.

I turned to Malcom, finally giving him my full attention.

'That's my mom.'

I hadn't exactly planned to say those words, and the shock on Malcom's face mirrored my own.

He stepped back, sizing me up.

'Wow, that must suck,' he said, 'having a mom who people want to … uh, *look at.*'

I raised my eyebrows at the unexpected sympathy.

'It does suck,' I said.

And it must suck to be sixteen with a baby on the way, I didn't say.

Malcolm started to leave, hesitated, turned back.

'I submitted a video, you know.'

I couldn't keep the surprise out of my voice. 'Which one?'

But he only grinned and walked away.

As he left, he brushed shoulders with a vision coming from the other direction. Two months had passed since I'd first worked up the courage to talk to Isabel, and words still failed me at the sight of her.

She cast a confused look over her shoulder as she reached me.

'I thought you hated that guy.'

'I do ... I did.'

'Oh.'

She nodded.

I rocked back on my heels.

A silence fell.

There had been a lot of awkward silences between the two of us in the past few weeks. My grounding kept me from seeing her outside of school, and her parents weren't exactly impressed by my legal troubles. That left us only the spare seconds in the hallway between classes, which wasn't ideal for winning her back. Eventually, Isabel had suggested we just be friends for now. I hoped 'for now' didn't mean 'forever.'

I glanced down the row of cars. Misty was four back. I could see through the windshield that she was cursing at the driver in front of her.

'I have your letter,' Isabel said, digging in her backpack. She produced a long thin envelope and pressed it into my hand. 'I hope it helps.'

I already knew what was inside. Our lawyer had recommended we all get character references to submit to the judge hearing our case, and Isabel had agreed to write mine. We were hoping for a plea agreement that would knock the charges down from child pornography to sexting – because apparently that was a crime too – and help keep us all out of jail. Still, the lawyer had told us to expect to spend the summer doing a shitload of community service, and despite a lot of shouting protests from our parents, he also said there was no way we were getting out of this without being labeled 'sex offenders.'

Gross.

No wonder Isabel just wanted to be friends.

'This means a lot,' I said. 'Really. *Gracias.*'

'You're welcome, Eli.' She rested a hand on my arm, and I felt a familiar tingle where our skin touched.

She opened her mouth to say something else, but she hesitated a second too long, and whatever it was fell into the void between us. She glanced over my shoulder, and I knew Misty's car was there.

Isabel dropped her hand, the connection broken.

I thanked her again, in English and Spanish, and watched her leave.

'Is that the famous Isabel?' Misty asked as I flopped into the passenger seat. 'Are you getting back together?'

I was saved from answering by a knock at the window. The back door opened, and Zach poked his head in.

'Can you give me a ride?'

I twisted in my seat.

'I thought you were supposed to get a ride with Seth.'

'Mouse got home early. Seth went to see him – said he'll be over after.'

I nodded, a tickle in my throat keeping me from making words.

Mouse's parents had sent him to a special facility for treatment – not so much because of what he'd done in the auditorium but because of what came after. He went practically catatonic – not talking or eating, and staying in bed all day, even when he was awake. Forty-eight hours of that, and his parents had called in the pros.

'How's he doing?' Misty asked as she steered the car out of the lot.

Zach shrugged. 'Good, I guess.'

'We wouldn't know,' I mumbled. The tickle in my throat now pricked at the back of my eyes.

All our parents were still sorting out what we'd done, and Mouse's parents had decided to keep everyone at a distance until they figured out who to blame. The one exception was Seth, because he had saved Mouse's life with his tackle. I liked to think I had helped too, but it seemed kind of petty to point it out.

Misty took her hand off the wheel to touch my shoulder. 'You'll see him soon.'

'Seth said he'd fill us in tonight,' Zach said.

He and Seth had been getting on surprisingly well since Zach had taken Mouse's spot on our ACC team. Mouse's parents refused to let him participate, and I guess I didn't blame them. I was shocked my dad hadn't done the same. I think he was afraid that even if we did score the plea deal, Haver wouldn't let me back for junior year, so the idea that I could get a job from the competition gave him hope that he wasn't raising a total delinquent.

Not that we had any chance of winning at this point. We'd decided to forfeit the real-world category, and we'd only had a few weeks to get Zach up to speed. I doubted we'd get noticed by any recruits for internships, let alone jobs, but I didn't mention that to Dad. His grounding rules were 'no computers and no friends, pretty much ever,' and the one exception was practise for the ACC, which was why Zach was allowed to come home with us now.

No one cared about winning anymore anyway. Seth had just committed to Stanford in the fall, pending the outcome of our case, so he was less uptight about competing, and Zach saw the whole thing as practise for next year. As for me, the only reason I was still in it was for the time with my friends, which I knew might be limited.

What they didn't know – what nobody knew – was that

even if we didn't get fried for Friends of Bishop, I'd already decided to confess to a much bigger bomb. I'd written the confession into admissions essays for MIT and Caltech. The essays were already printed and stuffed into big envelopes, along with early applications.

In the essays, I detailed my involvement, not just with the Haver High Hack (as the media was now calling it), but also Game Zap and Haver PD. It had been painful to type up that last one, but afterward I'd felt such a wash of relief. I used my own mistakes to illustrate the need for ethical hacking – my proposed major.

It was almost funny. I'd finally decided to go to college, and here I was, probably setting myself up to go to prison instead.

*

Two weeks later, I stood on the shore of Lake Michigan, the Chicago skyline at my back, leaning into the wind rushing off the water. The flat expanse in front of me was a welcome contrast to the twisty lines of code that had filled my vision almost every day for weeks.

The ACC was just hours away, and Seth and Zach were already at the convention centre, gathering our badges and sizing up the competition. Seth was giddy with the news that our plea deal had been approved by the court, and we would not face additional charges for violating cybermonitoring laws.

For him and Zach, the weekend was a celebration – for me, a last gasp of freedom.

I may have been off the hook for the Haver High Hack, but I had decided to expand my other confessions beyond my college admissions essays.

I checked my phone. Three minutes to launch.

A body appeared at my side, bouncing too much to be anybody but Mouse.

'You made it,' I said, smiling down at him.

His eyes were on the water. 'Wouldn't miss it.'

There was regret in his voice, and I knew he wished he was competing.

'Next year,' I told him.

Mouse shook his head. 'Nah, I don't think so. Competition makes me jumpy.'

He looked up at me and winked.

I laughed. 'Okay, then. Maybe freshman year.'

Mouse had applied for MIT early admission too, a fact he confided to me when his parents finally let him out of the house. He'd decided to major in computer science, but he assured us all he still had every intention of becoming a mahout when he was done.

'Not then either,' Mouse said. 'You'll have to go for the gold this year.'

'We forfeited an entire portion. There's no way we can win.'

'Cyberdefence Skills are seventy per cent of the final score. It's possible.'

'It's a pipe dream.' I laughed, but Mouse's face was serious.

'You have to try. For Jordan.'

The laughter died on my lips. We'd all been afraid to even mention Jordan's name in front of Mouse – for fear of a suicidal relapse. But he was telling me something now. I heard it in his voice and saw it in his face.

I nodded. *Living* seemed a much more fitting tribute to his friend.

'Okay,' I said, slinging an arm around Mouse's shoulder. 'Let's go win it for Jordan.'

'Yeah, right!' he said, his face breaking open now in a mischievous grin. 'I said *try*. You don't think you can really win it without me, do you?'

I pushed him toward the water. 'No, I don't.'

As I watched him skip to a stop, laughing, I wished with everything in me that I *would* somehow end up at MIT with him and Zach or at Stanford with Seth. I wished for a future of ivy halls instead of iron bars. I wished for forgiveness from Dad and Misty. And I wished for one last chance with a girl I didn't deserve. If I was lucky, by this time next year, I'd be away at school with a reason to minor in Spanish.

But I didn't want any of it without a clean slate.

I glanced down at my phone once more.

Time's up.

A new website had just been quietly launched into the world.

But the quiet would not last. As the ACC got under way, that site would infiltrate every phone, laptop, and tablet connected to the convention centre's Wi-Fi. It would pop up on competition big screens and flood judges' computer terminals.

It was a simple site with a singular purpose.

Confession.

My college admissions essay would be up for all the world to see, and then come what may, be it pardon or prison. That was actually a line from the essay. I was kind of proud of it.

I couldn't write the code for what was ahead, but I was learning to accept a little chaos in my life.

It was too late to unplug.

Acknowledgements

It has been a long journey to this book, so it is fitting that I have more people to thank for *The Chaos of Now* than anything else I have ever written.

The biggest thanks go to my mother and father, Michael & Holly, and my mother and father in-law, John & Donna, who all spent extra time taking care of my newborn twins so that I could make time to write. This story would not have made it to the page without you. It takes a village to raise two babies . . . and a book!

To that end, I also owe a world of thanks to my husband for being a true co-parent and allowing me time and space to write. At times, I know you felt like a single dad and gave up a lot of weekend fun so that I could run away for hours to write. You are the best father and my best friend.

I am blessed to have the insight of two amazing editors.

Thank you to Mary Kate Castellani, who gave me the toughest editorial note of all when she fearlessly pointed out that the entire story was built on a conceit that wasn't working. Thank you to Alice Swan, who told me years ago, in the very first sample pages, that the story would be stronger with a smaller cast of characters. You were both SO right!

Thank you, always, to my agent, Jennifer Laughran. I am incredibly grateful, four books in, to still be with the very best in the biz. The best decision I've ever made as a writer was to choose the agent who would guide me through all the big decisions that came after. I would be lost without you. And a huge thanks as well to Taryn Fagerness, for tirelessly championing my books overseas.

Thank you, Dani Calotta and Jeanette Levy, for one of my favourite covers ever! Thanks to Toni Rumore and Diane Aronson for your attention to detail. Who knew there was a right way to spell na-na na-na boo-boo? Thank you, Claire Stetzer, Courtney Griffin, Brittany Mitchell, Anna Bernard, Emily Ritter and everyone at Bloomsbury, for always taking good care of me. Many thanks to Leah Thaxton, Hannah Love, Natasha Brown, Emma Eldridge and the entire Faber family.

I am not a digital native, so I had to rely heavily on coders and other internet experts to tell me when I'd ventured into total gibberish with my cyber speak. Thank you, especially, to Germain Kirk for your insight and advice. Any errors left in this book are mine, alone. Thanks to Guadalupe Garcia McCall for checking my Spanish. Her input was invaluable, and any remaining bungled translations are my own doing. Thank you, also, to Meg Medina for connecting me with Guadalupe and, though she doesn't know it, for inspiring the image of the 'no bully zone' sign ever present in this story.

Thank you, as ever, to Gemma Cooper, my beta reader from the very beginning and a friend for life. Thanks also to Amy Dominy and Bill Konigsburg, who helped me talk through the different versions of this plot and for keeping me accountable and on track. Without our regular meetings, I never would have finished!

This is my first book written away from home. Thank you to Nosh in Phoenix and to Wildflower in Tempe for letting me take up space at your tables 3-4 times a week and to Changing Hands for not kicking me out of the tiny table in the back corner when I sometimes stayed past the time limit.

Thank you to my readers, who have been with me since *Butter*. Sometimes, when life gets crazy, I forget why I write, and then one of you pops up to remind me. You all rock.

Finally, to my girls, Grace and Harper – this was the most difficult story I've ever written, because it too often took me away from you. I hope when you are old enough to read it, you'll see I wrote it *for* you. Thank you so much for sharing your Mommy with this book.

From the novelist being
compared to R. J. Palacio and John Green

DEAD ENDS

Erin Lange

Dane Washington and Billy D couldn't be more
different. Dane is clever and popular, but he's also a
violent rebel. Billy D has Down's Syndrome, plays by the
rules and hangs out with teachers in his lunch break.

But Dane and Billy have more in common than they
think – both their fathers are missing. Maybe they'll just
have to suck up their differences and get on with helping
each other find some answers.

'A powerful and courageous novel.' *BookTrust*

I can't take another year in this fat suit, but I can end this year with a bang. If you can stomach it, you're invited to watch . . . as I eat myself to death.

-Butter

Butter is a lonely 423-pound boy. Desperate, he pledges to stream a live video of him eating himself to death and becomes instantly popular. And that feels good. But what happens when Butter reaches his suicide deadline?

The rebel, the bully, the geek, the pariah.

These four were never destined to like each other. But they're speeding down the motorway together. In a stolen police car. Running from the law . . .

Well, it's one way to make friends.